Future Power

RANDOM HOUSE ⌂ NEW YORK

Future
Power

A Science Fiction
Anthology

**EDITED, WITH INTRODUCTION
AND COMMENTARY BY**

Jack Dann

AND

Gardner Dozois

ACKNOWLEDGEMENT is made for permission to print the following material:

"The Diary of the Rose" by Ursula K. Le Guin. Copyright © 1976 by Ursula K. Le Guin.

"The Country of the Kind" by Damon Knight. Copyright © 1954 by Fantasy House, Inc. Reprinted by permission of the author.

"Smoe and the Implicit Clay" by R. A. Lafferty. Copyright © 1976 by R. A. Lafferty.

"She Waits for All Men Born" by James Tiptree, Jr. Copyright © 1976 by James Tiptree, Jr.

"The Day of the Big Test" by Felix C. Gotschalk. Copyright © 1976 by Felix C. Gotschalk.

"Contentment, Satisfaction, Cheer, Well-Being, Gladness, Joy, Comfort, and Not Having to Get Up Early Any More" by George Alec Effinger. Copyright © 1976 by George Alec Effinger.

"Coming-of-Age Day" by A. K. Jorgensson. Copyright © 1965 by A. K. Jorgensson. Reprinted by permission of the author and his agent.

"Thanatos" by Vonda N. McIntyre. Copyright © 1976 by Vonda N. McIntyre.

"The Eyeflash Miracles" by Gene Wolfe. Copyright © 1976 by Gene Wolfe.

The editors would like to thank the following people for their help and support: Pamela Sargent, Robert Silverberg, Harlan Ellison, Virginia Kidd, David Harris, Susan Casper, Marcia Kresge

For
the days
of
Sea Cliff
and
the Anchorage

"Things are more like they are today than they have ever been before."

—Dwight D. Eisenhower

CONTENTS

INTRODUCTION

Jack Dann and Gardner Dozois

IF you look in Webster's, you'll find power defined as, among other things, "the ability to control others." Up until a few years ago, the execution of this type of power has been a relatively simple, if unsavory, thing. There was *Force Majeur*—the power of the sword, the torch, the mailed fist, the blitzkrieg waiting in the wings; there were statesmanship and diplomacy, the power of gamesmanship, with ambassadors playing at draughts with the destiny of nations; there were politics and the rule of law, which all too often have become the power of the favor and the dollar. These things have not changed in kind since the beginning of history— World War II or the Punic Wars, the U.N. or the Court of Victoria, Hammurabi or Perry Mason, the exercise of power is the same. But as drastically as science and technology have changed the quality of our everyday life, they have also created new ways to power, and new powers.

Modern technology has created new and undreamed of capabilities for the "control of others"; *1984* is already upon us, ten years early, and if you look around, you'll discover that we caught up with *Brave New World* quite some time ago. We have techniques for the invasion of privacy in use today that as far outstrip 1984's telescreens as a supersonic jet outstrips an oxcart. With the development of observation satellites, microminiaturized bugging devices, laser technology and sophisticated optical techniques such as infrared and image intensification, there is literally no place on earth that can not be put under someone's interested eye, at least potentially. Newspeak? Today's specialists in psychological warfare would consider it childishly crude. Commercial advertising alone is a billion-dollar business, and new and more subtle methods to manipulate opinion are constantly being developed. Drugs, to pacify those who are controlled? Unlimited eroticism, for that same purpose? Look out your window, walk down your street, see an X-rated movie. Best of all, watch television, the soma of the McLuhan age.

And there are new capacities for control every year, new powers of man over man. Can you be sure that someone won't use them someday? Do you really know who's watching you, and why? You may be in someone's dossier at this moment—in fact, it is very likely that you are if you have a credit card or a driver's license, or have been in the Army, or have gone to college or to a psychiatrist. Are you *sure* that you're not?

Ominous as all this is, it is entirely possible that within the next fifty years new capabilities for control, new powers, will exist that go almost beyond the reach of imagination. Subliminal techniques may be wedded to behavioral conditioning to create a really efficient method of controlling people—without them ever being aware of it. Until now, the power of suggestion has mostly been a toy of Madison Avenue ad men, but in the future it may make armies and atom bombs equally obsolete. Within the foreseeable future, methods may be developed to control human emotions artificially, to induce rage or joy or fear or passivity at will, possibly at long distance. Drugs and hypnotism and microsurgery may give us the power to wipe a man's memory blank and then write upon it as we wish, to edit his life's experience, to shape his personality to our own ends. It may be possible for an experimental psychologist—

or a dictator—to make a person sane or insane at the turning of a switch. *In vitro* techniques—the use of artificial wombs—may enable us to educate—or condition—children even before birth. Sophisticated genetic science may give us the power to create living creatures—and human beings—to order, or to implant detailed specifications for unborn generations within the chromosomes themselves, breeding specific characteristics into our progeny with pinpoint accuracy. But which characteristics and to whose specifications? It is possible right now to monitor bodily functions from a distance—pacemakers in the heart, for instance—and it may someday be possible to *control* all of these functions, also from a distance: to stop the heart or the lungs of a transgressor, or to pinch off the flow of blood to the brain. Biological feudalism may be the condition of the future.

All of this is pretty frightening. And the average citizen *is* scared. He or she is already suffering from Future Shock—as is in no small way indicated by the very fact that Toffler's book has sold over 5 million copies. The future—and, more importantly, the quality of life in the future—has become a major cause of concern for many people. And in examining the prospects for that future, they may find much honest justification for apprehension and fear.

Unfortunately, that very fear often engenders a head-into-the-shell reaction that is actually counterproductive: the situation worsens in proportion to the number of people who abnegate their responsibility in dealing with it. So the potential for abuse grows. The impulse to make problems go away by ignoring them is probably a universal human reaction. It is also almost universally useless.

The most publicized example of the head-into-the-shell reaction is the 'back-to-nature' mystique. A moment's glance at an almanac—world population 3.7 billion, only about 1.6 hectares of arable land presently in use, with perhaps only half again as many hectares which are capable of being developed—and a moderate amount of common sense should demonstrate to almost anyone that the "back-to-nature" idea is unworkable and unreachable on any large scale, at least by the expedient of junking our technological civilization. The only thing now that will enable us to return to "simpler days" is the collapse of civilization and the death of most of our population. Some radical thinkers greet this prospect with aplomb, and even look forward to it eagerly. It seems doubtful, however, that these same people—even should they somehow happen to survive a cataclysm that could instantaneously destroy at least 31 percent of the American population alone—would really enjoy the "simpler life" once they had inescapably achieved it, with its attendant hardship, hunger, disease and death, and no city to go home to when they had tired of getting their hands in the dirt.

We tend to forget how thin a barrier exists between ourselves and the enormous, implacable forces of nature, a barrier created by tiny, almost imperceptibly slow increments, by thousands of small victories won over the course of thousands of years. Shatter that barrier, take away the thousands of small incremental victories of man over environment, and we find ourselves faced with conditions basically no different than those faced by our Neolithic ancestors—a hundred thousand years of progress wiped away in an afternoon. The Neolithic world is not gone; we have only momentarily abolished our susceptibility to it, banished it to wait behind the thinnest of glass partitions. As Ben Bova recently reminded us (*Analog*, September 1974): "To envision a human being without technology is to envision a dead naked ape, not a happy noble savage."

Much of the confusion among fearful people arises from a misunderstanding of what technology is, what it does, how it affects our lives. Is technology a computer or a screen window, a hydrogen bomb or a stone ax, a nuclear reactor or a bone needle? Does it affect your life more by putting you out of work through automation, or by killing the mosquitoes in the marshland behind your house—or by providing those of you who are myopic with eyeglasses and large type to enable you to read this page? In his essay "Frankenstein Phobia" (*Analog*, May 1974), Joe Allred points out that: "A large part of the problem causing the anti-science hysteria is inability to distinguish between *research* and *development*. It is *research* to discover the chemical information that iron and carbon combine to produce the harder substance, steel. It is *development* to make steel and turn it into either plowshares or swords. We may choose to ignore steel and live without plowshares in order to avoid the sins of swords, but whatever laws are passed and however many books are burned, steel will still be the result of combining iron and carbon no matter who makes it for whatever purpose."

Disturbingly, those who make the decisions—swords or plowshares—as to the application of technology—and too frequently even those scientists and technicians who are involved in making some aspect of it possible—quite often do not understand the consequences of what they are doing, consequences that can be enormously complicated and difficult to perceive, and which can interlock with an infinite number of other things. Often they are not even aware that there is such a thing as technological/social cause and effect. Even when they are aware, they sometimes don't give a damn.

John S. Lambert (*The New Prometheans*, Harper & Row) reminds us that "Western civilized man is a Stone Age organism trying to exercise 21st century power in a world of 18th century institutions which are based on medieval humanistic principles." Only recently has any extensive effort been made to assume conscious control of the world mechanism through preplanning and forecasting—only recently, in fact, has anyone even realized that it is possible to drive that particular car at all. Regretfully, this insight so far has mostly been a mixed blessing. Too often incomplete and erroneous planning has driven the car right over an unseen cliff—as the building of the Aswan Dam inadvertently triggered a widespread upsurge of deadly schistosomiasis along the Upper Nile, a region traditionally almost free of the disease, because the increased irrigation of the area made possible by the dam has also greatly increased the snail population, and snails carry schistosomiasis.

Incomplete knowledge of any sort is clearly an invitation to disaster. In the case of the anti-science and head-in-the-shell movements, it increases the very real danger of mismanagement and abuse of modern technology, not only by fogging the real issues, but by encouraging concerned people to pour their energies into attempted solutions that are completely infeasible instead of into projects that might have some chance of coping with conditions as they are.

We must also remember that not everyone regards the future with dread. Many look forward to the technology of the future, and long for it to be used to better order our lives. Some of the more rabid of these people might almost be said to be suffering from "pro-science hysteria," since in their idealistic yearning for such an "ordering" of the world they tend to sweep any moral or ethical considerations under the rug, and to ignore the question of whether the quality of life would then be better or worse. Such rosy optimism can also cloud the complexity of the issues and increase the danger of abuses. It tends to smooth over difficulties and to persuade people to buy a future filled with such technological encroachments without even looking at the price tag—in fact, to pursue the metaphor, unbridled enthusiasm is as effective as uninformed fear in preventing any intelligent "comparison shopping" between possible futures.

Isaac Asimov, in an article ("By the Numbers," *Fantasy and Science Fiction,* May 1973) attacking the hypocrisy of those who claim to yearn for a simple society while enjoying the benefits of a complex one, makes the point that tyranny is the fault of people, not technology. In arguing for an entirely computerized, cashless society in which detailed and complete dossiers are kept on *everybody* for the sake of increased efficiency and absolute identification, Asimov says: "The truth is that no government is ever at a loss for methods of controlling its population. No computer is needed, no codes, no dossiers. . . . Some of the most repressive and efficiently despotic governments have had very little in the way of technology at their service. . . . Did the Spanish Inquisition use computers to track down heretics?"

This is a valid point. But once a government is given that technological capacity—and the potential that goes with it for repression much more total and inescapable than any heretofore possible—can we really afford to assume that the government will use its new powers only to make our lives more comfortable and efficient? And if it does, then at what cost? We may end up trading what remnants of privacy and freedom remain to us for the advantage of more easily calculated income tax returns.

Polls taken in the shadow of Watergate indicate that most Americans no longer believe that their government is even minimally honest, let alone trustworthy and benign. Benign enough to be trusted with the power to control every facet of our lives? And the same is uncomfortably true of most governments around the world. Is it unreasonable to suspect that a despotic government would use such technology to create an *even more* intolerable despotism? The Spanish Inquisition didn't need computers to ferret out heretics, of course, but if it had had them, and the whole range of technology and information/behavioral sciences that go with them, then perhaps it would still be putting people to the Question today. Even a genuinely benevolent government might gradually, with the best and most humane intentions, end up squelching personal freedoms in the name of increased service and efficiency. Again, as always, the use to which technology is put depends on the intentions of those using it.

In this light, it is perhaps significant that Skinner's *Beyond Freedom and Dignity*—a book espousing the theory that human behavior should be consciously controlled and altered by social technicians through manipulation of the social surround—became a best seller at about the same time that some school systems were practicing the mandatory administration of amphetamines to unruly "hyperactive" children, police and governmental agencies were discussing the creation of a central data pool that would allow computerized access to—and accumulation of—dossiers on just about anybody, and Watergate was first becoming a household word.

Paranoia? Perhaps. Or perhaps not.

It becomes obvious that the exercise of power in the future—indeed, even of power in the 1970's, although most politicians have not yet realized it—will be a complicated, interlocking thing, affecting those who practice it as much as those upon whom it is practiced. Power does not have to be personalized, after all, nor directed by malice or ambition. It may not be necessary to imagine a conscious conspiracy, a dictatorship or a police state at all. As our machine civilization becomes increasingly complex, we become increasingly dependent on it, and it becomes correspondingly fragile. It is interesting to consider, for instance, that computers have *already* taken over. We could no more do without them now than we could do without electricity.

Remember Frank Herbert's aphorism from *The God Makers?* "The more god, the more devil; the more flesh, the more worms; the more property, the more anxiety; the more control, the more that needs control."

So will it be with the godlike powers of future technology: we will use them because we have them, and because by then we will have to use them to keep the shaky edifice of our civilization intact. And simply because we will *want* to use them. Power is a two-edged sword. We are owned by our possessions as surely as we own them, and it would seem that the ability to do something is almost synonymous with the necessity to do it. So we can't stop. We can only go on, hoping that when we reach the future—if indeed we ever do—the right powers will be in the right hands, and that those hands will know what to do with them.

Technology is a tool that can enable us to cope with the mindless, relentless forces of the universe. Or it can substitute for those

dead and hungry forces, and do an even more efficient job of anni-
hilating us. It can be the black wall through which no one can
break. Or it can lead us to undreamed-of freedom.

In his book *The Private Future* (Random House), Martin Pawley
gives us one version of the ultimate fate of Western man: "Alone in
a centrally heated, air-conditioned capsule, drugged, fed with
music and erotic imagery, the parts of his consciousness separated
into components that reach everywhere and nowhere, the private
citizen of the future will have become one with the end of effort
and the triumph of sensation divorced from action. When the bar-
barians arrive they will find him, like some ancient Greek sage, lost
in contemplation, terrified and yet fearless, *listening* to himself."
This is the future of increased technological encroachment on the
traditional humanistic values, and of varying degrees of control
over the everyday lives of individual citizens. This future assumes
that too much control will be ultimately bad for mankind, stifling
his spirit, even though the individuals involved might not be aware
of it under a comfortable "benign" despotism.

Or perhaps the Skinnerians are right, and mankind really does
need to be scientifically programmed and controlled for its own
good. As Skinner himself said in *Beyond Freedom and Dignity*
(Knopf): "What we need is a technology of behavior. We could
solve our problems quickly enough if we could adjust the growth of
the world's population as precisely as we adjust the course of a
spaceship, or improve agriculture and industry with some of the
confidence with which we accelerate high-energy particles, or move
toward a peaceful world with something like the steady progress
with which physics has approached absolute zero."

This future assumes that control will be positive, will provide the
social tools to achieve the kind of socially well-adjusted utopia that
people have always claimed to want—although whether they really
do want it or not is debatable—and have never been able to estab-
lish. It is interesting to note that this future coincides in many respects with the sort of future proposed by many prominent
ecologists—zero population growth, control of industrialization and
technology, alleviation of aggression and war through social/
psychological/spiritual methods, a "Spaceship Earth" ecology which
balances consumption of resources with their replacement—although
to many of these same ecologists the name of Skinner is anathema.

Perhaps the difference between the Skinnerian future and the
ecologists' "Spaceship Earth" future lies in the degree of social con-

trol each would postulate, how deeply into our everyday lives each
would reach, how benign are the governments administering the
control, and, in the final analysis, how much faith the scenerianists
are willing to put in human nature—the ecologists taking the 'idealistic' view that mankind will cooperate voluntarily, enthusiastically
and intelligently in building the utopia, the world becoming one integrated commune; the Skinnerians taking the "realistic" view that
mankind will have to be manipulated and coerced into accepting
the utopian lifestyle by methods so subtle that most of its citizens
will not even be aware that they are being so controlled. Perhaps
we also should ask ourselves at this point how much we really
would enjoy utopia should we ever achieve it. In his essay "Science
Fiction and a World in Crisis" (*Science Fiction, Today and Tomorrow*, edited by Reginald Bretnor, Harper & Row), Frank Herbert
points out that the usual vision of utopia—"public kitchens, public
clothing repair shops, public laundries, etc., and guidelines for public behavior"—is virtually synonymous with military life, and that
most people do not consider the military to be an utopian experience. It is perhaps also significant that in neither the Skinnerian future nor the "Spaceship Earth" future does space travel play a very
significant part, if indeed it continues to exist at all.

Or we may blow ourselves up in a thermonuclear war, or poison
ourselves to death with the excreta and pollution of a careless industrial world. Or a series of natural calamities and escalating systems failures may knock us back four or five hundred years, as Ro-
berto Vacca has proposed in his book *The Coming Dark Age*
(Doubleday). Such a dark age might be inescapable, as our
drained planet might prove to be far too poor in resources to enable
human beings to build another highly advanced technological civilization once they have destroyed the present one. In a *Gallery* interview (August 1974), Isaac Asimov said: "I think the world will
be driven by catastrophe. . . . In the end, we won't get away scot-
free. We can't. I'm hoping that we manage to pull through with
only a mild catastrophe. By a mild catastrophe, I mean one from
which we can recover. A serious catastrophe is one from which we
can't recover. . . . A *new* dark age will strike the entire earth."

Future history may be a race between education and catastrophe,
as H. G. Wells predicted. So far it is hard to tell who is winning. In
his essay "The Future Isn't What It Used to Be" (*Hawaii 2000*, The
University Press of Hawaii), Arthur C. Clarke comments: "This is
the first age that's ever paid much attention to the future, which is

a little ironic since we may not have one. . . . In the race against catastrophe of which H. G. Wells warned us, the last lap has already begun. If we lose it, the world of 2000 will be much like ours, with its problems and evils and vices enlarged—perhaps beyond endurance." In this future, technological encroachment will probably cease to be a problem, although despotism almost certainly will not, and it is possible that such a despotism would use whatever advanced technology still remained to shore itself up.

In another future, we may avoid both catastrophe and a social control that would have a dampening-out effect on technology. In this future, technology would continue to advance at the same fantastic rate, things would get stranger and stranger, and the possibilities would become almost limitless. Fusion power may be developed to solve our energy problems, or, as some scientists believe, even the awesome energies of black holes may someday be used in the service of man. Climate control may totally regulate our weather, preventing the disastrous storms and droughts that now afflict the earth. We may develop superintelligent computers, or greatly augment our own intelligence through mechanical/electronic link-ups between a computer and a human brain. We may create many different kinds of cyborgs, from people who have been rebuilt after disastrous accidents all the way to protected mind-centers with organic/mechanical mobile effectors that may enable us to extend our perceptions far beyond those environments tolerable to humans. Technology may enable us to create non-polluting, self-contained cities or even floating, mobile cities which could be moved about the earth at will. In an odd way, the "back-to-nature" dream may be possible to realize through advanced technology: instead of cities we might have thousands of individual homes scattered throughout a large region of rural countryside, each self-sufficient as to heat, food and energy, and all connected by a communications net. We may be able to extend our life spans by hundreds, perhaps thousands, of years. In *Man Into Superman* (St. Martin's Press) R. C. W. Ettinger presents the thesis that technology will make us immortal, for all practical purposes, and give us virtually divine power. We may spread our civilization through the solar system and on to the stars, and even rearrange planets to suit our own purposes.

In his book *The Next Ten Thousand Years* (Saturday Review Press), Adrian Berry states that "centuries from now, our most sophisticated computers will be but scrap metal and our fastest aircraft will attract the same amused interest as does a dugout canoe in a museum of anthropology. . . . Economic progress and technology are going to continue, not merely for decades, not even for centuries, but for millennia. . . . Space itself will be exploited. Jupiter, the largest of these planets, will be dismantled and its fragments displaced to capture the sun's radiation more efficiently. But even these great projects will be a mere beginning." This is the future of unlimited technological advance. Its enthusiasts seldom bother to speculate on how much technological encroachment will go along with the advances, and it is hard to predict how much control over our everyday lives we might have to endure to achieve it.

The phrase "The future will decide" has taken on a pregnant new meaning.

This book contains many different futures, a wide spectrum of possibilities, ranging from the black nightmare world created by Vonda N. McIntyre to the gray everything-rubbed-to-the-same-smoothness "benign" society depicted by George Alec Effinger, to the screwy cultures explored by Felix C. Gotschalk and R. A. Lafferty, which—in spite of some obvious drawbacks—seem like they would be rather pleasant places in which to live. But the one quality that almost all the authors and their stories share is a healthy wariness toward the future and what it is going to do to us, as well as what we are going to do to it. This attitude is neither one of hysterical despair or of foolish optimism. Instead, it is a questioning with open eyes, an inquiry, a new refusal to accept the easy prepackaged answers, pro or con. It seems that many science fiction writers have, unlike Fitzgerald's Gatsby, stopped believing in "the green light, the orgiastic future that year by year recedes before us." If so, then neither do they believe in the inevitability of Hell— at least one of our own making.

Future Power

THE DIARY OF THE ROSE

Ursula K. Le Guin

If power is a two-edged sword, then power over the mind is a weapon that may cut down the wielder as easily as the victim, a scalpel that could turn in the hand to savage the surgeon. If we could control the mind, or even spy on it, we could use that power to cure the hopelessly insane, or to obliterate dissent. To perform miracles or to suppress all hope, to create Heaven or Hell. This duality of choices is well understood and often remarked upon. It is less frequently realized, or admitted, that these two choices are not mutually exclusive. It is possible that such a power would be used simultaneously for the most noble and basest of purposes, and that the one will be used to justify the other. Heaven and Hell can be mixed, and once mingled, it may be as impossible to separate them again as it is to unscramble eggs.

Here, one of the foremost writers in the genre—Ursula K. Le

Guin, winner of the National Book Award in children's literature and both the Nebula and Hugo awards—gives us a glimpse of a world of well-rationalized banality, a gray and pious world where beauty and truth can only be encountered in small windowless rooms, a world in which the individual is only a soft machine to be rewired and repaired.

We are the ground in which the future will take seed. We may well ask ourselves what kind of flowers will grow from our soil. Do you believe that they will be roses?

EDITORS' NOTE: THIS IS AN ORIGINAL STORY, PUBLISHED HERE FOR THE FIRST TIME.

30 August. Dr. Nades recommends that I keep a diary of my work. She says that if you keep it carefully, when you reread it you can remind yourself of observations you made, notice errors and learn from them, and observe progress in or deviations from positive thinking, and so keep correcting the course of your work by a feedback process.

I promise to write in this notebook every night, and reread it at the end of each week.

I wish I had done it while I was an assistant, but it is even more important now that I have patients of my own.

As of yesterday I have six patients, a full load for a scopist, but four of them are the autistic children I have been working with all year for Dr. Nades' study for the Nat'l Psych. Bureau (my notes on them are in the cli psy files). The other two are new admissions:

Ana Jest, 46, bakery packager, md., no children, diag. depression, referral from city police (suicide attempt).

Flores Sorde, 36, engineer, unmd., no diag., referral from TRTU (psychopathic behavior—Violent).

Dr. Nades says it is important that I write things down each night just as they occurred to me at work: it is the spontaneity that is most informative in self-examination (just as in autopsychoscopy). She says it is better to write it, not dictate onto tape, and keep it quite private, so that I won't be self-conscious. It is hard. I never wrote anything that was private before. I keep feeling as if I was really writing it for Dr. Nades! Perhaps if the diary is useful I can show her some of it, later, and get her advice.

My guess is that Ana Jest is in menopausal depression and hormone therapy will be sufficient. There! Now let's see how bad a prognostician I am.

Will work with both patients under scope tomorrow. It is exciting to have my own patients; I am impatient to begin. Though of course teamwork was very educational.

31 August. Half-hour scope session with Ana J. at 8:00. Analyzed scope material, 11:00 to 17:00. N.B.: Adjust right-brain pickup next session! Weak visual Concrete. Very little aural, weak sensory, erratic body image. Will get lab analyses tomorrow of hormone balance.

It is amazing how banal most people's minds are. Of course the poor woman is in severe depression. Input in the Con dimension was foggy and incoherent, and the Uncon dimension was deeply open, but obscure. But the things that came out of the obscurity were so trivial! A pair of old shoes, and the word "geography"! And the shoes were dim, a mere schema of a pair-of-shoes—maybe a man's, maybe a woman's; maybe dark blue, maybe brown. Although definitely a visual type, she does not see anything clearly. Not many people do. It is depressing. When I was a student in first year I used to think how wonderful other people's minds would be, how wonderful it was going to be to share in all the different worlds, the different colors of their passions and ideas. How naïve I was!

I realised this first in Dr. Ramia's class when we studied a tape from a very famous, successful person, and I noticed that the subject had never looked at a tree, never touched one, did not know any difference between an oak and a poplar, or even between a daisy and a rose. They were all just "trees" or "flowers" to him, apprehended schematically. It was the same with people's faces, though he had tricks for telling them apart: mostly he saw the name, like a label, not the face. That was an Abstract mind, of course, but it can be even worse with the Concretes, whose perceptions come in a kind of undifferentiated sludge—bean soup with a pair of shoes in it.

But aren't I "going native"? I've been studying a depressive's thoughts all day and have got depressed. Look, I wrote up there, "It is depressing." I see the value of this diary already. I know I am over-impressionable.

Of course, that is why I am a good psychoscopist. But it is dangerous.

No session with F. Sorde today, since sedation had not worn off. TRTU referrals are often so drugged that they cannot be scoped for days.

REM scoping session with Ana J. at 4:00 tomorrow. Better go to bed!

1 September. Dr. Nades says the kind of thing I wrote yesterday is pretty much what she had in mind, and invited me to show her this diary again whenever I am in doubt. Spontaneous thoughts—not the technical data, which are recorded in the files anyhow. Cross nothing out. Candor all-important.

Ana's dream was interesting but pathetic. The wolf who turned into a pancake! Such a disgusting, dim, hairy pancake, too. Her visuality is clearer in dream, but the feeling tone remains low (but remember: *you* contribute the affect—don't read it in). Started her on hormone therapy today.

F. Sorde awake, but too confused to take to scope room for session. Frightened. Refused to eat. Complained of pain in side. I thought he was unclear what kind of hospital this is, and told him there was nothing wrong with him physically. He said, "How the hell do you know?" which was fair enough, since he was in strait jacket, due to the V notation on his chart. I examined and found bruising and contusion, and ordered an X-ray, which showed two ribs cracked. Explained to patient that he had been in a condition where forcible restraint had been necessary to prevent self-injury. He said, "Every time one of them asked a question, the other one kicked me." He repeated this several times, with anger and confusion. Paranoid delusional system? If it does not weaken as the drugs wear off, I will proceed on that assumption. He responds fairly well to me, asked my name when I went to see him with the X-ray plate, and agreed to eat. I was forced to apologize to him, not a good beginning with a paranoid. The rib damage should have been marked on his chart by the referring agency or by the medic who admitted him. This kind of carelessness is distressing.

But there's good news too. Rina (Autism Study Subject 4) saw a first-person sentence today. Saw it: in heavy black primer print, all at once in the high Con foreground: *I want to sleep in the big room.* (She sleeps alone because of the feces problem.) The sentence stayed clear for over five seconds. She was reading it in her mind just as I was reading it on the holoscreen. There was weak subverbalization, but not subvocalization, nothing on the audio. She has not yet spoken, even to herself, in the first person. I told Tio about it at once and he asked her after the session, "Rina, where do you want to sleep?" "Rina sleep in the big room." No pronoun, no conative. But one of these days she will say *I want*—aloud. And on that build a personality, maybe, at last: on that foundation. I want, therefore I am.

There is so much fear. Why is there so much fear?

4 September. Went to town for my two-day holiday. Stayed with B. in her new flat on the north bank. Three rooms to herself!!! But I don't really like those old buildings, there are rats and roaches, and it feels so old and strange, as if somehow the famine years were still there, waiting. Was glad to get back to my little room here, all to myself but with others close by on the same floor, friends and colleagues. Anyway I missed writing in this book. I form habits very fast. Compulsive tendency.

Ana much improved: dressed, hair combed, was knitting. But session was dull. Asked her to think about pancakes, and there it came filling up the whole Uncon dimension, the hairy, dreary, flat-wolf-pancake, while in the Con she was obediently trying to visualise a nice cheese blintz. Not too badly: colors and outlines already stronger. I am still willing to count on simple hormone treatment. Of course they will suggest ECT, and a co-analysis of the scope material would be perfectly possible, we'd start with the wolf-pancake, etc. But is there any real point to it? She has been a bakery packager for twenty-four years and her physical health is poor. She cannot change her life situation. At least with good hormone balance she may be able to endure it.

F. Sorde: rested but still suspicious. Extreme fear reaction when I said it was time for his first session. To allay this I sat down and talked about the nature and operation of the psychoscope. He listened intently and finally said, "Are you going to use only the psychoscope?"

I said yes.

He said, "Not electroshock?"

I said no.

He said, "Will you promise me that?"

I explained that I am a psychoscopist and never operate the electroconvulsive therapy equipment, that is an entirely different department. I said my work with him at present would be diagnostic, not therapeutic. He listened carefully. He is an educated person and understands distinctions such as "diagnostic" and "therapeutic." It is interesting that he asked me to *promise*. That does not fit a paranoid pattern, you don't ask for promises from those you can't trust. He came with me docilely, but when we entered the scope room he stopped and turned white at sight of the apparatus. I made Dr. Aven's little joke about the dentist's chair, which she always used with nervous patients. F.S. said, "So long as it's not an electric chair!"

I believe that with intelligent subjects it is much better not to make mysteries and so impose a false authority and a feeling of helplessness on the subject (see T. R. Olma, *Psychoscopy Technique*). So I showed him the chair and electrode crown and explained its operation. He has a layman's hearsay knowledge of the psychoscope, and his questions also reflected his engineering education. He sat down in the chair when I asked him. While I fitted the crown and clasps he was sweating profusely from fear, and this evidently embarrassed him, the smell. If he knew how Rina smells after she's been doing shit-paintings. He shut his eyes and gripped the chair arms so that his hands went white to the wrist. The screens were almost white too. After a while I said in a joking tone, "It doesn't really hurt, does it?"

"I don't know."

"Well, does it?"

"You mean it's on?"

"It's been on for ninety seconds."

He opened his eyes then and looked around, as well as he could for the head clamps. He asked, "Where's the screen?"

I explained that a subject never watches the screen live, because the objectification can be severely disturbing, and he said, "Like feedback from a microphone?" That is exactly the simile Dr. Aven used to use. F.S. is certainly an intelligent person. N.B.: Intelligent paranoids are dangerous!

He asked, "What do you see?" and I said, "Do be quiet, I don't want to see what you're saying, I want to see what you're thinking," and he said, "But that's none of your business, you know," quite gently, like a joke. Meanwhile the fear-white had gone into dark, intense, volitional convolutions, and then, a few seconds after he stopped speaking, a rose appeared on the whole Con dimension: a full-blown pink rose, beautifully sensed and visualized, clear and steady, whole.

He said presently, "What am I thinking about, Dr. Sobel?" and I said, "Bears in the zoo." I wonder now why I said that. Self-defense? Against what? He gave a laugh and the Uncon went crystal-dark, relief, and the rose darkened and wavered. I said, "I was joking. Can you bring the rose back?" That brought back the fear-white. I said, "Listen, it's really very bad for us to talk like this during a first session, you have to learn a great deal before you can co-analyze, and I have a great deal to learn about you, so no more jokes, please? Just relax physically, and think about anything you please."

There was flurry and subverbalization on the Con dimension, and the Uncon faded into gray, suppression. The rose came back weakly a few times. He was trying to concentrate on it, but couldn't. I saw several quick visuals: myself, my uniform, TRTU uniforms, a gray car, a kitchen, the violent ward (strong aural images—screaming), a desk, the papers on the desk. He stuck to those. They were the plans for a machine. He began going through them. It was a deliberate effort at suppression, and quite effective. Finally I said, "What kind of machine is that?" and he began to answer aloud but stopped and let me get the answer subvocally in the earphone: "Plans for a rotary engine assembly for traction," or something like that—of course the exact words are on the tape. I repeated it aloud and said, "They aren't classified plans, are they?" He said, "No," aloud, and added, "I don't know any secrets." His reaction to a question is intense and complex; each sentence is like a shower of pebbles thrown into a pool, the interlocking rings spread out quick and wide over the Con and into the Uncon, responses rising on all levels. Within a few seconds all that was hidden by a big signboard that appeared in the high Con foreground, deliberately visualized like the rose and the plans, with auditory reinforcement as he read it over and over: KEEP OUT! KEEP OUT! KEEP OUT!

It began to blur and flicker, and somatic signals took over, and soon he said aloud, "I'm tired," and I closed the session (12.5 min.).

After I took off the crown and clamps I brought him a cup of tea from the staff stand in the hall. When I offered it to him, he looked startled and then tears came into his eyes. His hands were so cramped from gripping the armrests that he had trouble taking hold of the cup. I told him he must not be so tense and afraid, we are trying to help him not to hurt him.

He looked up at me. Eyes are like the scope screen and yet you can't read them. I wished the crown was still on him, but it seems you never catch the moments you most want on the scope. He said, "Doctor, why am I in this hospital?"

I said, "For diagnosis and therapy."

He said, "Diagnosis and therapy of *what?*"

I said he perhaps could not now recall the episode, but he had behaved strangely. He asked how and when, and I said that it would all come clear to him as therapy took effect. Even if I had known what his psychotic episode was, I would have said the same. It was correct procedure. But I felt in a false position. If the TRTU report was not classified, I would be speaking from knowledge and the facts. Then I could make a better response to what he said next: "I was waked up at two in the morning, jailed, interrogated, beaten up, and drugged. I suppose I did behave a little oddly during that. Wouldn't you?"

"Sometimes a person under stress misinterprets other people's actions," I said. "Drink up your tea and I'll take you back to the ward. You're running a temperature."

"The ward," he said, with a kind of shrinking movement, and then he said almost desperately, "Can you really not know why I'm here?"

That was strange, as if he has included me in his delusional system, *on "his side."* Check this possibility in Rheingeld. I should think it would involve some transference and there has not been time for that.

Spent pm analysing Jest and Sorde holos. I have never seen any psychoscopic realization, not even a drug-induced hallucination, so fine and vivid as that rose. The shadows of one petal on another, the velvety damp texture of the petals, the pink color full of sunlight, the yellow central crown—I am sure the scent was there if the apparatus had olfactory pickup—it wasn't like a mentifact but a real thing rooted in the earth, alive and growing, the strong thorny stem beneath it.

Very tired, must go to bed.

Just reread this entry. Am I keeping this diary right? All I have written is what happened and what was said. Is that spontaneous? But it was *important* to me.

5 *September.* Discussed the problem of conscious resistance with Dr. Nades at lunch today. Explained that I have worked with unconscious blocks (the children, and depressives such as Ana J.) and have some skill at reading through, but have not before met a conscious block such as F.S.'s KEEP OUT sign, or the device he used today, which was effective for a full twenty-minute session: a concentration on his breathing, bodily rhythms, pain in ribs, and visual input from the scope room. She suggested that I use a blindfold for the latter trick, and keep my attention on the Uncon dimension, as he cannot prevent material from appearing there. It is surprising, though, how large the interplay area of his Con and Uncon fields is, and how much one resonates into the other. I believe his concentration on his breathing rhythm allowed him to achieve something like "trance" condition. Though of course most so-called trance is mere occultist fakirism, a primitive trait without interest for behavioral science.

Ana thought through "a day in my life" for me today. All so gray and dull, poor soul! She never thought even of food with pleasure, though she lives on minimum ration. The single thing that came bright for a moment was a child's face, clear dark eyes, a pink knitted cap, round cheeks. She told me in post-session discussion that she always walks by a school playground on the way to work because "she likes to see the little ones running and yelling." Her husband appears on the screen as a big bulky suit of work clothes and a peevish, threatening mumble. I wonder if she knows that she hasn't seen his face or heard a word he says for years? But no use telling her that. It may be just as well she doesn't.

The knitting she is doing, I noticed today, is a pink cap.

Reading De Cams' *Disaffection: A Study,* on Dr. Nades' recommendation.

6 *September.* In the middle of session (breathing again), I said loudly: "Flores!"

Both psy dimensions whited out but the soma realization hardly changed. After four seconds he responded aloud, drowsily. It is not "trance," but autohypnosis.

I said, "Your breathing's monitored by the apparatus. I don't need to know that you're still breathing. It's boring."

He said, "I like to do my own monitoring, Doctor."

I came around and took the blindfold off him and looked at him. He has a pleasant face, the kind of man you often see running machinery, sensitive but patient, like a donkey. That is stupid. I will not cross it out. I am supposed to be spontaneous in this diary. Donkeys do have beautiful faces. They are supposed to be stupid and balky, but they look wise and calm, as if they had endured a lot but held no grudges, as if they knew some reason why one should not hold grudges. And the white ring around their eyes makes them look defenseless.

"But the more you breathe," I said, "the less you think. I need your cooperation. I'm trying to find out what it is you're afraid of."

"But I know what I'm afraid of," he said.

"Why won't you tell me?"

"You never asked me."

"That's most unreasonable," I said, which is funny, now that I think about it, being indignant with a mental patient because he's unreasonable. "Well, then, now I'm asking you."

He said, "I'm afraid of electroshock. Of having my mind destroyed. Being kept here. Or only being let out when I can't remember anything." He gasped while he was speaking.

I said, "All right, why won't you think about that while I'm watching the screens?"

"Why should I?"

"Why not? You've said it to me, why can't you think about it? I want to see the color of your thoughts!"

"It's none of your business, the color of my thoughts," he said angrily, but I was around to the screen while he spoke, and saw the unguarded activity. Of course it was being taped while we spoke, too, and I have studied it all afternoon. It is fascinating. There are two subverbal levels running aside from the spoken words. All sensory-emotive reactions and distortions are vigorous and complex. He "sees" me, for instance, in at least three different ways, probably more—analysis is impossibly difficult! And the Con-Uncon correspondences are so complicated, and the memory traces and current impressions interweave so rapidly, and yet the whole is unified in its complexity. It is like that machine he was studying, very intricate but all one thing in a mathematical harmony. Like the petals of the rose.

When he realized I was observing he shouted out, "Voyeur! Damned voyeur! Let me alone! Get out!" and he broke down and cried. There was a clear fantasy on the screen for several seconds of himself breaking the arm and head clamps and kicking the apparatus to pieces and rushing out of the building, and there, outside, there was a wide hilltop, covered with short dry grass, under the evening sky, and he stood there all alone. While he sat clamped in the chair sobbing.

I broke session and took off the crown, and asked him if he wanted some tea, but he refused to answer. So I freed his arms, and brought him a cup. There was sugar today, a whole box full. I told him that and told him I'd put in two lumps.

After he had drunk some tea he said, with an elaborate ironical tone, because he was ashamed of crying, "You know I like sugar? I suppose your psychoscope told you I liked sugar?"

"Don't be silly," I said, "everybody likes sugar if they can get it."

He said, "No, little doctor, they don't." He asked in the same tone how old I was and if I was married. He was spiteful. He said, "Don't want to marry? Wedded to your work? Helping the mentally unsound back to a constructive life of service to the Nation?"

"I like my work," I said, "because it's difficult, and interesting. Like yours. You like your work, don't you?"

"I did," he said. "Goodbye to all that."

"Why?"

He tapped his head and said, "Zzzzzzt!—All gone. Right?"

"Why are you so convinced you're going to be prescribed electroshock? I haven't even diagnosed you yet."

"Diagnosed me?" he said. "Look, stop the play-acting, please. My diagnosis was made. By the learned doctors of the TRTU. Severe case of disaffection. Prognosis: Evil! Therapy: Lock him up with a roomful of screaming thrashing wrecks, and then go through his mind the same way you went through his papers, and then burn it . . . burn it out. Right, Doctor? Why do you have to go through all this posing, diagnosis, cups of tea? Can't you just get on with it? Do you have to paw through everything I am before you burn it?"

"Flores," I said very patiently, "*you're* saying 'Destroy me'—don't you hear yourself? The psychoscope destroys nothing. And I'm not using it to get evidence, either. This isn't a court, you're not on trial. And I'm not a judge. I'm a doctor."

He interrupted. "If you're a doctor, can't you see that I'm not sick?"

"How can I see anything so long as you block me out with your stupid KEEP OUT signs?" I shouted. I did shout. My patience *was* a pose and it just fell to pieces. But I saw that I had reached him, so I went right on. "You look sick, you act sick—two cracked ribs, a temperature, no appetite, crying fits—is that good health? If you're not sick, then prove it to me! Let me see how you are inside, inside all that!"

He looked down into his cup and gave a kind of laugh and shrugged. "I can't win," he said. "Why do I talk to you? You *look* so honest, damn you!"

I walked away. It is shocking how a patient can hurt one. The trouble is, I am used to the children, whose rejection is absolute, like animals that freeze or cower or bite in their terror. But with this man, intelligent and older than I am, first there is communication and trust and then the blow. It hurts more.

It is painful writing all this down. It hurts again. But it is useful. I do understand some things he said much better now. I think I will not show it to Dr. Nades until I have completed diagnosis. If there is any truth to what he said about being arrested on suspicion of disaffection (and he is certainly careless in the way he talks), Dr. Nades might feel that she should take over the case, due to my inexperience. I should regret that. I need the experience.

7 September.   Stupid! That's why she gave you De Cams' book. Of course she knows. As Head of the Section she has access to the TRTU dossier on F.S. She gave me this case deliberately.

It is certainly educational.

Today's session: F.S. still angry and sulky. Intentionally fantasized a sex scene. It was memory, but when she was heaving around underneath him he suddenly stuck a caricature of my face on her. It was effective. I doubt a woman could have done it, women's recall of having sex is usually darker and grander and they and the other do not become meat-puppets like that, with switchable heads. After a while he got bored with the performance (for all its vividness there was little somatic participation, not even an erection) and his mind began to wander. For the first time. One of the drawings on the desk came back. He must be a designer, because he changed it, with a pencil. At the same time there was a tune going on the audio, in mental pure-tone; and in the Uncon lapping over into the interplay area, a large, dark room seen from a child's height, the window sills very high, evening outside the windows, tree branches darkening, and inside the room a woman's voice, soft, maybe reading aloud, sometimes joining with the tune. Meanwhile the whore on the bed kept coming and going in volitional bursts, falling apart a little more each time, till there was nothing left but one nipple. This much I analyzed out this afternoon, the first sequence of over 10 sec. that I have analyzed clear and entire.

When I broke session, he said, "What did you learn?" in the satirical voice.

I whistled a bit of the tune.

He looked scared.

"It's a lovely tune," I said. "I never heard it before. If it's yours, I won't whistle it anywhere else."

"It's from some quartet," he said, with his "donkey" face back, defenseless and patient. "I like classical music. Didn't you—"

"I saw the girl," I said. "And my face on her. Do you know what I'd like to see?"

He shook his head. Sulky, hangdog.

"Your childhood."

That surprised him. After a while he said, "All right. You can have my childhood. Why not? You're going to get all the rest anyhow. Listen. You tape it all, don't you? Could I see a playback? I want to see what you see."

"Sure," I said. "But it won't mean as much to you as you think it will. It took me eight years to learn to observe. You start with your own tapes. I watched mine for months before I recognized anything much."

I took him to my seat, put on the earphone, and ran him 30 sec. of the last sequence.

He was quite thoughtful and respectful after it. He asked, "What was all that running-up-and-down-scales motion in the, the background I guess you'd call it?"

"Visual scan—your eyes were closed—and subliminal proprioceptive input. The Unconscious dimension and the Body dimension overlap to a great extent all the time. We bring the three dimensions in separately, because they seldom coincide entirely anyway, except in babies. The bright triangular motion at the left of the holo was probably the pain in your ribs."

"I don't see it that way!"

"You don't see it; you weren't consciously feeling it, even, then. But we can't translate a pain in the rib onto a holoscreen, so we give it a visual symbol. The same with all sensations, affects, emotions."

"You watch all that at once?"

"I told you it took eight years. And you do realize that that's only a fragment? Nobody could put a whole psyche onto a four-foot screen. Nobody knows if there are any limits to the psyche. Except the limits of the universe."

He said after a while, "Maybe you aren't a fool, Doctor. Maybe you're just very absorbed in your work. That can be dangerous, you know, to be so absorbed in your work."

"I love my work, and I hope that it is of positive service," I said. I was alert for symptoms of disaffection. He smiled a little and said, "Prig," in a sad voice.

Ana is coming along. Still some trouble eating. Entered her in George's mutual-therapy group. What she needs, at least one thing she needs, is companionship. After all, why should she eat? Who needs her to be alive? What we call psychosis is sometimes simply realism. But human beings can't live on realism alone.

F.S.'s patterns do not fit any of the classic paranoid psychoscopic patterns in Rheingeld.

The De Cams book is hard for me to understand. The terminology of politics is so different from that of psychology. Everything seems backwards. I must be genuinely attentive at P.T. sessions Sunday nights from now on. I have been lazy-minded. Or, no, but as F.S. said, too absorbed in my work—and so inattentive to its context, he meant. Not thinking about what one is working *for*.

10 September. Have been so tired the last two nights I skipped writing this journal. All the data are on tape and in my analysis notes, of course. Have been working really hard on the F.S. analysis. It is very exciting. It is a truly unusual mind. Not brilliant, his intelligence tests are good average, he is not original or an artist, there are no schizophrenic insights, I can't say what it is, I feel honored to have shared in the childhood he remembered for me. I

can't say what it is. There was pain and fear of course, his father's
death from cancer, months and months of misery while F.S. was
twelve, that was terrible, but it does not come out pain in the end,
he has not forgotten or repressed it but it is all changed, by his love
for his parents and his sister and for music and for the shape and
weight and fit of things and his memory of the lights and weathers
of days long past and his mind always working quietly, reaching
out, reaching out to be whole.

There is no question yet of formal co-analysis, it is far too early,
but he cooperates so intelligently that today I asked him if he was
aware consciously of the Dark Brother figure that accompanied several Con memories in the Uncon dimension. When I described it as
having a matted shock of hair, he looked startled and said,
"Dokkay, you mean?"

That word had been on the subverbal audio, though I hadn't
connected it with the figure.

He explained that when he was five or six, Dokkay had been his
name for a "bear" he often dreamed or daydreamed about. He said,
"I rode him. He was big, I was small. He smashed down walls, and
destroyed things, bad things, you know, bullies, spies, people who
scared my mother, prisons, dark alleys I was afraid to cross,
policemen with guns, the pawnbroker. Just knocked them over.
And then he walked over all the rubble on up to the hilltop. With
me riding on his back. It was quiet up there. It was always evening,
just before the stars come out. It's strange to remember it. Thirty
years ago! Later on he turned into a kind of friend, a boy or man,
with hair like a bear. He still smashed things, and I went with him.
It was good fun."

I write this down from memory as it was not taped; session was
interrupted by power outage. It is exasperating that the hospital
comes so low on the list of Government priorities.

Attended the Pos. Thinking session tonight and took notes. Dr. K.
spoke on the dangers and falsehoods of liberalism.

11 September.   F.S. tried to show me Dokkay this morning but failed. He laughed and said aloud, "I can't see him any
more. I think at some point I turned into him."

"Show me when that happened," I said, and he said, "All right,"
and began at once to recall an episode from his early adolescence.
It had nothing to do with Dokkay. He saw an arrest. He was told

that the man had been passing out illegal printed matter. Later on he saw one of these pamphlets, the title was in his visual bank, "Is There Equal Justice?" He read it, but did not recall the text or managed to censor it from me. The arrest was terribly vivid. Details like the young man's blue shirt and the coughing noise he made and the sound of the hitting, the TRTU agents' uniforms, and the car driving away, a big gray car with blood on the door. It came back over and over, the car driving away down the street, driving away down the street. It was a traumatic incident for F.S. and may explain the exaggerated fear of the violence of national justice justified by national security which may have led him to behave irrationally when investigated and so appeared as a tendency to disaffection—falsely, I believe.

I will show why I believe this. When the episode was done I said, "Flores, think about democracy for me, will you?"

He said, "Little doctor, you don't catch old dogs quite that easily."

"I am not catching you. Can you think about democracy or can't you?"

"I think about it a good deal," he said. And he shifted to right-brain activity, music. It was the chorus of the last part of the Ninth Symphony by Beethoven, I recognised it from the Arts term in high school. We sang it to some patriotic words. I yelled, "Don't censor!" and he said, "Don't shout, I can hear you." Of course the room was perfectly silent, but the pickup on the audio was tremendous, like thousands of people singing together. He went on aloud, "I'm not censoring. I'm thinking about democracy. That is democracy. Hope, brotherhood, no walls. All the walls unbuilt. You, we, I make the universe! Can't you hear it?" And it was the hilltop again, the short grass and the sense of being up high, and the wind, and the whole sky. The music was the sky.

When it was done and I released him from the crown I said, "Thank you."

I do not see why the doctor cannot thank the patient for a revelation of beauty and meaning. Of course the doctor's authority is important, but it need not be domineering. I realize that in politics the authorities must lead and be followed, but in psychological medicine it is a little different, a doctor cannot "cure" the patient, the patient "cures" himself with our help, this is not contradictory to Positive Thinking.

. . .

14 September. I am upset after the long conversation with F.S. today and will try to clarify my thinking.

Because the rib injury prevents him from attending work therapy he is restless. The Violent ward disturbed him deeply, so I used my authority to have the V removed from his chart and have him moved into Men's Ward B, three days ago. His bed is next to old Arca's, and when I came to get him for session they were talking, sitting on Arca's bed. F.S. said, "Dr. Sobel, do you know my neighbor, Professor Arca of the Faculty of Arts and Letters of the University?" Of course I know the old man—he has been here for years, far longer than I—but F.S. spoke so courteously and gravely that I said, "Yes, how do you do, Professor Arca?" and shook the old man's hand. He greeted me politely as a stranger—he often does not know people from one day to the next.

As we went to the scope room F.S. said, "Do you know how many electroshock treatments he had?" and when I said no he said, "Sixty. He tells me that every day. With pride." Then he said, "Did you know that he was an internationally famous scholar? He wrote a book, *The Idea of Liberty,* about twentieth-century ideas of freedom in politics and the arts and sciences. I read it when I was in engineering school. It existed then. On bookshelves. It doesn't exist any more. Anywhere. Ask Dr. Arca. He never heard of it."

"There is almost always some memory loss after electroconvulsive therapy," I said, "but the material lost can be relearned, and is often spontaneously regained."

"After sixty sessions?" he said.

F.S. is a tall man, rather stooped, even in the hospital pajamas he is an impressive figure. But I am also tall, and it is not because I am shorter than he that he calls me "little doctor." He did it first when he was angry at me and so now he says it when he is bitter but does not want what he says to hurt me, the me he knows. He said, "Little doctor, quit faking. You know the man's mind was deliberately destroyed."

Now I will try to write down exactly what I said, because it is important. "I do not approve of the use of electroconvulsive therapy as a general instrument. I would not recommend its use on my patients except perhaps in certain specific cases of senile melancholia. I went into psychoscopy because it is an integrative rather than a destructive instrument."

That is all true, and yet I never said or consciously thought it before.

"What will you recommend for me?" he said.

I explained that once my diagnosis is complete, my recommendation will be subject to the approval of the Head and Assistant Head of the Section. I said that so far nothing in his history or personality structure warranted the use of ECT, but that after all we had not got very far yet.

"Let's take a long time about it," he said, shuffling along beside me with his shoulders hunched.

"Why? Do you like it?"

"No. Though I like you. But I'd like to delay the inevitable end."

"Why do you insist that it's inevitable, Flores? Can't you see that your thinking on that one point is quite irrational?"

"Rosa," he said—he has never used my first name before—"Rosa, you can't be reasonable about pure evil. There are faces reason cannot see. Of course I'm irrational, faced with the imminent destruction of my memory—my self. But I'm not inaccurate. You know they're not going to let me out of here un—" He hesitated a long time and finally said, "unchanged."

"One psychotic episode—"

"I had no psychotic episode. You must know that by now."

"Then why were you sent here?"

"I have some colleagues who prefer to consider themselves rivals, competitors. I gather they informed the TRTU that I was a subversive liberal."

"What was their evidence?"

"Evidence?" We were in the scope room by now. He put his hands over his face for a moment and laughed in a bewildered way. "Evidence? Well, once at a meeting of my section I talked a long time with a visiting foreigner, a fellow in my field, a designer. And I have friends, you know, unproductive people, bohemians. And this summer I showed our section head why a design he'd got approved by the Government wouldn't work. That was stupid. Maybe I'm here for—for imbecility. And I read. I've read Professor Arca's book."

"But none of that matters, you think positively, you love your country, you're not disaffected!"

He said, "I don't know. I love the idea of democracy, the hope, yes, I love that. I couldn't live without that. But the country? You mean the thing on the map, lines, everything inside the lines is good and nothing outside them matters? How can an adult love such a childish idea?"

"But you wouldn't betray the nation to an outside enemy."

He said, "Well, if it was a choice between the nation and humanity, or the nation and a friend, I might. If you call that betrayal. I call it morality."

He *is* a liberal. It is exactly what Dr. Katin was talking about on Sunday.

It is classic psychopathy: the absence of normal affect. He said that quite unemotionally—"I might."

No. That is not true. He said it with difficulty, with pain. It was I who was so shocked that I felt nothing—blank, cold.

How am I to treat this kind of psychosis, a *political* psychosis? I have read over De Cams' book twice and I believe I do understand it now, but still there is this gap between the political and the psychological, so that the book shows me how to think but does not show me how to *act* positively. I see how F.S. should think and feel, and the difference between that and his present state of mind, but I do not know how to educate him so that he can think positively. De Cams says that disaffection is a negative condition which must be filled with positive ideas and emotions, but this does not fit F.S. The gap is not in him. In fact, that gap in De Cams between the political and the psychological is exactly where *his* ideas apply. But if they are wrong ideas, how can this be?

I want advice badly, but I cannot get it from Dr. Nades. When she gave me the De Cams she said, "You'll find what you need in this." If I tell her that I haven't, it is like a confession of helplessness and she will take the case away from me. Indeed, I think it is a kind of test case, testing me. But I need this experience, I am learning, and besides, the patient trusts me and talks freely to me. He does so because he knows that I keep what he tells me in perfect confidence. Therefore I cannot show this journal or discuss these problems with anyone until the cure is under way and confidence is no longer essential.

But I cannot see when that could happen. It seems as if confidence will always be essential between us.

I have got to teach him to adjust his behavior to reality, or he will be sent for ECT when the Section reviews cases in November. He has been right about that all along.

. . .

9 *October.* I stopped writing in this notebook when the material from F.S. began to seem "dangerous" to him (or to myself). I just reread it all over tonight. I see now that I can never show it to Dr. N. So I am going to go ahead and write what I please in it. Which is what she said to do, but I think she always expected me to show it to her, she thought I would want to, which I did, at first, or that if she asked to see it I'd give it to her. She asked about it yesterday. I said that I had abandoned it, because it just repeated things I had already put into the analysis files. She was plainly disapproving but said nothing. Our dominance-submission relationship has changed these past few weeks. I do not feel so much in need of guidance, and after the Ana Jest discharge, the autism paper, and my successful analysis of the T. R. Vinha tapes she cannot insist upon my dependence. But she may resent my independence. I took the covers off the notebook and am keeping the loose pages in the split in the back cover of my copy of Rheingeld, it would take a very close search to find them there. While I was doing that I felt rather sick at the stomach and got a headache.

Allergy: A person can be exposed to pollen or bitten by fleas a thousand times without reaction. Then he gets a viral infection or a psychic trauma or a bee-sting, and next time he meets up with ragweed or a flea he begins to sneeze, cough, itch, weep, etc. It is the same with certain other irritants. One has to be sensitized.

"Why is there so much fear?" I wrote. Well, now I know. Why is there no privacy? It is unfair and sordid. I cannot read the "classified" files kept in her office, though I work with the patients and she does not. But I am not to have any "classified" material of my own. Only persons in authority can have secrets. Their secrets are all good, even when they are lies.

Listen. Listen, Rosa Sobel. Doctor of Medicine, Deg. Psychotherapy, Deg. Psychoscopy. Have you gone native?

Whose thoughts are you thinking?

You have been working two to five hours a day for six weeks inside one person's mind. A generous, integrated, sane mind. You never worked with anything like that before. You have only worked with the crippled and the terrified. You never met an equal before.

Who is the therapist, you or he?

But if there is nothing wrong with him what am I supposed to cure? How can I help him? How can I save him?

By teaching him to lie?

. . .

(*Undated*) I spent the last two nights till midnight re-
viewing the diagnostic scopes of Professor Arca, recorded when he
was admitted, eleven years ago, before electroconvulsive treatment.

This morning Dr. N. inquired why I had been "so far back in the
files." (That means that Selena reports to her on what files are
used.) (I know every square centimeter of the scope room but all
the same I check it over daily now.) I replied that I was interested
in studying the development of ideological disaffection in intel-
lectuals. We agreed that intellectualism tends to foster negative
thinking and may lead to psychosis, and those suffering from it
should ideally be treated, as Professor Arca was treated, and
released if still competent. It was a very interesting and harmonious
discussion.

I lied. I lied. I lied. I lied deliberately, knowingly, well. She lied.
She is a liar. She is an intellectual too! She is a lie. And a coward,
afraid.

I wanted to watch the Arca tapes to get perspective. To prove to
myself that Flores is by no means unique or original. This is true.
The differences are fascinating. Dr. Arca's Con dimension was
splendid, architectural, but the Uncon material was less well integrated and less interesting. Dr. Arca knew very much more, and the
power and beauty of the motions of his thought was far superior to
Flores'. Flores is often extremely muddled. That is an element of
his vitality. Dr. Arca is an—was an Abstract thinker, as I am, and so
I enjoyed his tapes less. I missed the solidity, spatiotemporal realism, and intense sensory clarity of Flores' mind.

In the scope room this morning I told him what I had been
doing. His reaction was (as usual) not what I expected. He is fond
of the old man and I thought he would be pleased. He said, "You
mean they saved the tapes, and destroyed the mind?" I told him
that all tapes are kept for use in teaching, and asked him if that
didn't cheer him, to know that a record of Arca's thoughts in his
prime existed: wasn't it like his book, after all, the lasting part of a
mind which sooner or later would have to grow senile and die anyhow? He said, "No! Not so long as the book is banned and the tape
is classified! Neither freedom nor privacy even in death? That is the
worst of all!"

After session he asked if I would be able or willing to destroy his diagnostic tapes, if he is sent to ECT. I said such things could get misfiled and lost easily enough, but that it seemed a cruel waste, I had learned from him and others might, later, too. He said, "Don't you see that I will not serve the people with security passes? I will not be used, that's the whole point. You have never used me. We have worked together. Served our term together."

Prison has been much in his mind lately. Fantasies, daydreams of jails, labor camps. He dreams of prison as a man in prison dreams of freedom.

Indeed, as I see the way narrowing in I would get him sent to prison if I could, but since he is *here* there is no chance. If I reported that he is in fact politically dangerous, they will simply put him back in the Violent ward and give him ECT. There is no judge here to give him a life sentence. Only doctors to give death sentences.

What I can do is stretch out the diagnosis as long as possible, and put in a request for full co-analysis, with a strong prognosis of complete cure. But I have drafted the report three times already and it is very hard to phrase it so that it's clear that I know the disease is ideological (so that they don't just override my diagnosis at once) but still making it sound mild and curable enough that they'd let me handle it with the psychoscope. And then, why spend up to a year, using expensive equipment, when a cheap and simple instant cure is at hand? No matter what I say, they have that argument. There are two weeks left until Sectional Review. I have got to write the report so that it will be really impossible for them to override it. But what if Flores is right, all this is just play-acting, lying about lying, and they have had orders right from the start from TRTU, "Wipe this one out"—

(*Undated*) Sectional Review today.

    If I stay on here I have some power, I can do some good   No no no but I don't I don't even in this one thing even in this what can I do now how can I stop

(*Undated*) Last night I dreamed I rode on a bear's back up a deep gorge between steep mountainsides, slopes going steep up into a dark sky, it was winter, there was ice on the rocks

. . .

(*Undated*) Tomorrow morning will tell Nades I am resigning and requesting transfer to Children's Hospital. But she must approve the transfer. If not, I am out in the cold. I am in the cold already. Door locked to write this. As soon as it is written will go down to furnace room and burn it all. There is no place any more.

We met in the hall. He was with an orderly.

I took his hand. It was big and bony and very cold. He said, "Is this it now, Rosa—the electroshock?" in a low voice. I did not want him to lose hope before he walked up the stairs and down the corridor. It is a long way down the corridor. I said, "No. Just some more tests—EEG probably."

"Then I'll see you tomorrow?" he asked, and I said yes.

And he did. I went in this evening. He was awake. I said, "I am Dr. Sobel, Flores. I am Rosa."

He said, "I'm pleased to meet you," mumbling. There is a slight facial paralysis on the left. That will wear off.

I am Rosa. I am the rose. The rose, I am the rose. The rose with no flower, the rose all thorns, the mind he made, the hand he touched, the winter rose.

THE COUNTRY OF THE KIND

Damon Knight

Here is the triumph of the Skinnerian future: calm, quiet, serene, cool as pale-blue shadows on a pale-blue day. Here is, in Skinner's own words, "a world in which people live together without quarreling," a world in which everyone has been forever freed to "enjoy themselves and contribute to the enjoyment of others in art, music, literature, and games." It is a very civilized world, a very healthy, active, bright-eyed and bushy-tailed world, a polite world where the loudest sounds are laughter. A world in which people change houses, cars, and lovers as casually as they change their clothes. A summer resort world full of tennis players and hobbyists and placid happy men.

But beneath the unruffled surface of this shallow future sea swim all the old cold creatures, burning like ice: rage, murder, lust, horror, ecstasy, beauty, true art. And perhaps the oldest and

*hairiest animal of all swims there as well, down in the blue-black
depths, skimming the muddy bottom and looking up toward the
hidden sky, banished but not gone, locked out but not yet forgotten
—our humanity.*

*As critic, writer, and editor, Damon Knight has set what is per-
haps one of the very highest literary standards in the genre, and
"The Country of the Kind" is Knight at the top of even his own
high standard.*

THE attendant at the car lot was daydreaming when I
pulled up—a big, lazy-looking man in black satin chequered down
the front. I was wearing scarlet, myself; it suited my mood. I got
out, almost on his toes.

"Park or storage?" he asked automatically, turning around. Then
he realized who I was, and ducked his head away.

"Neither," I told him.

There was a hand torch on a shelf in the repair shed right behind
him. I got it and came back. I knelt down to where I could reach
behind the front wheel, and ignited the torch. I turned it on the
axle and suspension. They glowed cherry red, then white, and
fused together. Then I got up and turned the flame on both tires
until the rubberoid stank and sizzled and melted down to the pavement. The attendant didn't say anything.

I left him there, looking at the mess on his nice clean concrete.

It had been a nice car, too; but I could get another any time. And
I felt like walking. I went down the winding road, sleepy in the afternoon sunlight, dappled with shade and smelling of cool leaves.
You couldn't see the houses; they were all sunken or hidden by
shrubbery, or a little of both. That was the fad I'd heard about; it
was what I'd come here to see. Not that anything the dulls did
would be worth looking at.

I turned off at random and crossed a rolling lawn, went through
a second hedge of hawthorn in blossom, and came out next to a big
sunken games court.

The tennis net was up, and two couples were going at it, just
working up a little sweat—young, about half my age, all four of
them. Three dark-haired, one blond. They were evenly matched,
and both couples played well together; they were enjoying themselves.

I watched for a minute. But by then the nearest two were beginning to sense I was there, anyhow. I walked down onto the court, just as the blonde was about to serve. She looked at me frozen across the net, poised on tiptoe. The others stood.

"Off," I told them. "Game's over."

I watched the blonde. She was not especially pretty, as they go, but compactly and gracefully put together. She came down slowly, flat-footed without awkwardness, and tucked the racket under her arm; then the surprise was over and she was trotting off the court after the other three.

I followed their voices around the curve of the path, between towering masses of lilacs, inhaling the sweetness, until I came to what looked like a little sunning spot. There was a sundial, and a birdbath, and towels lying around on the grass. One couple, the dark-haired pair, was still in sight farther down the path, heads bobbing along. The other couple had disappeared.

I found the handle in the grass without any trouble. The mechanism responded, and an oblong section of turf rose up. It was the stair I had, not the elevator, but that was all right. I ran down the steps and into the first door I saw, and was in the top-floor lounge, an oval room lit with diffused simulated sunlight from above. The furniture was all comfortably bloated, sprawling and ugly; the carpet was deep, and there was a fresh flower scent in the air.

The blonde was over at the near end with her back to me, studying the autochef keyboard. She was half out of her playsuit. She pushed it the rest of the way down and stepped out of it, then turned and saw me.

She was surprised again; she hadn't thought I might follow her down.

I got up close before it occurred to her to move; then it was too late. She knew she couldn't get away from me; she closed her eyes and leaned back against the paneling, turning a little pale. Her lips and her golden brows went up in the middle.

I looked her over and told her a few uncomplimentary things about herself. She trembled, but didn't answer. On an impulse, I leaned over and dialed the autochef to hot cheese sauce. I cut the safety out of circuit and put the quantity dial all the way up. I dialed *soup tureen* and then *punch bowl*.

The stuff began to come out in about a minute, steaming hot. I took the tureens and splashed them up and down the wall on either side of her. Then when the first punch bowl came out I used the empty bowls as scoops. I clotted the carpet with the stuff; I made streamers of it all along the walls, and dumped puddles into what furniture I could reach. Where it cooled it would harden, and where it hardened it would cling.

I wanted to splash it across her body, but it would've hurt, and we couldn't have that. The punch bowls of hot sauce were still coming out of the autochef, crowding each other around the vent. I punched *cancel*, and then *sauterne (swt., Calif.)*.

It came out well chilled in open bottles. I took the first one and had my arm back just about to throw a nice line of the stuff right across her midriff, when a voice said behind me: "Watch out for cold wine."

My arm twitched and a little stream of the wine splashed across her thighs. She was ready for it; her eyes had opened at the voice, and she barely jumped.

I whirled around, fighting mad. The man was standing there where he had come out of the stair well. He was thinner in the face than most, bronzed, wide-chested, with alert blue eyes. If it hadn't been for him, I knew it would have worked—the blonde would have mistaken the chill splash for a scalding one.

I could hear the scream in my mind, and I wanted it.

I took a step toward him, and my foot slipped. I went down clumsily, wrenching one knee. I got up shaking and tight all over. I wasn't in control of myself. I screamed, "You—you—" I turned and got one of the punch bowls and lifted it in both hands, heedless of how the hot sauce was slopping over onto my wrists, and I had it almost in the air toward him when the sickness took me—that damned buzzing in my head, louder, louder, drowning everything out.

When I came to, they were both gone. I got up off the floor, weak as death, and staggered over to the nearest chair. My clothes were slimed and sticky. I wanted to die. I wanted to drop into that dark furry hole that was yawning for me and never come up; but I made myself stay awake and get out of the chair.

Going down in the elevator, I almost blacked out again. The blonde and the thin man weren't in any of the second-floor bedrooms. I made sure of that, and then I emptied the closets and bureau drawers onto the floor, dragged the whole mess into one of the bathrooms and stuffed the tub with it, then turned on the water.

I tried the third floor: maintenance and storage. It was empty. I turned the furnace on and set the thermostat up as high as it would go. I disconnected all the safety circuits and alarms. I opened the freezer doors and dialed them to defrost. I propped the stairwell door open and went back up in the elevator.

On the second floor I stopped long enough to open the stairway door there—the water was halfway toward it, creeping across the floor—and then searched the top floor. No one was there. I opened book reels and threw them unwinding across the room; I would have done more, but I could hardly stand. I got up to the surface and collapsed on the lawn: that furry pit swallowed me up, dead and drowned.

While I slept, water poured down the open stair well and filled the third level. Thawing food packages floated out into the rooms. Water seeped into wall panels and machine housings; circuits shorted and fuses blew. The air conditioning stopped, but the pile kept heating. The water rose.

Spoiled food, floating supplies, grimy water surged up the stair well. The second and first levels were bigger and would take longer to fill, but they'd fill. Rugs, furnishings, clothing, all the things in the house would be waterlogged and ruined. Probably the weight of so much water would shift the house, rupture water pipes and other fluid intakes. It would take a repair crew more than a day just to clean up the mess. The house itself was done for, not repairable. The blonde and the thin man would never live in it again.

Serve them right.

The dulls could build another house; they built like beavers. There was only one of me in the world.

The earliest memory I have is of some woman, probably the cresh-mother, staring at me with an expression of shock and horror. Just that. I've tried to remember what happened directly before or after, but I can't. Before, there's nothing but the dark formless shaft of no-memory that runs back to birth. Afterward, the big calm.

From my fifth year, it must have been, to my fifteenth, everything I can remember floats in a pleasant dim sea. Nothing was terribly important. I was languid and soft; I drifted. Waking merged into sleep.

In my fifteenth year it was the fashion in love-play for the young people to pair off for months or longer. "Loving steady," we called it. I remember how the older people protested that it was unhealthy; but we were all normal juniors, and nearly as free as adults under the law.

All but me.

The first steady girl I had was named Elen. She had blonde hair, almost white, worn long; her lashes were dark and her eyes pale green. Startling eyes: they didn't look as if they were looking at you. They looked blind.

Several times she gave me strange startled glances, something between fright and anger. Once it was because I held her too tightly, and hurt her; other times, it seemed to be for nothing at all.

In our group, a pairing that broke up sooner than four weeks was a little suspect—there must be something wrong with one partner or both, or the pairing would have lasted longer.

Four weeks and a day after Elen and I made our pairing, she told me she was breaking it.

I'd thought I was ready. But I felt the room spin half around me till the wall came against my palm and stopped.

The room had been in use as a hobby chamber; there was a rack of plasticraft knives under my hand. I took one without thinking, and when I saw it I thought, *I'll frighten her*.

And I saw the startled, half-angry look in her pale eyes as I went toward her; but this is curious: she wasn't looking at the knife. She was looking at my face.

The elders found me later with the blood on me, and put me into a locked room. Then it was my turn to be frightened, because I realized for the first time that it was possible for a human being to do what I had done.

And if I could do it to Elen, I thought, surely they could do it to me.

But they couldn't. They set me free: they had to.

And it was then I understood that I was the king of the world . . .

The sky was turning clear violet when I woke up, and shadow was spilling out from the hedges. I went down the hill until I saw the ghostly blue of photon tubes glowing in a big oblong, just outside the commerce area. I went that way, by habit.

Other people were lining up at the entrance to show their books and be admitted. I brushed by them, seeing the shocked faces and feeling their bodies flinch away, and went on into the robing chamber.

Straps, aqualungs, masks and flippers were all for the taking. I stripped, dropping the clothes where I stood, and put the underwater equipment on. I strode out to the poolside, monstrous, like a being from another world. I adjusted the lung and the flippers, and slipped into the water.

Underneath, it was all crystal blue, with the forms of swimmers sliding through it like pale angels. Schools of small fish scattered as I went down. My heart was beating with a painful joy.

Down, far down, I saw a girl slowly undulating through the motions of sinuous underwater dance, writhing around and around a ribbed column of imitation coral. She had a suction-tipped fish lance in her hand, but she was not using it; she was only dancing, all by herself, down at the bottom of the water.

I swam after her. She was young and delicately made, and when she saw the deliberately clumsy motions I made in imitation of hers, her eyes glinted with amusement behind her mask. She bowed to me in mockery, and slowly glided off with simple, exaggerated movements, like a child's ballet.

I followed. Around her and around I swam, stiff-legged, first more child-like and awkward than she, then subtly parodying her motions; then improving on them until I was dancing an intricate, mocking dance around her.

I saw her eyes widen. She matched her rhythm to mine, then, and together, apart, together again we coiled the wake of our dancing. At last, exhausted, we clung together where a bridge of plastic coral arched over us. Her cool body was in the bend of my arm; behind two thicknesses of vitrin—a world away!—her eyes were friendly and kind.

There was a moment when, two strangers yet one flesh, we felt our souls speak to one another across that abyss of matter. It was a truncated embrace—we could not kiss, we could not speak—but her hands lay confidingly on my shoulders, and her eyes looked into mine.

That moment had to end. She gestured toward the surface, and left me. I followed her up. I was feeling drowsy and almost at peace, after my sickness. I thought . . . I don't know what I thought.

We rose together at the side of the pool. She turned to me, removing her mask: and her smile stopped, and melted away. She stared at me with a horrified disgust, wrinkling her nose.

"*Pyah!*" she said, and turned, awkward in her flippers. Watching her, I saw her fall into the arms of a white-haired man, and heard her hysterical voice tumbling over itself.

"But don't you remember?" the man's voice rumbled. "You should know it by heart." He turned. "Hal, is there a copy of it in the clubhouse?"

A murmur answered him, and in a few moments a young man came out holding a slender brown pamphlet.

I knew that pamphlet. I could even have told you what page the white-haired man opened it to; what sentences the girl was reading as I watched.

I waited. I don't know why.

I heard her voice rising: "To think that I let him *touch* me!" And the white-haired man reassured her, the words rumbling, too low to hear. I saw her back straighten. She looked across at me . . . only a few yards in that scented, blue-lit air; a world away . . . and folded up the pamphlet into a hard wad, threw it, and turned on her heel.

The pamphlet landed almost at my feet. I touched it with my toe, and it opened to the page I had been thinking of:

> . . . sedation until his fifteenth year, when for sexual reasons it became no longer practicable. While the advisors and medical staff hesitated, he killed a girl of the group by violence.

And farther down:

> The solution finally adopted was threefold.
> 1. A *sanction*—the only sanction possible to our humane, permissive society. Excommunication: not to speak to him, touch him willingly, or acknowledge his existence.
> 2. A *precaution*. Taking advantage of a mild predisposition to epilepsy, a variant of the so-called Kusko analog technique was employed, to prevent by an epileptic seizure any future act of violence.
> 3. A *warning*. A careful alteration of his body chemistry was affected to make his exhaled and exuded wastes emit a strongly pungent and offensive odor. In mercy, he himself was rendered unable to detect this smell.
> Fortunately, the genetic and environmental accidents which combined to produce this atavism have been fully explained and can never again . . .

The words stopped meaning anything, as they always did at that point. I didn't want to read any farther; it was all nonsense, anyway. I was the king of the world.

I got up and went away, out into the night, blind to the dulls who thronged the rooms I passed.

Two squares away was the commerce area. I found a clothing outlet and went in. All the free clothes in the display cases were drab: those were for worthless floaters, not for me. I went past them to the specials, and found a combination I could stand—silver and blue, with a severe black piping down the tunic. A dull would have said it was "nice." I punched for it. The automatic looked me over with its dull glassy eye, and croaked, "Your contribution book, please."

I could have had a contribution book, for the trouble of stepping out into the street and taking it away from the first passer-by; but I didn't have the patience. I picked up the one-legged table from the refreshment nook, hefted it, and swung it at the cabinet door. The metal shrieked and dented, opposite the catch. I swung once more to the same place, and the door sprang open. I pulled out clothing in handfuls till I got a set that would fit me.

I bathed and changed, and then went prowling in the big multi-outlet down the avenue. All those places are arranged pretty much alike, no matter what the local managers do to them. I went straight to the knives, and picked out three in graduated sizes, down to the size of my fingernail. Then I had to take my chances. I tried the furniture department, where I had had good luck once in a while, but this year all they were using was metal. I had to have seasoned wood.

I knew where there was a big cache of cherry wood, in good-sized blocks, in a forgotten warehouse up north at a place called Kootenay. I could have carried some around with me—enough for years—but what for, when the world belonged to me?

It didn't take me long. Down in the workshop section, of all places, I found some antiques—tables and benches, all with wooden tops. While the dulls collected down at the other end of the room, pretending not to notice, I sawed off a good oblong chunk of the smallest bench, and made a base for it out of another.

As long as I was there, it was a good place to work, and I could eat and sleep upstairs, so I stayed.

I knew what I wanted to do. It was going to be a man, sitting, with his legs crossed and his forearms resting down along his calves. His head was going to be tilted back, and his eyes closed, as if he were turning his face up to the sun.

In three days it was finished. The trunk and limbs had a shape that was not man and not wood, but something in between: something that hadn't existed before I made it.

Beauty. That was the old word.

I had carved one of the figure's hands hanging loosely, and the other one curled shut. There had to be a time to stop and say it was finished. I took the smallest knife, the one I had been using to scrape the wood smooth, and cut away the handle and ground down what was left of the shaft to a thin spike. Then I drilled a hole into the wood of the figurine's hand, in the hollow between thumb and curled finger. I fitted the knife blade in there; in the small hand it was a sword.

I cemented it in place. Then I took the sharp blade and stabbed my thumb, and smeared the blade.

I hunted most of that day, and finally found the right place—a niche in an outcropping of striated brown rock, in a little triangular half-wild patch that had been left where two roads forked. Nothing was permanent, of course, in a community like this one that might change its houses every five years or so, to follow the fashion; but this spot had been left to itself for a long time. It was the best I could do.

I had the paper ready: it was one of a batch I had printed up a year ago. The paper was treated, and I knew it would stay legible a long time. I hid a little photo capsule in the back of the niche, and ran the control wire to a staple in the base of the figurine. I put the figurine down on top of the paper, and anchored it lightly to the rock with two spots of all-cement. I had done it so often that it came naturally; I knew just how much cement would hold the figurine steady against a casual hand, but yield to one that really wanted to pull it down.

Then I stepped back to look: and the power and the pity of it made my breath come short, and tears start to my eyes.

Reflected light gleamed fitfully on the dark-stained blade that hung from his hand. He was sitting alone in that niche that closed him in like a coffin. His eyes were shut, and his head tilted back, as if he were turning his face up to the sun.

But only rock was over his head. There was no sun for him.

Hunched on the cool bare ground under a pepper tree, I was looking down across the road at the shadowed niche where my figurine sat.

I was all finished here. There was nothing more to keep me, and yet I couldn't leave.

People walked past now and then—not often. The community seemed half deserted, as if most of the people had flocked off to a surf party somewhere, or a contribution meeting, or to watch a new house being dug to replace the one I had wrecked. . . . There was a little wind blowing toward me, cool and lonesome in the leaves.

Up the other side of the hollow there was a terrace, and on that terrace, half an hour ago, I had seen a brief flash of color—a boy's head, with a red cap on it, moving past and out of sight.

That was why I had to stay. I was thinking how that boy might come down from his terrace and into my road, and passing the little wild triangle of land, see my figurine. I was thinking he might not pass by indifferently, but stop: and go closer to look: and pick up the wooden man: and read what was written on the paper underneath.

I believed that sometime it had to happen. I wanted it so hard that I ached.

My carvings were all over the world, wherever I had wandered. There was one in Congo City, carved on ebony, dusty-black; one on Cyprus, of bone; one in New Bombay, of shell; one in Chang-teh, of jade.

They were like signs printed in red and green, in a color-blind world. Only the one I was looking for would ever pick one of them up, and read the message I knew by heart.

TO YOU WHO CAN SEE, the first sentence said, I OFFER YOU A WORLD. . . .

There was a flash of color up on the terrace. I stiffened. A minute later, here it came again, from a different direction: it was the boy, clambering down the slope, brilliant against the green, with his red sharp-billed cap like a woodpecker's head.

I held my breath.

He came toward me through the fluttering leaves, ticked off by pencils of sunlight as he passed. He was a brown boy, I could see at this distance, with a serious thin face. His ears stuck out, flickering pink with the sun behind them, and his elbow and knee pads made him look knobby.

He reached the fork in the road, and chose the path on my side. I huddled into myself as he came nearer. *Let him see it, let him not see me*, I thought fiercely.

My fingers closed around a stone.

He was nearer, walking jerkily with his hands in his pockets, watching his feet mostly.

When he was almost opposite me, I threw the stone.

It rustled through the leaves below the niche in the rock. The boy's head turned. He stopped, staring. I think he saw the figurine then. I'm sure he saw it.

He took one step.

"Risha!" came floating down from the terrace.

And he looked up. "Here," he piped.

I saw the woman's head, tiny at the top of the terrace. She called something I didn't hear; I was standing up, tight with anger.

Then the wind shifted. It blew from me to the boy. He whirled around, his eyes big, and clapped a hand to his nose.

"Oh, what a stench!" he said.

He turned to shout, "Coming!" and then he was gone, hurrying back up the road, into the unstable blur of green.

My one chance, ruined. He would have seen the image, I knew, if it hadn't been for that damned woman, and the wind shifting . . . They were all against me, people, wind and all.

And the figurine still sat, blind eyes turned up to the rocky sky.

There was something inside me that told me to take my disappointment and go away from there, and not come back.

I knew I would be sorry. I did it anyway: took the image out of the niche, and the paper with it, and climbed the slope. At the top I heard his clear voice laughing.

There was a thing that might have been an ornamental mound, or the camouflaged top of a buried house. I went around it, tripping over my own feet, and came upon the boy kneeling on the turf. He was playing with a brown and white puppy.

He looked up with the laughter going out of his face. There was no wind, and he could smell me. I knew it was bad. No wind, and the puppy to distract him—everything about it was wrong. But I went to him blindly anyhow, and fell on one knee, and shoved the figurine at his face.

"Look—" I said.

He went over backwards in his hurry: he couldn't even have seen the image, except as a brown blur coming at him. He scrambled up, with the puppy whining and yapping around his heels, and ran for the mound.

I was up after him, clawing up moist earth and grass as I rose. In the other hand I still had the image clutched, and the paper with it.

A door popped open and swallowed him and popped shut again in my face. With the flat of my hand I beat the vines around it until I hit the doorplate by accident and the door opened. I dived in, shouting, "Wait," and was in a spiral passage, lit pearl-gray, winding downward. Down I went headlong, and came out at the wrong door—an underground conservatory, humid and hot under the yellow lights, with dripping rank leaves in long rows. I went down the aisle raging, overturning the tanks, until I came to a vestibule and an elevator.

Down I went again to the third level and a labyrinth of guest rooms, all echoing, all empty. At last I found a ramp leading upward, past the conservatory, and at the end of it voices.

The door was clear vitrin, and I paused on the near side of it looking and listening. There was the boy, and a woman old enough to be his mother, just—sister or cousin, more likely—and an elderly woman in a hard chair holding the puppy. The room was comfortable and tasteless, like other rooms.

I saw the shock grow on their faces as I burst in: it was always the same, they knew I would like to kill them, but they never expected that I would come uninvited into a house. It was not done.

There was that boy, so close I could touch him, but the shock of all of them was quivering in the air, smothering, like a blanket that would deaden my voice. I felt I had to shout.

"Everything they tell you is lies!" I said. "See here—here, this is the truth!" I had the figurine in front of his eyes, but he didn't see.

"Risha, go below," said the young woman quietly. He turned to obey, quick as a ferret. I got in front of him again. "Stay," I said, breathing hard. "Look—"

"Remember, Risha, don't speak," said the woman.

I couldn't stand any more. Where the boy went I don't know; I ceased to see him. With the image in one hand and the paper with it, I leaped at the woman. I was almost quick enough; I almost reached her; but the buzzing took me in the middle of a step, louder, louder, like the end of the world.

. . .

It was the second time that week. When I came to, I was sick and too faint to move for a long time.

The house was silent. They had gone, of course . . . the house had been defiled, having me in it. They wouldn't live here again, but would build elsewhere.

My eyes blurred. After a while I stood up and looked around at the room. The walls were hung with a gray close-woven cloth that looked as if it would tear, and I thought of ripping it down in strips, breaking furniture, stuffing carpets and bedding into the oubliette . . . But I didn't have the heart for it. I was too tired. Thirty years . . . They had given me all the kingdoms of the world, and the glory thereof, thirty years ago. It was more than one man alone could bear, for thirty years.

At last I stooped and picked up the figurine, and the paper that was supposed to go under it—crumpled now, with the forlorn look of a message that someone has thrown away unread.

I sighed bitterly.

I smoothed it out and read the last part.

YOU CAN SHARE THE WORLD WITH ME. THEY CAN'T STOP YOU. STRIKE NOW—PICK UP A SHARP THING AND STAB, OR A HEAVY THING AND CRUSH. THAT'S ALL. THAT WILL MAKE YOU FREE. ANYONE CAN DO IT.

Anyone. Someone. Anyone.

SMOE AND THE IMPLICIT CLAY

R. A. Lafferty

*R. A. Lafferty is an Oklahomian gnome with the imagina-
tion and erudition of ten distinguished futurologists on a drunk,
and he writes the damnedest stories in this or any other genre. It is
always dangerous, though, to dismiss any of Lafferty's nuthatch futures—often they have more truth to them than their more sober
brothers, and stand a disquieting chance of coming true.*

*Here he gives us a ringside seat for a battle between the sentient,
cigar-smoking computer Epikt, and—a planet full of invisible Indians and buffalo hokey.*

*This story may be read, if you so wish, as a demonstration that
even all the technological gimmickry of a scientific Inquisition
might not prevail against us if we were of sufficient mettle—or of
sound enough clay.*

EDITORS' NOTE: THIS IS AN ORIGINAL STORY, PUBLISHED HERE FOR THE FIRST TIME.

1

> *There is belief that the Indians had fast cars before the flood.*
> *They remembered them more than did other people when man-*
> *kind was reconstituted, and more than other people they knew*
> *what to do with them.*
>
> —THE REEFS OF EARTH

"DONNERS, I called you in here on a hunch, just as I called in the latest (Oh God!) computer on a hunch," Colonel Crazelton of the Inquisition said. Crazelton always seemed like a volcano waiting its turn to erupt. "We have a problem, or we are going to create a problem for the purpose of getting it solved. There's been a cloud on the mind of every computer and man who's touched this case, and I'll have no peace till it's cleared. If only I could get straight answers to straight questions. Who was there, Donners? That's the straight question."

"Who was *where*, Crazelton? I've heard that question 'Who was there?' or 'Who was already there?' several times since I walked into these Sepulchres today. I think that the walls are mumbling the questions. Dammit, Crazelton, what are you trying to ask me?"

"I'm trying to ask you whether there was ever anyone already there when you got there. You've been on initial landing parties to more than a hundred worlds. Was there ever anyone already there when you got there?"

"Anyone? Or anything?"

"Anyone preferably. Any human or near human. Any person. Who was there first?"

"Well, there's an old serviceman's legend that 'Kilroy was here' first. And he did get around for several centuries there, I suppose. He's worn down to a wraith now though. Likely he was always a projection. And yes, of course projections can write short declarations or claims or taunts on walls or whatever. They've often done it. I've caught several glimpses of Kilroy myself. He is not at all a nonentity as has been claimed. He's really an imposing figure, for all his haziness: a tall, rangy wraith with a far-off look in his eye."

"Kilroy isn't the one, Donners," Colonel Crazelton said. "The new computer that we have working on the job now has assembled a bucket of information on Kilroy. He agrees that Kilroy has a far-off look in his eyes, which may be why he failed to see someone who was right under his nose. And Kilroy may have *set* this peculiar nonseeing pattern, if he is as ancient as has been claimed for him. But our new computer (Are they so much smarter than man anyhow?) says that the answer we are looking for now is 'Who was there when Kilroy got there?' And this new computer on the job said that he wanted to interview the man who had been on more initial landings than any other. That's you, Donners, and I had already sent for you before the computer put in his request."

"I suppose I'm the one then, Crazelton. I've been around a lot. You have a *new* computer on this ill-defined job?" Donners had developed a grotesque facial tic and an oddity of speech and manner. Many of the space pioneers get a little bit odd.

"We have had five computers on this job before this one," Colonel Crazelton admitted. "None of them could state the problem cogently or even be sure that there was a problem. But they all thought that there was a cloud on the records and that it went clear back to the beginning. It bothered them. They were like old punch-drunk fighters trying to brush imaginary flies or cobwebs or clouds out of their eyes. And each of those first five computers was larger, more intelligent, more advanced, and more sophisticated than the one before it. We couldn't go any further in that direction. There aren't any machines more intelligent or more advanced or more sophisticated than those five. So we decided that—"

"—that you had been going in the wrong direction, Crazelton?" Donners finished for him. "So you got one that was less intelligent, less sophisticated, less advanced than these. You got one that was used to imaginary flies and cobwebs and clouds, not bothered at all by them. You got a machine like—"

"Like Epikt. In fact we got Epikt."

"Oh God!" Epikt was the ktistec machine associated with the Institute for Impure Science. He was a showboat and a comedian. Except for his brains and flexibility and intuitions he wasn't much of an improvement over humans.

"And Epikt said that he wanted to check out the man who had

been on more initial landings than any other. And when I told him
that you were that man he said—"

"He said 'Oh God!'"

"Yes."

"Colonel Crazelton, what's the name of that gadget that's hanging with its nose over the edge of your ashtray? I've seen them before. They remind me of someone. But I can't remember their
names."

"Oh, there it is! I couldn't see it a while ago. I thought someone
had swiped it. Very often I can't see it and think that it's been
stolen or misplaced. It's a Smoe. They are made out of unbaked
clay, I think. They were first in vogue about two hundred years
ago. Interesting little conversation pieces, except that you always
forget that they're there, or forget to see them. It hangs by its nose
over the edge of anything and pops those one-way eyes at you. Just
a little statuette, a head only, and the nose is the handle of the
head."

"Oh, yeah. I always forget what you call them. I think I've got a
couple of them somewhere, but I never seem to notice them. I've
known guys that look just like that: not known them very well
though."

Epikt, the intelligent ktistec machine, arrived at the Inquisition Sepulchres. (And the Sepulchres weren't as gloomy as all
that, just big, statued, white slabs of buildings, functional really.)
Epikt arrived in the form of one of his hasty extensions. This Epikt-
extension was duded out in walrus mustaches, sky-blue eyes as big
as plates, and a paunch that would measure two meters around.
Watch out for him when he uses a big paunch, or anything big and
bulky. That means that he is carrying quite a few of his brains
with him. All the leading computers can make working extensions
of themselves, but most of them don't go so heavy on the whimsy
when they do it.

"Ah, Donners, to business first," Epikt said as he drew on a cigar
through an arty cigar holder. "And after we have solved our business, then you may be permitted to regale me with a few tall tales.
I have a photograph here. It is of yourself and those who accompanied you on one of your initial landings. It is Donners' World, in
fact. Can you name me the five people who appear in this picture,
Donners?"

"Sure, Epikt. There's myself, and Bernheim, Marin, Procop, Scarble."

"Five persons, Donners?"

"Certainly. We were a five-man team."

"Point out the five in this picture, Donners."

"Why, there's myself. There's Bernheim. There's Marin. There's Procop, who we had to report as disappearing completely: but who can say whether he stayed disappeared? There's Scarble, who later got cobwebs on the brain from the giant spiders. Five men." Donners looked at the picture for a moment longer as though he would name something else. Then he shrugged his shoulders. He looked at Epikt the showboat machine. The cigar holder that Epikt was using was in the shape of a Smoe, a big-nosed Smoe. "Have Smoes come back?" Donners asked. "I seem to be seeing more of them lately."

"That you're seeing more of them doesn't mean that there are more of them," Epikt cautioned. "I wish you could get away from that human logic of yours. Back to the picture: who's the sixth man there, Donners?"

"Sixth man? There isn't any sixth man. I wish you would let things alone!" Donners exploded suddenly. "Yes, Epikt, I see where you're pointing. But that's only—well, that's only the fellow who was there, I mean, his name was—Epikt, I don't believe that he had any name! He used to tickle me though. I remember once when he said—but how could he have? How could I remember an impossibility? And why do I feel funny?"

"That thing in the picture is a nonoptical illusion, Donners," the Epikt-extension said, "and sometimes the nonoptics do make the head swim. Luckily this picture was taken on biofilm so it could be analyzed as to the composition of the pictured objects. And they have been analyzed. He isn't a sixth man, Donners, though he looks mighty like one with the light and arrangement of the picture. But he's just a big outcropping of clay."

"Just a pile of clay there? Are you sure, Epikt?"

"Of course I'm sure," said the machine Epikt. "Am I a man that I should have doubts?"

Colonel Crazelton walked through. "Is everything going all right?" he asked.

"No, I don't believe that it is," Donners said. "Epikt, now that I look back on it, it just seems that he was *more* than a lump of clay.

And yet I don't have any memory of him at all. I have something else of him, but it isn't memory."

"The analysis shows that it is just a lump of clay, Donners," Epikt said.

"All right then. Clay it is. Why not make it dust so it'd be easier swept away or under? Clay is always a little sticky. But it's all simple and neat, is it, Epikt?"

"No, not really, Donners," Epikt said. His cigar holder, the Smoe-form, seemed to be puffing away independently of Epikt. "Similar lumps of clay have turned up in more than a hundred pictures from more than a hundred discovery worlds. And they sure do look like men. Tricky light and arrangement that! Very tricky, to be on more than a hundred worlds. Not only do they all look like men, sort of, but they all look like brothers."

"The brotherhood of clay, I suppose," said Colonel Crazelton. "Well, why shouldn't there be?"

"And all the lumps of clay have one thing in common, Epikt," Donners mused.

"What's that?" Epikt asked.

"They all like to get their picture taken," said Donners. "Hey, that's right. I never knew one of them that didn't like to get in on a picture."

"How was this one taken, Donners?" Epikt asked, and the Smoe cigar holder grimaced and mugged, believing itself to be of the invisible clay. "There's a hundred ways you could have done it, Donners, but how *did* you activate the picture-snapping in this one? All five of you were in the picture, and the lump of clay also."

"Oh, his wife took the picture," Donners said in a flat voice.

"*Whose* wife, Donners?" the Epikt-extension asked archly. Epikt had forgotten to put eyebrows on this extension of his; but now he created them, and he created them arched.

"Do you realize what you have just said, Donners?" Colonel Crazelton demanded.

"Would I have said it if I had?" Donners asked with a spread-out-hands gesture. "Ah, ah, what shall I say now? Is this all there is to losing one's mind, Epikt? What do you think, Colonel? Just have it blow up on you with a little 'poof' like that? Dammit, it was the piece-of-clay's wife: that's who took the picture! Wait, wait, it only hurts for a moment and then it will pass. It's gone now, guys. I don't remember how that picture was taken. I really don't. And I bet I'm not going to remember it either."

The Epikt-extension gazed at Donners thoughtlessly. This Epikt-form looked a little like an old Beardsley drawing: those mustaches, those big plate-sized eyes, that *outré* cigar holder, that huge girth, all a bit Turkish looking. And down in the corner of the imagined Beardsley picture that was Epikt there had to be a hardly noticed small smudge. It would be seen only on about the third sweep of the eye. Who could say what it was? Who could say more about it than that it was made of clay?

"Donners, you were one of the party that returned to a particular world to pick up Procop," the Epikt was saying, and the Smoe-form cigar holder was mugging and ughing (what's so strange? If Epikt could make a droll extension of himself he could also put enough of himself in a cigar holder to show animation and mockery), "and you found that he had disappeared completely. And the instrumentation, which could discover any animation whatsoever on that world, could not discover any trace of him. He was clear gone, was he, Donners?"

"Absolutely, Epikt, he was clear gone."

"But two moments ago you asked 'Who can say whether he stayed disappeared?' Just what did you mean by that?"

"I don't know, Epikt." Donners was a little bit flustered with himself. "I hate people who put awkward words in my mouth, and I hate myself when I do it. And I wish the Inquisition would go back to using humans for its questioners. Ah, it seems as if I used to see Procop after that, every time I was back on Procop's World; but I never saw him to notice him much or to think about him. He was a bit like those lumps of clay. There's something about him that still comes to me, if I don't think about it too closely, but that something that comes sure isn't memory."

"Donners, I said that we would attend to business first, and then that you might be permitted to regale me with a few tall tales," the Epikt-article said. "But aren't you mixing the two things up in a pretty sloppy manner now?"

"Yes. Mixing them up inextricably, Epikt. There isn't any other way. I can't tell you anything else about this stuff. I don't know anything else. It's a nice day, Epikt and Crazelton. Let's go fishing, or—"

"Or what, man-article?" Epikt asked him. "What else is it a nice day for?" But they were already gathering themselves up and walk-

ing out of the Inquisitional Sepulchres. "Come along, Crazelton.
Donners says that it's a nice day."

"All right," Colonel Crazelton said. "This is an oblique business
and we won't solve it by direct examination in here. Yes, what else
is it a nice day for, Donners?"

"Oh, it's a nice day for a quick trip off-world," Donners ventured.
"Maybe to one of our early landings in the Cercyon belt. We might
just notice something there that was missed before. We might even
notice the answer to the Crazelton Problem."

"Taxi!"—there was a dampish, muddy voice—"Hey, maxi-taxi, go
anywhere. Even go to Procop's World."

Epikt, Donners, and Crazelton piled into the maxi-taxi.

"How come we take a maxi-taxi without any driver?" Crazelton
asked. "That isn't very good practice, is it? Or is there a driver?"

"Oh, sure, I'm the driver," the hackie said. "Lots of people say
that I don't make a very good appearance." Oh, sure, there was a
driver, but he wasn't the sort of a man who would be much noticed.
That hackie wore a slouch hat with a beaded headband on the outside of it, and he wore his hair in two long, black braids. The rest
of him was less conventional though.

And he really gunned that maxi on the takeoff. He set it to roaring and screeching, and he left a trail of flame fifty kilometers long
below him.

"Things like that are bad for the streets," Crazelton told the
hackie. "Hey, quit blinking on and off like that. It makes you hard
to see."

"I don't blink on and off," the hackie said. "I'm just a low-resolution kind of guy."

"It's dangerous to drive like that," Crazelton lectured. "A takeoff
like that from a local traffic area can well crisp a pedestrian to a
cinder. It would even burn up a cruising car with all the people in it.
It's unmannerly to drive like that."

"Hey, I know it, but it sure is fun," the hackie said. "Hey, will
this maxi ever dig out!"

"Did the driver say to Procop's World?" Donners asked. "Why
not go to Donners' world? That's the one I know best, and that's
where the picture was taken."

"No, we'll go to Procop's World," the Epikt-form said. "We have
an early picture from there too. Besides, Procop might have become
undisappeared in the meanwhile, and we might run into him. Now

then, Donners, before you diverted me I was accusing you of mixing up tall tales with the business at hand."

"Yes, and I said that it couldn't be helped, that they were tangled together too tightly to be separated. What we are really investigating is the shaggiest of tales. And you are a computer and don't even know how to state the problem in its right area."

"Ah, Donners, that lump of clay on Donners' World, what was it he said one time that tickled you?" Epikt asked, and the Epikt cigar holder cupped a hand to ear as if to hear it too.

"Ah, clay-face said a thousand things at a thousand times. But this one that comes to mind—"

"Yes?"

"He said 'Hey, you know what the toothless termite said when he came into the Shaggy Star Bar?'"

2

The Malayans said in the old times that when men got to the moon they would find a Chinaman already there running a store. The old Germans said that when the afterlife was reached there would be a Wendt on every good stream already running a mill. The Spanish said that it would be a Catalan already running a fulling mill. The Gascons said that whenever a strange world was reached one would find a Gypsy there with a blind horse and a jar of salve that would give vision to that horse only until it could be sold. Well, what will we find to be already there when we come arriving at new worlds? What is common to the Chinese and Wendts and Catalans and Gypsies? What is the least common denominator of humanity? What is the most fundamental clay of them all?

—THE BACK-DOOR OF HISTORY,
ARPAD ARUNTINOV

The Idumeneans said that, as to humanity, God created the fundamental clay only; that this clay was not animated in the beginning, but that human life was implicit in it. They said that at various later dates fifteen archangels, Michael, Gabriel, Raphael, Israphael, Uriel, Jeremiel, Ninip, Uzziel, Ithuriel, Zephon, Abdiel, Zophiel, Urim, Urania, Thimmim, came by and formed the implicit clay into particular races, the races to which they would be the guardians. This seems to be a primitive and simplistic theory, almost a myth. Paranormal research has proved the accuracy of it, however; and this Idumenean thesis cannot now be doubted.

Fifteen archangels formed fifteen races out of that clay. But are there not sixteen races of men in all? Whence comes the sixteenth? Did the implicit clay still contain another race after the fifteen had been activated from it? Would this make the sixteenth to be the oldest or the youngest of the races? Was this sixteenth people really the first and original, our Paternal Clay, our Heritage? What is the name of this race from which we may all descend?

—SERMONS OF JOHN KING SPENCER

"Well, what *did* the toothless termite say when he came into the Shaggy Star Bar?" the distraught Colonel Crazelton asked after the silence had hung there for a long minute.

"He said 'Is the bartender here?'" Donners finished it.

3

What then did Columbus discover? And why was he the first one able to see them? Had they changed? Or had he and his mariners taken an irreversible step for all of us? Or is it irreversible? Are they often seen even now? At first meeting, it took me five minutes to notice one of them. And I'm told that such experience is common—common, but seldom noted.

—LETTERS OF DONALD BARON
BANTING

"Take your time, Colonel," the maxi-taxi driver said. "It'll come to you."

4

The Census Bureau says that, on the basis of numbered facts and listed names, there are a few more than two and a half million Indians in this country. But the Bureau also says that, on the authority of its most sophisticated instrumentation, there

*are an additional thirty million Indians living in this country,
usually and unaccountably invisible; and that there may be a
hundred million buffalo not usually figured in the count of live-
stock. And Barnaby Sheen of Oklahoma Seismograph Co. says
that, on the basis of his own instrumentation (even more sophisticated and even more suspect) there may be ten times these
numbers of "low resolution" (quasi-invisible) men and beasts.*

—CONTROLLED FLASH, THE
PICTORIAL MAGAZINE OF THE
STATISTICAL INDUSTRY (REPRINTED
IN THE WEEKLY FREELOADER)

*The Census Bureau's instrumentation is getting too damn so-
phisticated. And Barnaby Sheen is Mr. Brain Damage himself.*

—LETTERS TO THE EDITOR, THE
WEEKLY FREELOADER

On Procop's World, Colonel Crazelton became very
nervous.

"Where has that maxi-taxi driver gone?" he cried. "He's either
blinked out again, or he's gone. If he goes off and leaves us here on
this world, it will be pretty inconvenient."

"I'm here, Colonel," that hackie said. "I don't blink off. It's all
your own eyes. And I told you that I was a pretty low-resolution
fellow."

"Epikt, quit clowning!" Crazelton snapped as though searching a
target to attack. "What's so smart about smoking a cigar that's ten
centimeters from your mouth? Any stage trickster could do that."

"I'm smoking it with a Smoe cigar holder, Colonel," Epikt said.
"There isn't any ten-centimeter gap. How come you have so much
trouble seeing Smoes? The hackie here looks like a Smoe, and you
have trouble seeing him too. Do you also have trouble about not
hearing things?"

"No. I hear too many things that aren't there," Colonel Crazelton
complained. "I hear a stomping now, and a lowing, but it isn't the
same as proper cattle lowing. It's possible that such sounds on
Earth would be unnoticed amid the regular background noise, but
here the background is slighter. And I hear, oh, no, that's all imaginary. Epikt, give me everything that you have on the property of
invisibility of unbaked clay; and on bison; and on Smoe physiog-

nomy; and on apperceptions that bypass memory and sense reception; and on anything else that you think might be germane. We should have stopped off and loaded up a few more of your brains before leaving Earth."

"No, Colonel Crazelton, I have plenty brains along," said Epikt the dapper machine. "This isn't a very cerebral mission. Unbaked clay often hides from the eye by merging into the background. That's all that anybody knows about the property of invisibility of unbaked clay. But it should come through clear to the other senses; you should be able to hear it and smell it."

"Am I unbaked clay?" the maxi-taxi driver asked. Yeah, he had a big, hooked, Smoe nose on him, and very low resolution.

"You're half-baked, Hackie," Donners said. "Let's go have a drink. I think there's an old friend of mine motioning to me over there." And Donners and the maxi-taxi driver ambled off.

And Kilroy was seen crossing the landscape, a tall, rangy wraith with a far-off look in his eyes.

"He is everywhere," Crazelton said. "Is he generic, do you suppose? And where would Donners and the maxi-taxi driver go to get a drink here on an uninhabited world, Epikt? Hear it and smell it, you ask? Ah, that's what I'm doing: but I don't trust my ears and nose much more than I do my eyes. Epikt, my basic training was in zoology. And, well, I took my very basic training in a zoo. I know what that has to be: that stamping, that lowing (not a conventional cattle lowing), dammit, the booming, the belching, the rattling of hooves (they'd rattle even on velvet), the smell of them, and the plain *multitudinousness* of them! Epikt, there has to be a test. Are they here on this uninhabited world, or are they not?"

"Sure, they're bound to be here," that machine Epikt said. "How would the clay-faced Smoes live without them? You have to remember, though, that buffalo are low-resolution animals. They are clay-colored. And they are probably made out of unbaked clay. Yes, Colonel, the buffalo is also of the implicit clay. It is nearly everywhere in great numbers, and it is nearly always invisible."

"I don't mean buffalo. I mean particular bison," the puzzled Crazelton said. "It was bison we had in the zoo. I'll never forget them."

"No, you don't mean particular bison," Epikt corrected the colonel. "Bison is a weasel word. Colonel Crazelton, a buffalo just *can't* be particular. He's *the* generalized beast. He's the ancestral clay from which all the other beasts are formed."

"I don't even understand the ancestral clay from which all the people are formed," Crazelton said. "Are the clay people the Jews?"

"Jews? Those Reuben-come-latelies? What, with the toy noses on them? No, Colonel, they're not red-leg enough to be the original clay people. But there *is* a test for your buffalo, whether they're real or not. It's the hokey. That can't be faked. If it is real, then it must have come from real and present animals, however merged with their background they are. Remember the hokey, Colonel. Notice the hokey. Look out for the hokey! Oh, oh, too late. It does come through pretty pungent, doesn't it, Crazelton?"

"It sure does, Epikt. Mighty pungent, mighty pervading. And it shouldn't be all that hard to see. Yeah, I'll be a bit smelly for a while, Epikt."

"I smell something too," Epikt gasped. "Something completely other than all this. I knew those Smoe-faces could make fast cars out of something, but I sure did not know that they could make—whoof! Talk about a pile of junk! But just think of some of the things he could do if you managed him right! Hey, I got to get a closer glom of that guy." And Epikt had dashed off.

"Inexplicable, inexplicable," Colonel Crazelton said. "I have a feeling that things are beginning to come apart."

"Give me the boots," the woman said to Crazelton. "You wouldn't even know how to start to get the buffalo hokey off of them. You have to use powder-weed and feather-weed and snakebite-weed." She dumped Crazelton on his rump and pulled the boots off him. "And flimsy-rock and shoestone-rock and soap-medown-rock."

"What is your name?" Colonel Crazelton asked the woman. There was powder-weed dust in his eyes and he couldn't see her clearly.

"Joanna Sweetstomach," she said. The woman took Crazelton's boots and went off with them. Crazelton wondered only mildly about there being a woman on the uninhabited world. There were other sensations impinging on his senses.

There was another roaring, a booming, a belching, a whining, a rattling, a lowing of uncattle, a humming—the sweetest humming ever. And that humming strengthened and rose into a joyous scream.

"They're all stock cars," Kilroy said to Crazelton. "Special stock. Only the engines and bodies have been modified and jazzed up. Some of those machines ran in the demolition derby on Bernheim's World yesterday, and a couple of our hot-fire boys bought a couple of the wrecks and brought them here to fix up. They don't care a whole lot about derbies or formal races though. They just like to rev up the things and dig out with them and run them over the roughest ground there is."

"Cars, Kilroy? I thought they rode horses," Crazelton said.

"Oh, sure. They like to ride horses too. They put flint-shoes on them to make them spark when they run. But fast cars are the first love of all of us. You got to remember that we had fast cars way back when horses were still rabbit-sized."

"Are *you* one of the red-clay folk, Kilroy?" Colonel Crazelton asked him. Things were jumping their fences and breaking down their gates.

"Partly, partly," Kilroy said. "I go way back. Whatever was first, I've got some of it in me."

In the near distance, they heard the dapper voice of Epikt becoming less dapper.

"Bear grease and beaver brains, how corny can you get?" Epikt was sneering and shouting. "You should be arrested for impersonating a thinking machine. And your name isn't even a categorical descriptive name!"

"Feather-Spring-Go-Fast is my name," they heard something say in the lessening distance. Colonel Crazelton and that tall, rangy wraith with the far-away eyes and the name of Kilroy went into Wolf-Rib's Barrelhouse to have a few cool ones.

And then it was that the tight logic, the orderly rationality of the situation, really began to come to pieces. The Investigation was getting too big for its format.

When does a case have a beginning and middle and end?

When it has only one dimension.

But it was multidimensional inside Wolf-Rib's Barrelhouse. Donners and Procop and the maxi-taxi driver were boozing together with a few boozem buddies, and Crazelton had the term 'Revisional Clay' come to lodge suddenly in his mind.

There was a large Smoe figurine at the end of the bar. Its nose was hooked over the bar and the funny head was rocking and bobbling on its nosey pivot. Crazelton took it by the scalp lock to lift it and examine it. And it was too heavy to lift as casually as that. It was no Smoe figurine; it was a Smoe man, standing and alive, and drinking choc beer. It looked at Crazelton with hard little eyes. It hadn't been hanging with its nose hooked over the edge of the bar. It was simply of short stature, and that's where the nose had come to rest.

A woman was making parfleches out of fine, flexible leather or skin.

"What do you make them out of?" Crazelton asked her. "You haven't any deer on this world, and buffalo hide is too thick and stiff for such work."

"Old-man skin," the woman said. "I use that. It's just right."

"How do you get it?"

"Just take it off them. Those old men sure do holler and carry on though. All I take is the skin."

Another woman was fletching a lance. And a third woman came into Wolf-Rib's place. "Joanna Sweetstomach says that you promised to marry her," this woman told Colonel Crazelton. "Yeah, she says she's going to have you, or else she's going to keep the boots. She sure does like those boots, now that she's got the buffalo hokey off of them."

Ah, it was really going to pieces now.

Colonel Crazelton was suffering impressions of world after world after world of implicit clay that was almost being called into animation. These worlds bucked and buckled like drunken water. They were seas, and Colonel Crazelton was seasick. The worlds were clay-colored oceans, and they heaved with billions upon billions of half-animated Indians. Indians making up the heaving world-waves, with their buffalo and their small game! What else was roiling and boiling in that clay-sea? There were the fast and snazzy cars waiting for the archangel of cars to come and evoke them into metallic animation. There were the later horses, clay-maned, snorting out of that underfootness. There was the crowding, churning multitudinousness of it all.

"I'm breaking apart into pieces," Colonel Crazelton gasped. "Reason fails us, and what is left? No world is firm, no foundation is solid. I am falling endlessly into a bottomless pit." Crazelton felt himself mistreated by every implicit Indian everywhere.

"Naw. That's what I thought once," Procop reassured him. "I thought I'd had it till I'd bust. But you can't fall very far here, Colonel. The ground's mighty high all around here. You'll go native like I did; and when you do that, you'll go invisible for a little while. That's what's really known as being the 'Reversional Clay.' And Joanna Sweetstomach wouldn't be too bad to go native with."

"So Indians is the answer," Crazelton said softly and with some awe at the magnitude of the whole affair.

"What was the question?" one of those Smoe-faced Indians asked.

"Indians is the answer," the colonel repeated. "It's Indians who were already on every world before the initial landings were made. On old world it's Indians who were in Africa before the black men came, who were on the Weald before the blue-woad men came there, who were on the Yellow River (man, there's a lot of clay along the Yellow River!) before the yellow men came there. It's Indians who were already in every square rood of every earth from the beginning. We can't take a step anywhere without stepping on an implicit Indian face in the heaving clay, without stepping on a Smoe nose hooking up out of the nervous ground, without treading buffalo hump—oh, this is insanity! Let's away from here, Donners and Epikt, and make our dismal and earth-heaving report."

But Epikt was busy. Epikt was still giving unshirted ned to—to what? To a— "What slap-dash guys ever threw you together anyhow?" that Epikt was carrying on. "Knotted cords to count and calculate with! Porcupine quills for analysis and prediction! And for intelligence—beaver brains! Boy, are you a mess!" To an Indian brain-machine it was that Epikt was shoving scorn and harangue. An intelligent Indian machine! Who would have believed that possible?

"When I consider my own degree of sophistication, and then look at you—" Epikt tried to continue.

"Oh, stuff it, white-eye contraption!" said the Indian brain-machine, who was named Feather-Spring-Go-Fast. There was the smell of scorched clay in the barrelhouse, or at least the smell of exasperation.

"Epikt, is this all scientific?" Colonel Crazelton cried. "Can the very clay of all the worlds be made out of Indians and their animals?"

"Oh, sure, Colonel, why not?" Epikt answered. "They had to make it out of something. It looks like they made it out of the lowest thing they could think of. What's lower than the Indians and their animals and their—ugh—contraptions? Feather-Spring-Go-

Fast, you make me ashamed of being a machine. I bet your brains aren't even dynamically balanced."

"Hey, you ever wrestle an Indian?" a lady said to Crazelton as she came into the place. "It's all right. Joanna Sweetstomach says that she don't want you anyhow."

"No, no, I don't wrestle much any more," Crazelton said with a touch of embarrassment. "Epikt, this is all as amazing as it is taste-less," Crazelton said a very little moment later (there had been a bucking and screaming of fast cars in between, and they were all in Bum-Drum's Bar now). "When the first explorer crossed the first high range, Epikt, and wondered whether anyone could possibly have been there before him—Epikt, those ranges were made out of people and stuff that *had been there long* before him. He wasn't striding over new Earth under new Heaven. He was striding upon the upturned faces of those unevoked ancestors, and those faces had watched the new Heaven since it was really new."

"Something like that, Crazelton," said Epikt, not much willing to be distracted from his own pursuit. "Now then, little clap-trap Feather-Spring-Go-Fast, you don't even have—Hey, what do you think you're doing!"

"I think I can make something out of this," the proprietor Bum-Drum mumbled. Bum-Drum had just removed a piece from Epikt with that deft and wrenching movement as if he were tearing a wing off a chicken. "I'm fixing to invent a clock," Bum-Drum said, "if the people will only decide whether they want it to be forty-four- or forty-five-hour days. And this piece of you sure looks like a piece of a clock, Epikt."

"But that piece is necessary for my mental balance," Epikt protested. "With that piece gone, I'm likely to be a little erratic." Other persons came and pulled other pieces from Epikt, and he did become quite erratic.

"Hey, you ever do any romancing?" a lady said to Crazelton as she came into the place. "It's all right. Joanna Sweetstomach says that she don't want you anyhow."

"No, no, I don't romance much any more," Crazelton said with a touch of embarrassment.

"Epikt," Colonel Crazelton said a little moment later (there had been a jolting and noisy interlude when they all rode on young and half-broken horses, and they were now in the Skinny Wife Bar and Grill). "Epikt, what we see now, even with our new apperception, may be no more than the tip of the iceberg, than the nose of the

Smoe. No, that part's wrong. The nose makes up at least half the Smoe by bulk. But it isn't just the surface, it's the immeasurable depth also. You could dig a well forever and not come to the bottom of Indians."

"Hey, there's even a well of blue-eyed Indians," a fellow named Three Coonskins said. "Not a very big well, but there's a well for every kind of Indians. I bet I can make something out of that piece there." And Three Coonskins pulled an intricate piece off of Epikt.

"Protection, protection!" Epikt howled. "I'll report it to the sector police. You're taking vital pieces off of me!"

"Can the sector boys police every little piece of clay on every world?" Three Coonskins asked. "Here, I'll give you something in place of it." Three Coonskins pulled a piece of clay from his leg, blew on it to animate it, and set it into Epikt in place of the piece that he'd stolen. "Now you're part Indian," Three Coonskins told Epikt. But the new piece made Epikt even more irrational than he had been. He began to boast, and those fellows there will eat boasters alive. After a while they will.

"And now I take something to replace my replacement piece," Three Coonskins said, and he took Epikt's Smoe-form cigar holder. "And now I'll just have your cigars too. They're no good to you without a cigar holder. And I always liked to make a clean sweep."

"Come, Cabbie, come, Donners, come, Epikt," Colonel Crazelton was saying after another while (they had all ridden travois in the interval, and now they were in the Happy Rattle-Snake Bar), "we've solved the question of who was already on every world and continent when the first explorers got there. And we've raised, I'm sure, dozens of other questions. And now I find myself becoming highly nervous. I can take no more of this place. Let's go back to earth immediately."

"Donners and I are going native for a while," the maxi-taxi cabbie said, "like Procop here did. He says it's a lot of fun. Yeah, can't see us very well, can you, Colonel Weak-Eyes? It's fun to merge in with the background, with the ground itself."

"The renewal experience alone is worth it," said the once-more invisible Procop.

"I will settle with these clods before I go, Colonel," Epikt spoke madly. "Feather-Spring-Go-Fast, you're a fink and a fraud! And

that's really all of you? There isn't anything to you except what's
here? But the Main Me is elsewhere, and what you see here is only
one of many extensions of me. The Main Epikt has so many brains
that we dip them out by the bucketful whenever we want to provi-
sion a major mobile extension. But you, there is nothing to you except that silly lump over there."

"Last call, everybody!" Feather-Spring-Go-Fast sang out. "Anybody want any last piece of him?" And the folks there (the action
had now moved to the Wet Dog Tavern) began to pick Epikt clean
of interesting pieces. And he made the mistake of being defiant and
boastful.

"Destroy this mortal coil here before you, and I still exist in a
finer place," Epikt bantered them. Whoof, that mortal coil wasn't
going to last very long, the way they began to cut it up.

"Help, help, murder, murder," the frightened Epikt howled then.
But a big Indian reached into him and took out his howler and
rowler, and thereupon that Epikt extension was muted forever. And
the remnants of him were quickly taken, down to the smallest
piece.

"I am alone and deserted," Colonel Crazelton said after another while. "How ever will I get back to Earth?"

"Oh, I'll take you," a lean Indian said. "I always liked Earth. I
wonder if Prairie Dog's Pancake Palace is still there on Earth, just
over the Osage line from T-Town."

"Yes. I imagine that Prairie Dog's is one of the enduring places.
But that vehicle won't go to Earth, will it?"

"It sure doesn't look like it. It's worn out and the back-end of it is
shot. I made it myself, and I'm not a very good mechanic. I can't
even get insurance on it any more, or I'd heap it. But it's gone to
Earth before, and I bet it'll do it again. Let's have a couple for the
road, and then we'll hit that sky-road."

They had them for the road at Joe Shawnee's Sky-High Club,
and at the Pit Stop, the Boar Coon, the Wooden-Legged Buffalo
Bistro and Brasserie, and at the Stuck Buck Bar. Then they flew to
Earth.

The agreeable Indian left Colonel Crazelton off at the Institute
for Impure Science. Then he went to Prairie Dog's Pancake Palace,
which was just across the Osage line from the Institute.

"Indians, Indians!" Colonel Crazelton cried as he burst into the Institute.

"To the loopholes, everyone!" the great Institute Director Gregory Smirnov ordered. "We'll give those red-spleens a whiff of grapeshot. Aw, wait a minute. Whose side are we on anyhow?"

"The answer is Indians," Colonel Crazelton said. "Indians is what was already there whenever the first discoverers got there."

"Well, of course we were there," Valery said. "Why wouldn't we have been there?"

"You are Indians?" Crazelton asked.

"Isn't everybody?" Glasser inquired.

"Of course we're all Indians at the Institute," Gregory said. "And almost everywhere else. Always, everywhere, under every condition, you should assume that people and things are Indian, unless it is clearly stated that they are something else."

"You didn't think that yellow or black or white guys would carry on like we do, did you?" Aloysius Shiplap asked. "So now you are straight about everything, are you, Crazelton?"

"Not quite, Shiplap, oh, not quite! I've just developed a new phobia. I can't take a step, not a step. Oh, how will I live if I'm afraid to step anywhere?"

"Why, Colonel, I kind of like it," Valery said. "Grind my heels into them! I like it!"

"What is the difficulty, Crazelton?" Director Smirnov asked.

"I like it too," Aloysius gloated. "That's why I go walking so much. That's why I wear calks on my shoes."

"Just what is this phobia, Crazelton?" Smirnov asked again.

"Oh, the faces, the faces! It's the billions of faces, Smirnov, staring up at me from the implicit clay, through the pavements, through the structures, through the sidewalks. Wherever I step I'm stepping on those waiting faces. Oh, I can't do it. I can't step anywhere. What will I do? I would be a murderer and oppressor in my feet and legs!"

"I say that those who won't have the fun don't deserve it," Valery said sharply.

Aloysius Shiplap was whistling the old drag tune "Cut off my legs and call me shorty."

And down in the bowels of the Institute Building, the Main Epikt was building a new mobile extension with spikes on its boots. You wouldn't believe the grin on the Main Epikt, or the spikes that he was putting on those boots!

SHE WAITS FOR ALL MEN BORN

James Tiptree, Jr.

> *Rilke says that one has "one's death within one, as a fruit its kernel."*
>
> *We are possibly the only species in the world who can look into a mirror or a reflecting pool and see the grinning skull that waits behind the flesh. We may be the only species that must live out each day with the conscious knowledge that we have also spent that day in dying. It may be that we alone among Earth's creatures can extrapolate youth into naked bone and offal. Certainly we alone look up at the stars at night and say "If I die before I wake."*
>
> *If so, then the "dumb brutes" of the fields and forests, living in an eternal present, share in a kind of immortality—perhaps the only kind possible—from which man is forever excluded. If so, if man alone lives in anticipation and retrospect, past and future, then we are doubly alone on this lonely planet.*

Except for death itself, which is a constant companion to us, closer than a shadow, more intimate than flesh. We can understand why Rilke thought that inside a pregnant woman there are always growing "two fruits: a child and a death."

This circular dance with death provides the impetus for all that we do, all that we create, from fugues to fusion. We build to escape death, and we do not succeed, and the cultures and things we create remain behind when we are gone, like the sturdy shell of a dead snail. No one has ever succeeded in escaping death, not in countless millennia of human history, but we keep trying anyway. The evidence is overwhelming that we will not succeed—but that means nothing compared to the bone-deep awareness of the imminence of death that keeps whispering hurry, hurry.

All systems of control are built upon these two things: the awareness of death, and the false intuition that we can escape it. No other despotism is so complete and inescapable, no tyranny as awful. Technology may eventually offer us one much-touted way out of the trap—the possibility of corporeal immortality. But "immortality" may be a misnomer. Such "immortality" would probably be only a postponement of death; perhaps it would last for thousands of years, perhaps for hundreds of thousands or even millions, but at least the patiently waiting death will probably catch up with even the most changed and ingeniously guarded of men.

Here, Nebula and Hugo winner James Tiptree, Jr.—considered by many to be one of the two or three best short story writers in the genre—shows us a totally different possibility, and a chilling new kind of victory over death.

EDITORS' NOTE: THIS IS AN ORIGINAL STORY, PUBLISHED HERE FOR THE FIRST TIME.

> Pale, beyond porch and portal,
> Crowned with calm leaves she stands
> Who gathers all things mortal
> With pale, immortal hands.

> Swinburne

IN the wastes of nonbeing it is born, flickers out, is born again and holds together, swells and spreads. In lifelessness it lives, against the gray tide of entropy it strives, improbably persists, gath-

*ering itself into ever richer complexities until it grows as a swelling
wave. As a wave grows it grows indeed, for while its crest surges
triumphant in the sunlight its every particle is down-falling forever
into dark, is blown away into nothing in the moment of its leap. It
triumphs perishing, for it was not born alone. Following it into
being came its dark twin, its Adversary, the shadow which
ceaselessly devours it from within. Pitilessly pursued, attacked in
every vital, the living wave foams upward, its billion momentary
crests blooming into the light above the pain and death that claims
them. Over uncounted aeons the mortal substance strives, out-
reaches. Death-driven, it flees ever more swiftly before its Enemy
until it runs, leaps, soars into flashing flight. But it cannot outrace
the fire in its flesh, for the limbs that bear it are Death, and Death
is the wing it flies on. In the agony of its myriad members, victori-
ous and dying, Life drives upon the indifferent air . . .*

The burrow is dark. Pelicosaurus squats over her half-
grown pups, her dim node of awareness holding only the sensation
of their muzzles sucking the glandular skin of her belly among her
not-quite hair. From outside comes a thunderous eructation,
splashing. The burrow quakes. Pelicosaurus crouches, rigid; the
huddled pups freeze. All but one—a large female pup has squirmed
free, is nosing nervously toward the recesses of the burrow. She
moves in a half-crawl, her body slung from the weak reptilian
shoulder girdle.

More crashes outside. Earth showers down within the damp nest.
The mother only crouches tighter, locked in reflexive stasis. The
forgotten pup is now crawling away up a tunnel.

As she vanishes, the giant hadrosaur in the stream outside de-
cides to clamber out. Twenty tons of reptile hit the soft bank.
Earth, rocks and roots slam together, crushing Pelicosaurus and her
pups and all other bank-dwellers into an earthy gel, a trough of destruction behind the departing one. Leather wings clap; pterosaurs
are gathering to stab in the wreckage.

Farther up the bank beside a gymnosperm root, the lone pup
wriggles free. She cowers, hearing the hoarse grunts of the scavengers. Then an obscure tropism rises in her, an undefined urge toward space, toward up. Awkwardly she grips the bole of the gymnosperm with her forelimbs. A grub moves on the bark.
Automatically she seizes and eats it, her eyes blinking as she strives

to focus beyond. Presently she begins to clamber higher, carrying, in the intricacy of her genes, the tiny anomaly which has saved her. In the egg from which she grew a molecule has imperceptibly shifted structure. From its aberrant program has unfolded a minute relaxation of the species-wide command to freeze, a small tendency to action under stress. The pup that is no longer wholly Pelicosaur feels her ill-adapted hindlimb slip upon the branch, scrabbles for purchase, falls, and crawls weakly from the graveyard of her kind.

. . . So the wave of Life mounts under the lash of Death, grows, gathers force in unbounded diversity. Ever-perishing, ever-resurgent, it foams to higher, more complex victories upon the avalanche of its corpses. As a wave swells, it surges, swarming, striving ever more strongly, achieving ever more intricate strategies of evasion, flinging itself in wilder trajectories to escape its pain. But it bears its Enemy within it, for Death is the power of its uprush. Dying in every member, yet every moment renewed, the multiple-hearted wave of Life crests into strangeness . . .

Yelling, the hairless creature runs swiftly, knuckles to earth, and screams again as a rock strikes him. He swerves and scuttles, limping now; he is unable to avoid the hail of missiles flung by those stronger, more freely jointed arms. His head is struck. He goes down. The bipeds close around him. Shouting in still wordless joy they fall upon their brother with weak jaws and sharpened stones.

. . . The living, dying tumult mounts, fountains into culminate light. Its billion tormented fragments take on intenser being; it leaps as a great beast above the ravenings of its Adversary. But it cannot shake free, for the force of its life is Death, and its strength is as the strength of the deaths that consume it, its every particle is propelled by the potency of the dark Assailant. In the measure of its dying, dying Life towers, triumphs, and rolls resistless across the planet that bore it . . .

. . .

Two horsemen move slowly across the plain under the cold autumn rain. The first rider is a young boy on a spotted pony; he is leading a black-eared roan on which his father is riding slumped, breathing open-mouthed above the rifle-ball in his chest. The man's hand holds a bow, but there are no arrows; the Kiowas' stores and supplies were lost at Palo Duro Canyon and the last arrows were fired in the slaughter at the Staked Plains three days back, where his wife and oldest son were killed.

As they pass a copse of willows the rain eases for a moment. Now they can see the white man's buildings ahead: Fort Sill with its gray stone corral. Into that corral their friends and relatives have vanished, family by family, surrendering to their merciless enemy. The boy halts his pony. He can see them, a column of soldiers riding out of the fort. Beside him his father makes a sound, tries to raise his bow. The boy licks his lips; he has not eaten for three days. Slowly he urges his pony forward again.

As they ride on, faint sounds of firing come to them on the wet wind, from a field west of the fort. The white men are shooting the Kiowas' horses, destroying the life of their life. For the Kiowas, this is the end. They were among the finest horsemen the world has ever known, and this was their sacred occupation. Three centuries before, they had come down out of the dark mountains, had acquired horses and a god and burst out in glory to rule a thousand miles of range. But they never understood the grim, unrelenting advance of the U.S. Cavalry. Now they are finished. (1)

The Kiowas have been toughened by natural hardship, by millennia of death in the wilderness. But their death-strength is not enough. The pale soldiers before them are the survivors of more deadly centuries in the cauldrons of Europe, they drive upon the Indians with the might derived from uncountable generations of close-quarter murder in battle, deaths under merciless tyrannies, by famines and plagues. As it has happened before and before and before, the gray-faced children of the greater death roll forward, conquer and spread out across the land.

   . . . So the great Beast storms among the flames that devour it, the myriad lives of its being a crucible of always fiercer deaths and more ascendant life. And now its agonized onrush changes; what had been flight becomes battle. The Beast turns on the Enemy that savages it and strives to cast Death from its heart.

*Desperately it struggles, streaming from the wounds that are its life
it fights to save some fragment while Death slays whole members.
For Death is the twin of its essence, growing as Life grows, and the
fury of its attack mounts with the power that attacks it. Locked into
intimate battle, the Beast and its Enemy are now nearing a consum-
mating phase of pain. The struggle rages, breaches the norms of
matter. Time accelerates . . .*

As night comes over the Mediterranean the battered
freighter limps warily past the enemy ears on Cyprus. Rain and
darkness hide it; it creeps with all lights extinguished, every human
sound quenched. Only the throbbing of its engines and the
thrashing of its rusty screw remain to betray it to the blockaders. In
its body is the precious cargo, the huddled silent sparks of life. The
children. The living ones, the handfuls saved from the six million
corpses of the death camps, saved from the twenty million killed by
the Reich. In darkness and desperation it crawls on, leaking, the
crew not daring to work the creaking pumps. Hidden by the night
it steams mile by daring mile through the gauntlet of the blockade,
carrying the children to Palestine.

While on the other side of the world, in the morning of that same
night, a single bomber leaves its escort and bores steadily westward
through the high cold air. The *Enola Gay* is on course to
Hiroshima.

*. . . Pain-driven, death-sinewed, the convulsed Beast strives
against its Enemy. In ever-new torment it grows, rears itself to new
brilliancy, achieves ever-greater victories over Death, and is in turn
more fearfully attacked. The struggle flames unseen across the
planet, intensifying until it breaks from the bounds of earth and
flings portions of itself to space. But the Beast cannot escape, for it
carries Death with it and fuels Death with its fire. The battle
heightens, fills earth, sea and air. Then in supreme agony it fountains into a crest of living fire that is a darkness upon the
world . . .*

"Doctor, that was beautiful." The senior surgical nurse's
whisper barely carries beyond her mask.

The surgeon's eyes are on the mirror where the hands of the suturist can be seen delicately manipulating the clamped-back layers. *Lub-dub, lub-dub;* the surgeon's eyes go briefly to the biofeedback display, check the plasma exchange levels, note the intent faces of the anesthesiology team under their headsets, go back vigilantly to the mirror. Vigilant—but it is over, really. A success, a massive success. The child's organs will function perfectly now, the dying one will live. Another impossibility achieved.

The senior nurse sighs again appreciatively, brushing away a thought that comes. The thought of the millions of children elsewhere now dying of famine and disease. Healthy children too, not birth-doomed like this one but perfectly functional; inexorably dying in their millions from lack of food and care. Don't think of it. Here we save lives. We do our utmost.

The operating room is sealed against the sounds of the city outside, which yet comes through as a faint, all-pervading drone. Absently, the nurse notices a new sound in the drone: an odd high warbling. Then she hears the interns behind her stirring. Someone whispers urgently. The surgeon's eyes do not waver, but his face above the mask turns rigid. She must protect him from distraction. Careful that her clothing does not rustle, she wheels on the offenders. There is a far burst of voices from the corridor.

"Be quiet!" She hisses with voiceless intensity, raking the interns with her gray gaze. As she does so, she recalls what that continuous warbling tone is. Air-attack warning. The twenty-minute alert, meaning that missiles are supposed to be on their way around the world from the alien land. But this cannot be serious. It must be some drill—very laudable, no doubt, but not to be allowed to disturb the operating room. The drill can be held another time; it will take more than twenty minutes to finish here.

"Quiet," she breathes again sternly. The interns are still. Satisfied, she turns back, holding herself proudly, ignoring fatigue, ignoring the shrill faint whining, ignoring at the end even the terrible flash that penetrates the seams of the ceiling far above.

—And the riven Beast crashes, bursts together with its Enemy into a billion boiling, dwindling fragments that form and re-form under the fires of a billion radiant deaths. Yet it is still one, still joined in torment and unending vitality. With its inmost plasm laid bare to the lethal energies Life struggles more intensely still,

more fiercely attacks the Death that quenches its reborn momentary lives. The battle grows to total fury, until it invades the very substrata of being. A supreme paroxysm is reached; in ultimate agony the ultimate response is found. The Beast penetrates at last into its Adversary's essence and takes it to itself. In final transcendence. Life swallows Death, and forges the heart of its ancient Enemy to its own . . .

The infant between the dead thighs of its mother is very pale. Dismayed, the Healer frees it from the birthslime, holds it up. It is a female, and perfectly formed, he sees, despite the whiteness of its skin. It takes breath with a tiny choke, does not cry. He hands it to the midwife, who is covering the mother's corpse. Perhaps the pallor is natural, he thinks; all his tribe of Whites have heavy pale skins, though none so white as this.

"A beautiful baby girl," the midwife says, swabbing it. "Open your eyes, baby."

The baby squirms gently but its eyes remain closed. The Healer turns back one delicate eyelid. Beneath is a large, fully-formed eye. But the iris is snow-white around the black pupil. He passes his hand over it; the eye does not respond to light. Feeling an odd disquiet, he examines the other. It is the same.

"Blind."

"Oh, no. Such a sweet baby."

The Healer broods. The Whites are a civilized tribe, for all that they have lived near two great craters before they came here to the sea. He knows that his people's albinism is all too frequently coupled with optical defect. But the child seems healthy.

"I'll take her," says Marn, the midwife. "I still have milk, look."

They watch as the baby girl nuzzles Marn's breast and happily, normally, finds her food.

Weeks pass into months. The baby grows, smiles early, though her eyes remain closed. She is a peaceful baby; she babbles, chortles, produces a sound that is surely "Marn, Marn." Marn loves her fiercely and guiltily; her own children are all boys. She calls the pale baby "Snow."

When Snow begins to creep Marn watches anxiously, but the blind child moves with quiet skill, seeming to sense where things are. A happy child, she sings small songs to herself and soon pulls herself upright by Marn's leather trousers. She begins to totter alone and Marn's heart fears again. But Snow is cautious and adroit, she strikes few obstacles. It is hard to believe that she is blind. She laughs often, acquires only a few small bumps and abrasions which heal with amazing speed.

Though small and slight, she is an amazingly healthy baby, welcoming new experience, new smells, sounds, tastes, touches, new words. She speaks in an unchildishly gentle voice. Her dark world does not seem to trouble her. Nor does she show the stigmata of blindness; her face is very mobile, and when she smiles, the long white lashes tremble on her cheeks as if she is holding them closed in fun.

The Healer examines her yearly, finding himself ever more reluctant to confront that blank silver gaze. He knows he will have to decide if she should be allowed to breed, and he is dismayed to find her otherwise so thriving. It will be difficult. But in her third year the decision is taken from him. He feels very unwell at the time of her examination and shortly realizes that he has contracted the new wasting sickness which has been beyond his power to cure.

The daily life of the Whites goes on. They are a well-fed, Ingles-speaking, littoral people. Their year revolves around the massive catches of fish coming up from the sea-arm to spawn. Most of the fish are still recognizable as forms of trout and salmon. But each year the Whites check the first runs with their precious artifact, an ancient Geiger counter which is carefully recharged from their water-driven generator.

When the warm days come Snow goes with Marn and her sons to the beach where the first-caught will be ritually tested. The nets are downstream from the village, set in the canyon's mouth. The beaches open out to the sea-arm, surrounded by tall ice-capped crags. Fires burn merrily on the sands, there is music and children are playing while the adults watch the fishermen haul in the leaping, glittering nets. Snow runs and laughs, paddling in the icy stream edge.

"Fliers up there," the Netmaster says to Marn. She looks up at the cliffs where he points, searching for a flitting red shape. The Fliers have been getting bolder, perhaps from hunger. During the last winter they have sneaked into an outlying hut and stolen a child. No one knows exactly what they are. Some say they are big monkeys, some believe they are degenerated men. They are man-shaped, small but strong, with loose angry-looking folds of skin between their limbs on which they can make short glides. They utter cries which are not speech, and they are always hungry. At fish-drying times the Whites keep guards patrolling the fires day and night.

Suddenly there is shouting from the canyon.

"Fliers! They're heading to the town!"

Fishermen paddle swiftly back to shore, and a party of men go pounding upstream toward the village. But no sooner have they gone than a ring of reddish heads pops into sight on the near cliffs, and more Fliers are suddenly diving on the shore.

Marn snatches up a brand from a fire and runs to the attack, shouting at the children to stay back. Under the women's onslaught the Fliers scramble away. But they are desperate, returning again and again until many are killed. As the last attackers scramble away up the rocks Marn realizes that the blind baby is not among the other children by the fires.

"Snow! Snow, where are you?"

Have the Fliers snatched her? Marn runs frantically along the beach, searching behind boulders, crying Snow's name. Beyond a rocky outcrop she sees a Flier's crumpled legs and runs to look.

Two Fliers lie there unmoving. And just beyond them is what she feared to find—a silver-pale small body in a spread of blood.

"Snow, my baby, oh, no—"

She runs, bends over Snow. One of the little girl's arms is hideously mangled, bitten nearly off. A Flier must have started to eat her before another attacked him. Marn crouches above the body, refusing to know that the child must be dead. She makes herself look at the horrible wound, suddenly stares closer. She is seeing something that makes her distraught eyes widen more wildly. A new scream begins to rise in her throat. Her gaze turns from the wound to the white, still face.

Her last sight is of the baby's long pale lashes lifting, opening to reveal the shining silver eyes.

Marn's oldest son finds them so; the two dead Fliers, the dead woman and the miraculously living, scarless child. It is generally agreed that Marn has perished saving Snow. The child cannot explain.

From that time little Snow the twice-orphaned is cared for among the children of the Netmaster.

She grows, though very slowly, into a graceful, beloved little girl. Despite her blindness she makes herself skilled and useful at many tasks; she is clever and patient with the endless work of mending nets and fish-drying and pressing oil. She can even pick berries, her small quick hands running through the thickets almost as well as eyes. She patrols Marn's old gathering paths, bringing back roots, mushrooms, bird's eggs and the choicest camass bulbs.

The new Healer watches her troubledly, knowing he will have to make the decision his predecessor dreaded. How serious is her defect? The old Healer had thought that she must be interdicted, not allowed to breed lest the blindness spread. But he is troubled, looking at the bright, healthy child. There has been so much sickness in the tribe, this wasting which he cannot combat. Babies do not thrive. How can he interdict this little potential breeder, who is so active and vigorous? And yet—and yet the blindness must be heritable. And the child is not growing normally; year by year she does not mature. He becomes almost reassured, seeing that Snow is still a child while the Netmaker's baby son is attaining manhood and his own canoe. Perhaps she will never develop at all, he thinks. Perhaps there will be no need to decide.

But slowly, imperceptibly Snow's little body lengthens and rounds out, until when the ice melts one year he sees that small breasts have budded on her narrow ribs. The day before she had been still a child; today she is unmistakably a baby woman. The Healer sighs, studying her tender, animated face. It is hard to see her as defective; the lightly closed eyes seem so normal. But two of the dead-born infants have been very pale and white-eyed. Is this a lethal mutation? His problem is upon him. He cannot resolve it; he determines to call a council of the tribe.

But his plan is never to be put to action. Someone else has been studying Snow too. It is the Weatherwoman's youngest son, who follows her to the fern-root grove.

"This is the kind you eat," Snow tells him, holding up the yellow fiddle-heads. He stares down at her delicious little body. Impossible to remember or care that she is thrice his age.

"I want—I want to talk to you, Snow."

"Umm?" She smiles up at his voice. His heart pounds.

"Snow . . ."

"What, Byorg?" Listening so intently, the silvery lashes quivering as if they will lift and open to him. Yet they do not, and pity for her blindness chokes him. He touches her arm, she comes against him naturally. She is smiling, her breathing quickened. He holds her, thinking how she must feel his touch in her dark world, her help-lessness. He must be gentle.

"Byorg?" she breathes. "Oh, Byorg—"

Trying to restrain himself he holds her more tightly to him, touching her, feeling her trembling. He is trembling too, caressing her beneath her light tunic, feeling her yielding, half trying to pull away, her breath hot on his neck.

"Oh, Snow—" Above the pounding of his blood he is vaguely conscious of a sound overhead, but he can think only of the body in his arms.

A harsh yowl breaks out behind him.

"Fliers!"

He whirls around too late—the red flapping figure has launched something at him, a spear—and he is staggering, grasping a bony shaft sunk in his own neck.

"Run, Snow!" he tries to shout. But she is there still, above him, trying to hold him as he falls. More Fliers pound past. As the world dims, he sees in last wonderment her huge eyes opening wide and white.

Silence.

Snow raises herself slowly, still open-eyed. She lets the dead boy's head down to the moss. Three dead Fliers sprawl around them. She listens, hears faintly the sound of screaming from the vil-lage. It is a major attack, she realizes. And Fliers have never used weapons before. Shivering, she strokes Byorg's hair. Her face is crumpled in grief but the eyes remain open, silver reflectors focused at infinity.

"No," she says brokenly. "No!" She jumps up, begins running to-ward the village, stumbling as she races open-eyed, as a blind per-son runs. Three Fliers swoop behind her. She screams and turns to face them. They drop in red, ragged heaps and she runs on, hearing the clamor of battle at the village walls.

The frantic villagers do not see her coming, they are struggling in a horde of Fliers who have infiltrated the side gate and broken loose among the huts. At the main gate the torches have started thatch fires; Fliers and Whites alike have fallen back. Suddenly there is redoubled shouting from the huts. Six Fliers are seen clum-sily hopping and gliding from roof to roof. They carry stolen in-fants.

Men and women clamber fiercely after them, shouting impreca-tions. A Flier pauses to bite savagely into his victim's neck, leaps onward. The evil band outrace their pursuers and launch themselves onto the outer wall.

"Stop them!" a woman shrieks, but there is no one there.

But as the Fliers poise to leap, something does halt them. Instead of sailing they are tumbling limply with their captives, falling on the ground below the walls. And other Fliers have stopped yowling and striking, they are falling too.

The villagers pause uncertainly and become aware of a stillness spreading from a point beside the gates.

Then they see her, the girl Snow, in the blue evening light. A slender white shape with her back to them, surrounded by a red ruin of dead Fliers. She is leaning bent over, dragged down by a shaft sticking in her side. Blood is flooding down her thighs.

Painfully she tries to turn toward them. They see her pull feebly at the spear in her belly. As they watch aghast she pulls the weapon out and drops it. And still stands upright, blood pouring down.

The Healer is nearest. He knows it is too late, but he runs toward her across the rank bodies of the Fliers on the ground. In the dimness he can see a shining loop of intestine torn and hanging from her mortal wound. He slows, staring. Then he sees the blood-flow staunch and cease. She is dead—but she stands there still.

"Snow—"

She lifts her head blindly, smiles with a strange, timid composure.

"You're hurt," he says stupidly, puzzled because the gaping flesh of her wound seems somehow radiant in the fading light. Is it—moving? He stops, staring fearfully, not daring to go closer. As he stares, the rent in which he has seen viscera seems to be filming over, is drawing itself closed. The white body before him is blood-stained but becoming whole before his unbelieving gaze. His eyes start from their sockets, he trembles violently. She smiles more warmly and stands straighter, pushing back her hair.

Behind them a last Flier yowls as it is run down.

Has he had an hallucination? Surely so, he tells himself. He must say nothing.

But as he thinks this he hears an indrawn gasp behind him. Another, others have seen this too. Someone mutters sibilantly. He senses panic.

Those Fliers, he thinks confusedly, how did they die? They show

no wounds. What killed them? When they came near her, did she—
what did she—

A word is being hissed behind him now, a word the Whites have
not heard for two hundred years. The muttered hissing is rising.
And then it is broken with wails. Mothers have found that the
saved children are lying too still among the Fliers who had cap-
tured them, are in fact not saved but dead.

"Witch! Witch! Witch!"

The crowd has become a menacing ring behind him, they are
closing warily but with growing rage upon the white, still girl. Her
blind face turns questioningly, still half smiling, not understanding
what threatens. A stone whizzes past her, another strikes her
shoulder.

"Witch! Killer witch!"

The Healer turns on them, holding up his arms.

"No! Don't! She's not—" But his voice is lost in the shouting. His
voice will not obey him, he too is terrified. More stones fly by from
the shadows. Behind him the girl Snow cries out in pain. Women
trample forward, shoving him aside. A man jumps past him with
uplifted spear.

"No!" the Healer shouts.

In full leap the man is suddenly slumping, is falling bonelessly
upon the dead Fliers. And women beyond him are falling too.
Screams mingle with the shouts. Hardly knowing what he does, the
Healer bends to the downed man, encounters lifelessness. No
breath, no wound; only death. And the woman beside him the same,
and the next, and all around—

The Healer becomes aware of unnatural quiet spreading through
the twilight. He lifts his head. All about him the people of his village have fallen like scythed grain. Not one is standing. As he
stares, a small boy runs from behind a hut—and is instantly struck
down. Unable to grasp the enormity, the Healer sees his whole village lying dead.

Behind him where the girl Snow stands alone there is silence too,
terror-filled. He knows she has not fallen; it is she who has done
this thing. The Healer is a deeply brave man. Slowly he forces himself to turn and look.

She is there upright among the dead, a slight, childish form
turned away from him, one hand pitifully clutching her shoulder.
Her face in profile is contorted, whether from pain or anger he cannot tell. *Her eyes are open.* He sees one huge silver orb glinting

wide, roving the silent village. As he stares, her head turns slowly around to where he stands. Her gaze reaches him.

He falls.

When the dawn fills the valley with gray light, a small, pale figure comes quietly from the huts. She is alone. In all the valley no breath sighs, no live thing stirs. The dawn gleams on her open silver eyes.

Moving composedly she fills her canteen from the well and places food in her simple backpack. Then she gazes for a last time on the tumbled bodies of her people, reaches out her hand and draws back again, her face without expression, her eyes blank and wide. She hoists her pack to her shoulders. Walking lightly, resiliently—for she is unwounded—she sets out on the path up the valley, toward where she knows another village lies.

The morning brightens around her. Her slight figure is tender with the promise of love, her face lifted to the morning breeze is sweet with life. In her heart is loneliness; she is of mankind and she goes in search of human companionship.

Her first journey will not be long. But it will be soon resumed, and resumed again, and again resumed and again, for she carries wasting in her aura, and Death in her open eyes. She will find and lose, and seek and find and lose again, and again seek. But she has time. She has all the time of forever, time to search the whole world over and over again. She is immortal.

Of her own kind she will discover none. Whether any like her have been born elsewhere she will never know. None but she have survived.

Where she goes Death goes too, inexorably. She will wander forever, until she is the last human, is indeed Humanity itself. In her flesh the eternal promise, in her gaze the eternal doom, she will absorb all. In the end she will wander and wait alone through the slow centuries for whatever may come from the skies.

. . . And thus the Beast and its Death are at last at one, as when the fires of a world conflagration die away to leave at their heart one imperishable crystal shape. Forged of life in death, the final figure of Humanity waits in perpetual stasis upon the spent, uncaring earth. Until, after unimaginable eons, strangers driven by their own agonies come from the stars to provide her unknown end. Perhaps she will call to them.

THE DAY OF THE BIG TEST

Felix C. Gotschalk

Although much of science fiction is concerned with creating far-future scenarios, even the wildest, galaxy-shaking space operas may actually be too conservative, may suffer from what Arthur C. Clarke has called "a failure of nerve" in prediction. We all wear the blinders of the present. History is littered with "what-might-have-beens." With the ease of hindsight we can gleefully catch our distinguished predecessors making fools of themselves: In 1899 the director of the U.S. Patent Office declared that "everything that can be invented has been invented." When the first steamships appeared, Professor Dionysius Lardner stated: "Men might as well expect to walk on the moon as cross the Atlantic in one of those steamships." It's but a short skip to the 'present' of 1956, a year before Sputnik 1, when Dr. Richard van der Riet Woolley said that "space travel is utter bilge."

The real world of the future will probably be neither the dystopia some fear or the utopia others dream of, but an amalgamation of both. Like the present it will probably seem to be both the best and worst of times, at least to those living in it. Like the present, its inhabitants may often find it hard to decide if it is a wonderful dream or a horrible nightmare—or both.

Here Felix C. Gotschalk gives us what seems to be a wildly improbable world, a world long ages in the future, almost unattainably distant. If anyone would care to bet on that, he might be well-advised to examine some relevant evidence—Kitty Hawk to Cape Kennedy in seventy years—before putting his money down. He might lose both his sanity and his shirt.

Most science-fiction futures are already yesterday.

Gotschalk's may be tomorrow.

EDITORS' NOTE: THIS IS AN ORIGINAL STORY, PUBLISHED HERE FOR THE FIRST TIME.

MY big fat mother-surrogate seemed worried about my appointment at the Princeton Educational Test Service Bureau, but I wasn't worried at all. I thought, what the hell, the Genetics Board had programmed me, the obstets, gynecs, and pediats all had their shot at me—and now that I was turning seven calendrical tiers in age, it was time for the good old ETS psychognomes to do their testing. I felt sharp as a razor, raring to go, but it wasn't time to leave yet, so I scudded over to the visoport and looked out over the Newark vista. It is a pretty view from our tower: lots of basic green turf, opaque domes and rhomboid towers, neat red leviton trenchways, and pearly air-tunnels. Beneath the turf are three layers of service decks for the city's energy pool, and beneath that, the mantle of plutonium extract, a huge grid, in constant and marvelous radioactive decay. Beneath the grid are the strata of previous ages: layers of space stations, ICBM's, 797's and huge varieties of aircraft, monorails, trains, autos, velocipedes, housing cubules, plasticrete freeways, cracking towers, entire factories, and high-rise apartments. The earthquake on the continental shelf created several of these layers. Deeper still are asphalt and concrete streets, utility poles and transmission wires, and even narrow cobblestone lanes and street lamps with kerosene wicks. Below that level, we're really not sure, because everything is homogenized and pyrolated and hot.

My short evolutionary reverie gets popped by Debbie asking me WHAT ARE YOU GAPING AT, YOU DUMMY, and then she laughs when I jump. Debbie is my sibling, she is ten tiers old, and she bitches a lot. I called her a split-tail strumpet and zapped across the room to my cubicle. I'm just starting a checker game with my pet (a really keen Afghan hound) when Mommy comes to tell me it's time to go.

My lovely fat materno-surrogate notches me in the airsled and double-checks the impact-neutralizer. She still looks a little sad and worried, but she gives me a big wet kiss, and irises the port to the outside. My sled lifts away from the tower and we're off. The asepsis satellites have drawn up all the smog and it is a fine bright day. I love low-altitude, high-speed sled rides. The topography flows beneath at about 500 mph, the gravity and centrifugal pulls are minimal, the visual perspective is grand, and the amber fluid in my semicircular canals barely even ripples. The total perceptual experience is exhilarating. I'm not old enough to fly visual, the flight plan to Princeton is all coded in, and I can already see the spidery geodesics and monoliths of Princeton in the distance. I'm having a snack of something new (pressurized pretzels shaped like supercubes) as my sled sidles up to a huge tower and clamps on. Sleds and flits and aviettes are all over the sides of the tower, like bees on a honeycomb. I sit still as a mouse as my impact pod gets tractor-beamed into a receptacle, and then I'm in a keen office, with springy warm carpets, crushed velvet drapes, and a ceiling of yellow fur. My pod de-fluxes and I walk out on to the carpet. I think it would be fun to walk on a carpet made of tits. Or better still to crawl across them.

This must be the psygnonomist coming now. Funny how people give off instant signals, I'm not sure I'm going to dig this guy, he looks vaguely supercilious, and I can't read his body language resolvedly.

"I'm Dr. LeGrand," he says, "and you must be Bradley IX from Newark." I'm something of a smart-ass, so I'm tempted to say something like NO, I'M A HOLOGRAPHIC ROBOT LOOKING FOR MY IONIZER, but I don't. I smile, and give off routine deference cues, and a spatter of ego-spunk. Immediately I wonder if he can read my subvocals, so I probe him, and am surprised at the lack of response. IF YOU CAN'T

SUBVOKE, HOW THE HELL DID YOU GET ASSIGNED TO PSYGNONOMY? I beam in, and it apparently doesn't register.

"Well, Bradley, how are you feeling today?" he asks, and his inflective nuances seem to say I DON'T GIVE A SHIT HOW YOU FEEL, JUST SO YOU DEFER TO ME. I am very sensitive to vocal timbre and expressive nuance.

"I'm a little scared, Doctor," I say, though I'm really not—is a dog afraid of a bone? The doctor smiles his bland, patented smile, that subtle blend of smugness and condescension. Wow, what spurious credibility his title confers on him! The witch doctor liveth still, even in our supra-advanced society.

"Tell me a little about yourself," he says, as if his overt interest in me constituted some high and explicit compliment. I WAS ONE OF EIGHT BOYS, I subvoke, AND MY PAW BROUGHT US WEST FROM KAINTUCK IN '59, and the subvocals still are not being picked up by him. So I rare back and luxuriate and beam in KISS MY ASS, YOU CHARLATAN. Wow, that ought to get him, that vector had an edge on it, and I threw in a little body English too. But it didn't seem to have any interactional effect. He could be faking or putting me on, and maybe he was clever and predatory, I couldn't figure him out. Remarkable too how my long silence didn't seem to bother him. If he acknowledged my silence, it would underscore his fleeting fall from superordinacy. And he doesn't even look up at me, just begins to fill in little cross-hatched slots with checkmarks. I lean forward, rather intrusive, into his Lewinian lifespace.

"My history is on the forms and cubes," I reply. "Beyond anecdotal samples of my tastes and activities, I have no basis for reply." The response seemed to ruffle him a shade. I seek out eye contact with him, and try to lock in, but his attention span is too short. YOU MEDICO-PSYCHOGNOMIC CREEP, I vector in, YOU'RE MISSING THE BALL GAME. HERE I AM OVER HERE—IN THE FLESH—LITTLE BRADLEY-BOO IX—

"I see you had a touch of epididymitus last year," Dr. LeGrand says, sounding very important, "of the what?"

"I beg your pardon?"

"Epididymitus of the *what?*" he says it again, for God's sake. Is he putting me on?

"Well, of the epididymis, of course!" I laugh, and see quickly that he is not sharing my jocularity, "You get appendicitis in the appendix, and epididymitus in the epididymis!"

He looks a little angry, and asks me the question I've been wanting to ask him: "Are *you* a doctor, Bradley?"

What the hell was I supposed to say? "Well, of course not, I'm just seven tiers old—"

"Well, then, let the doctors take care of things like that. You don't have to know about such things." I was starting to get pissed off.

"Medico-taxonomic information is public domain, is it not?" I ask, and, God, I wish my little voice wasn't so high-pitched.

"You don't understand such things—"

"The hell I don't!"

"Now, Bradley, you're misbehaving—"

"Misbehaving, my little ass!"—I feel my adrenals beginning to come loose—"So far, the signals are that I ought to be examining you. I'm not sure I'm in the right office. You act dumb. Are you humanoid?"

"I'm Baptist, but that's no concern of—"

"I'm not referring to denominational preference." Wow, this is unreal.

"What church do *you* go to?"

"I don't go to any goddamn church, the churches were burned years ago . . . Say, what the hell are you, some kind of anachronut? Are you a robot?"

"You *should.*"

"Should what?"

"Go to church." That does it. I'm not believing my orbs and audios. All I can figure is that this so-called Dr. LeGrand may be testing my frustration tolerance in some weird way. I decide to play it cognitively straight, play down my natural bent to be a smart-ass, and still not be a conforming patsy.

"Your remark—" I begin. "Hey, I just noticed, where's the semantic monitor?"

"Such things needn't concern you, Bradley."

"Well, they *do*, goddammit!" I flare up. "You're not making any sense. Your semantic chainings aren't even halfway linked up adequately. Talking to you is like talking to some dumb-ass household robot—"

Then—I guess I should have suspected it all along—good old Dr. LeGrand's face begins to show important changes: it's subtle again, but he begins to look alert, kind, understanding, supra-humanoid.

I'm human, but I have some bionic implants, and now LeGrand looks like he may have several. His visual agates have faceted surfaces, and some sort of sensor nacelle bulges slightly at his temporal lobe. He slaps his thigh loudly with his hand, and cuts loose a marvelous joyful guffaw. I think I know why he is acting this way, but the change elicits autonomic responses in me, and I think I must have looked stupid to him, with my mouth hanging open.

"Bradley, my boy, you're great!" LeGrand all but crows. He seems like a different person now, but then, who can stereotype anybody anymore?

"Do I know you?" I ask, hoping somehow that I do know him.

"I know your paterno—but wait, I have to make some adjustments here for halo effect. Just a minute and I'll explain everything." Hey, I see this new doctor as a keen guy. I am moderately empathic, and I feel flooded with self-worth reinforcement. For whatever reasons, this guy seems to dig me, and I feel it like a warm fire in a hearth. LeGrand spins his chaise, adjusts some dial settings on a console, and turns back to me.

"My name *is* LeGrand, for whatever connotative value that may have for you now, and you had me sized up right. These past few minutes have been what we call testing the limits. Not really fair to you, prodding your emotional reactivity like that, but something we have to do. I am the psygnonomist assigned to test your cognition. I happen to know your father, and I recognized you. Come, sit in the pod here, and we can get this done fairly quickly." He walks over to an egg-shaped pod about six feet high, and motions me into the seat, as casually and graciously as if welcoming me to his billet. The pod is opaque and sort of shimmery, like it was painted with mercury, and the seat is buttery-soft leatheroid or maybe even chamois, better than the seats in the ancient Benzes and Porsches.

"You know what *rapport* is, Bradley?"

"I know the stock definitive thing—like, harmony of relationship."

"Good. During psychometric test sessions, it's good for us—you and me—to have adequate or good rapport, and this can be a brittle, chancy, tenuous thing, or it can be easy as pie. I read your receptivity as adequate, even optimal; how do you read me?"

"Fine as silk," I say, and sure enough, whatever the interactional factors really are, for me it's like basking in a beneficent cone of light and warmth. The scent of personality! The sharing of person-ality! Nebulous as it sounds, it comes across like some tangible, complex, molecular aura. True-to-life personality aerosol! I read about a smell so strong it discolored walls. I've read ancient hard-cover books, and one of them said you could smell Groton and Har-vard and fledgeling ensign bars on a man, as well as PS 82, CCNY, and a PFC's fresh khakis. Who says we aren't caste-oriented and elitist? I don't. And I know damn well I am smart enough to get as-signed to a better part of the continent. Anyway, this new man, LeGrand, gives off signals like from some sunny California high school, maybe then USC or Stanford, an ROTC drop-out, and maybe Mensa.

"Now we'll do a rapport check, with masks and voice-codes," he says, and I guess my facial cues tell him that I don't know what he means. "It's good that our rapport matrix is optimal," he continues, "but we still have to do this as neutrally as possible, as objectively as we can. Here, put this on, it will feel good, and I'll put this one on." He hands me an aminoplast mask and fluxes one over his face. I flux mine on and look at him. It's amazing what a mask can do. I feel like a sniper behind a stone redoubt, all dug in, secure and au-tonomically cool. LeGrand's mask is neutral and pleasant. He palms a switch, and his voice comes out with really neat timbre and mellifluousness—hey, that was hard to say. I respond, and hear my own new voice, all programmed for nuancial objectivity.

"We read well on the rapport indices," he says. "Ready to start?"

"Affirm," I reply, feeling enthusiastic.

"First we'll whip through some prelims to get warmed up, and get some biog."

"Ready."

"What's your name or number?"

"Bradley Nine Beta Fox."

"What cartographic indices locate your billet?"

"Northwest quad, latitude 40° 43′ 17″, longitude 75° 50′ 22″, Zip 487776."

"Where were you parturated?"

"Atchafalaya Basin, demographic base #14."

"Where were your parents born?"

"Mater in Grove Park Trench, Illinois. Pater in Houma Marsh, Louisiana."

"Any grandparents living?"

"Yes. A Gee Mat and a Gee Pat, both in Geriat Dome 32 in Newark."

"Do you know anything about your GG Pats?"

"Nothing documented. I've been told they came from the Scottish Volcano Slopes."

"At what curricular level are you enrolled?"

"Fifteen point oh," I say, "third year collegiate." I shift and ease back in the great orthopedic seat. It's almost like being weightless, only better. The semantic monitor is purring along nicely, everything within plus or minus half a standard deviation. Ask Debbie the chronomet of day, and she'll give you some fecal response that will skew any monitor reading far out into the tail of the good ol' Gaussian curve. One day the monitor billed her out at 92 percent negative verbal content. I teased her about it, and she told me and the monitor both to go to hell—why can't talking to each other always be as nice and smooth as it is here with LeGrand?

"Do you have any siblings?" LeGrand asks. He must have read me, but then the question is routine. I probe him and get a cordial request not to do operant subvocals.

"Yilch. Affirm," I reply, "I have Debbie—or she has me. She is a negative little split-tail snip." I see the monitor's oscillobar rise into darker cross-hatches.

"Do you have intellective insight into the basis for the rivalry?"

"None beyond the Sturgeon Principle."

"State it please, for the record."

"Incest tropisms, liberally admixed with guilt."

"What is your paterno-surrogate's vocational or professional assignment?"

"He tells me he got Peter-Principled at a young age, and is a career paper-shuffler and cube-stacker."

"Your Mat?"

"A former model, pedagogue, and copulatress." LeGrand seems to smile through his pleasing physiognomy, but the smile is of admiration, not smirkdom.

"Fine, Brad," he says, "tell me if you feel any fatigue as we go along. Do you have any strong hobbies or special interests?"

"I like tennis. Singles. With holographic robot opponents."

"Who's your favorite opponent, if you have one?"

"I like bandy-legged Pancho Segura."

"Any other hobbies or interests?"

"Esoteric things like collecting water pipes, smoking black cigars, and I like chronographs, old books and tapes and cubes, cigar-store Indians, and pieces of old aircraft."

"Do you have any work quotas in your billet setting?"

"I'm supposed to keep the charbot oiled, but the old bitch is so mean, I usually have to call Dad to de-phase her, so we can get at her lube-latch."

"Do you have access to barter credits?"

"No set limits. My Pat lets me have credits within reason, and I did get an AKIA flitter for my birthday."

"Okay, Brad, here we go with some routine information questions, starting off easy, and getting harder as we go along." LeGrand snaps a cube in the refractor, and the questions appear in beautiful bright letters on a screen. He reads them aloud, easy things like:

> HOW MANY IMPLANTS OR PROSTHETES DO YOU HAVE?
> WHAT IS YOUR LONGEST DACTYL EXTENSOR CALLED?
> HOW MANY EXTREMITIES ARE THERE ON A LAPINE?
> FROM WHAT ANIMAL DO WE GET LYSERGINS?
> WHAT MUST YOU DO TO VAPORIZE SEWAGE?
> IN WHAT TAXONOMIC CUBE WOULD WE DIAL AMINO C-111?
> HOW MANY BARTER CREDITS IN A BASAL SCRIPT VOUCHER?
> HOW MANY CALENDRICAL TIERS IN A SUBLUNAR SPAN?

I zap through these questions handily, with split-second response times. Call it informational storage and retrieval capacity, fund of common facts, whatever you like, it's easy for me. It's amazing how a young kid can learn something useless, say, like the red ant population of Brazil, and remember the exact figure ten tiers later. Such a fleck of statistical nit! And things like the population of New Pompeii or Old York, the depth of the Los Angeles fault, or the height of the new Brevard Mountains. The questions get tougher though, just like LeGrand said they would:

> WHO DISCOVERED THE EQUATORIAL FORCE-FIELDS?
> WHAT IS A CEREBROMORPH?
> WHAT IS A CRYPTOGRAM?
> WHO WAS DWIGHT EISENHOWER?
> WHAT IS A DIVORCE?

I was stumped by the word Eisenhower, though I remembered some smoky plastic stuff called Eisenglass. And the word divorce—except for some face-value etiology, I drew a blank. Then I thought, suppose I was bilingual, or polyglot, what engrams would flicker around in the snug depths of my cognition if somebody asked me:

HOWL GRUNKLE SCHNACK EN ALLER VELT
PROVOLONE?

All those initial consonants, initial and medial vowels, blends, diphthongs (that word always breaks me up! what would you like to dip your thong in?). Anyway, I would assimilate that little nonsense chain, and reply something like:

YES, ASCOOBIE DOO DAVID BINKLEY BEARS ASS.

But then this is like bowing and wowing and onomatopoetic sport. The test situation is making me feel good, even cocky or overconfident so far, but I know my abilities. If I were fat and dumpy and cloddish, I might be worried, but I rank well on mesomorphy, physiognomy, metabolic rate, all that jazz, and I feel that I am a bright boy. So we launch off into what LeGrand calls practical reasoning questions:

WHAT IS THE THING TO DO IF YOUR FLEXOR PROSTHETE
ATROPHIES?
WHAT IS THE THING TO DO IF YOUR LEWINIAN LIFESPACE IS IN-
VADED BY A NEOPHYTE?
WHAT SHOULD YOU DO IF YOUR NUTRIENT CONSOLE
MALFUNCTS?
WHY IS IT BETTER TO BUILD PODS OF LAMNIPLAST THAN OF
PLASTICRETE?
WHY ARE MALADAPTIVE CITIZENS NEURONALLY ERASED?

Then I get asked all the math artifacts: the syntactics, the archaic ciphering, sequencing, integers, pyramidals, summations, differences, series, progressions—not far from out-and-out dactylonomy—all in the revered name of math. It's just syntactic sport to me. Then I get some good Boolean jazz, a pebble or two of calculus, the geodesic geometry I like so well—but also the differential equations that usually floor me. Finally, LeGrand asks me some touch-base questions about intuitional geometry and spherical trig. I've always had the same kinds of feelings about math in general; namely, that it should give us something as good or better than the abacus, and that it should provide models for physical events, like in a few seconds of pow and whammy, à la $e = mc^2$.

Now we're into verbal abstractions, and LeGrand chuckles a bit, saying that this will stretch my cognitive abilities more than any part of the tests. He then asks me how a blastula and a peristaltic block are *alike,* and I guess I gave him an incredulity signal, even through my mask. Then I get a Eureka gestalt, and see the paradigm: extracting similarities from overt dissimilitudes, and it's easy enough from there on in. Blastulas and blocks are nutrient masses, anybody knows that. He asks me a few more, and these are fun:

HOW IS A CLONE AND A HOLOBOT ALIKE?
HOW IS VODKA EXTRACT AND TEQUILA BLATTERS ALIKE?
HOW IS A SYNTHESIZER AND A LYRE ALIKE?
HOW IS A CUBE AND A TAPE ALIKE?
HOW IS A PARSEC AND A LIGHT-YEAR ALIKE?

Then we do some strictly rote stuff: chains of nonsense syllables I have to repeat, rhythmic beat patterns in audio-tones, and silly sentences like I LIKE APPLES COOKED IN TURPENTINE. The key to it seems to be audio-visual engramming: flaring, imprinting neon messages on a mental scoreboard, then reading them off aloud. I'm good at the digit spans too. I retain twenty digits forward and fifteen backward, and I think I could have done better with purely random numbers, or sequences with nice melodic-phonic cues.

"Now we'll do some word definitions," LeGrand says, as if he is going to award me a bon-bon. "Dial yourself a drink if you like—by the way, what irradiation regimen are you on?" I remember getting irradiated just this morning. "Enervation," I reply, "every twenty hours or so, equivalent to about ten mg. My mother says it's nothing atypical." I had a favorite aunt who waxed sluggish, and she got up to eighty mugs daily. Poor girl, her metaboles kept dying down, like trying to burn green wood. So I dial a tiny lime distillate and take a sip. It puckers my mouth and rectum. I dig astringency.

"Again, Brad, we'll start on easy words and go on to tougher ones. I'll say the words one at a time, and they will appear on your screen. You tell me what each word means. If you don't score within thirty seconds, a visual cue will appear on the trivid deck." So I rare back and wait, half expecting little ducks and bull's-eyes to start skittering across my visual field, and I'll have to blap them down with my verbal cork-gun. The words begin, and they are in fact simple at first: TELEPORTER, HACKBUTT, TOGA, VERBACUBE, ISOMORPH, ANTIGRAV, CATAMOUNT, AMOEBAFUR, CARBONAIZE, DOCK, FUSOTORCH, COGNIDISSONANT, MALADAPT, NON SEQUITUR, PEER, COBALT . . . I try for synonyms, but it is tough going. If words had neat, one-to-one corollaries, language facility would quickly double—a kind of handy meta-language. The test words start getting tougher now, more abstract, and the trivid deck analogies are fuzzier. But sometimes they are stupendously relevant; for example, LeGrand says "inn-treeg," INTRIGUE appears on my screen, and I muddle around for terms like plot, scheme, conspire, even wire-pulling, the thirty-second time limit slips past, and the trivid scene blooms on: it is Honoré Daumier's *Crispin and Scapin*, a beautiful little 3-D tableau of two rogues of the stage. And I think, how wonderfully clever and isomorphic! Who could objectivize a better plastic scene to function as a cue to this word INTRIGUE? The tie-in is neat and congruent—a very nice tight fit. The words spin through discernible categories: morphology, literature, fashion, history, medicine, physics, quantities, orderings, time, change. They begin to suggest pure thesauritic taxonomy—and I guess that's where it's really rooted anyhow. We finish up with some maddeningly obscure words, like POPE, COCA-COLA, WHISK BROOM, BALLPOINT, and XEROX. How can anybody be expected to know words that strange? I found out later that the Pope was a man in a funny hat, Coca-Cola some kind of fluid, a whisk broom a kind of cleaning device, ballpoint a calligraphic stylus, and Xerox, an archaic 2-D cloning mechanism.

I felt a shade glum finishing the vocabulary section with five consecutive failures, and LeGrand must have shot in some happy aerosol, because I began to feel better immediately, and for no good reason. "We'll take a break now, Brad," he says, taking off His mask. I deflux mine and wonder if I look like a peeled orange or onion. LeGrand clears all the visoports and the room floods with sunlight. I look out and down on the taut dorsal surfaces of an ancient Ercoupe reprod, and a tight wedge of delta-stab flitters. The sense of visual perspective is stunning. We're about one mile up, and the air is clear enough to see for about fifty miles. Last Christmas, the commune put tiny metal spangles in the asepsis satellites, and had them dropped at sunset. The billions of shiny fragments reflected in the light, and it was beautiful, pretty enough to make you want to cry. At eye-level, I can see some intra-megalop cruisers, all silver and shark-nosed. At the three-thousand-foot stratum, all the intra-meg flits, and a few nostalgia reprods—hey, a Stinson Reliant! Below that, it's all hell and traffic patterns, with thousands of filmy-winged flitters jockeying over the domes and in-and-out-the-windows of the decks and slabs and silos, like swarms of bees turned loose in a 3-D maze of pearly translucent pipelines. I look up and see a mag-rocket at about 10,000 feet, and, of course, we have traject rockets of various sizes and ranges, as well as the whole retinue of craft for what is loosely termed space travel. I'm only seven, so I'm no world traveler. Our kindergarten did take the twice-around-the-globe outing once, from about fifty miles up, and I remember seeing great things, like Lake Titicaca, the Himalayas, Siberia, Atlantis, and the Marianas Trench. They put us to sleep during blastoff and recovery, though. I guess some of us might have thrown up or shit our pants. I finish my drink and walk back to the testing pod.

"The next few tests won't require you to talk very much, Bradley," Doctor LeGrand says, positioning himself behind a small lucoid table, "they'll be picture puzzle, design things you can do with your hands and eyes. As you probably know, smartness—cognition, intelligence, cranial wattage—whatever we variously call it, goes beyond the measure of mere verbal facility." The fictive world of symbols, I think, thinking of peers who talk a good game, but remain suspiciously full of shit. "We'll start with this set of cubes," he continues. "In each cube-scene, an important part is missing. Look carefully at each scene, and tell me what important part is missing." An electrolysis wand materializes. I make a move to size it up from different angles, but LeGrand says this is not necessary—that the scene will be posed accurately in 2-D angle-faces. Anyway, it's obvious that the focal lobe of the wand is missing, so I say that. My response does not get any reinforcement, a few seconds pass, and new scenes come on the trivid deck: a chaise without a cantilever stem, a lamprey without a rasp, and a cyborg with no audio-slits. Then I see a pterodact missing its trim tabs, an ingress port without a vesicular membrane, and a podiat web minus some digits. They're all fairly obvious so far, and LeGrand keeps saying "Now, what important part is missing?" A helioflit sans its vertical rotor stumps me, I get it at thirty-four seconds, but no score. Close, but no psychometric cigar. Some short-suited whist plaques come on, a thumbprint lock missing its ratchet-pawl, and an icky Mediterranean lobster lacks its gracefully waving antenna shafts. I'm stumped by a strange, boxlike structure, with a steep-pitched dome, or canopy, or roof, or whatever they used to be called (the word "house" nudges at my consciousness, but I don't say it). And there's a bovine quadruped with an udder-and-teat structure that I can't quite fathom. I think it is unfair to test kids on such strange and unique things; but then, it's all a matter of public information. It's all in the archives, waiting for anybody to dial it out. A girl in our billet asked me if I had ever seen the Deep Throat trivid cube. She knew about an animal called GIRAFFE, and wondered if the cube was about them. I didn't know, so I dialed the cube, and it was about fellatio. Wow, that was eons before prostate kickers, pelvic floor innervators, and orgasm conduits. A guy on the deck just below ours turned pube the other day, the Synod issued him his prostate kicker, and he stayed hooked into it for three whole days. He told me he had about 4,500 orgiastic surges before he disconduited. I can't wait till I get mine.

Next, LeGrand gives me some supercube matrices to replicate. This is fun, stacking colored luminescent cubes in varying configurations to match the ones staged on the trivid deck. I even get a time bonus on one of them. Next comes scrambled cube sequences of routine behavior samples, and I have to reorder them so they tell the right story. One of the best tests is assembling holographic sculpture-puzzles: I have to put the right muscle slabs on a neat humanoid skeleton standing about one foot high—hey, Ken and Barbi and GI Joe from ages past. I flux on the traps, lats, and delts, then the pecs and the abdoms, biceps, triceps, forearms, then down to the thighs and calves—a real Adonis-doll. Then comes a churningly kinesthetic Pegasus equine, with pumping legs and cloven hooves, a neck like a thick porcelain chess piece, and a mane flying in the imaginary wind. So I put him altogether too. A global Janus face follows, and I feel like a real life plastisculptor. The last one is an old terracar. LeGrand violated the test instructions and told me it was a Porsche Steamcar from about the 1990's. And then he tells me the test is finished.

The transduct starts some happy convoluted clavier music, the compositor thrusts out brittle histograms, and LeGrand begins to collate the results of all the tests I took. He shakes my hand and that feels good. His koala smiles at me, and so does his lab assistant and his secretary. He tells me I am a fine boy, walks me over to the flit-port, and waves at me through the vesicle as I lift off and away from the building. Hey, he didn't tell me how I did on the tests . . .

Good old worrywart Mater had already punched in the codes for the flight home, so I couldn't do any extra sightseeing. I did get into a brief race with a pretty girl in a flowery orange flitter. She flew right up beside me and blinked her umbicular zircon. I felt immature because I didn't have a penile flagstaff to hoist, or an innovative orgasm regimen to beam over to her. So all I did was wave, and say I'm only seven tiers old.

"The dummy's back," Debbie calls over her shoulder to Mater, as I iris the ingress-port.

"He's Mother's big boy," Mater says, coming to me and hugging me. My nasal ridge gets mashed in her pectoral cleavage and I blush a little. Daddy was not home yet.

"Well, how did you do, darling?" she asks.

"Horrible, I bet," Debbie snickers.

"Shut up, Deb," Mater says casually, cutting her eyes at Debbie's console. Debbie knows that Mater will shut off her power if she doesn't behave. Implants are fun, but you have to stay on the charging pod an hour every day to feel top-flight.

"He didn't tell me any scores, but he said I was a good boy. The tests were easy enough, and the trip was fun—"

"Didn't he tell you your mental age?" Debbie asks, more earnestly than she usually talks.

"Silence, Deborah," Mater says.

"No, wait," I cut in, "let her talk."

"No quotients, centiles, stanines, DQ's, IQ's, MQ's, grade levels—nothing?"

"Wherever did you learn all that?" Mater gasps at Debbie.

"Dianne told me. She's eight."

"Wait again," I say, seeing a heavy, mental, velvet gestalt-curtain starting to roll open into the stage wings. "I know my grade level. It's 15.0. If my chrono age is seven, then my mental age must be whatever is required for a 15.0 grade placement."

"Dianne told me you need 18–0 mental age to get to 14.2 grade level. That's where her brother is."

"So mine must be about 19 or 20," I say, excitedly, doing a quick mental 7 X 3, and wondering if my IQ is really about 210.

"Well anyway, you're my smart stud boy," Mater says, and she grabs me again, "and you know a lot, you got plenty common sense, you count good, and not much gets by you. And you know big words. I just hope you're smart enough to get us reassigned to a better part of this goddamn continent." The central console flashes, and Mater all but trips over herself to get to it. A cube-plaque slips out and she notches it quickly in the refractor. The very first word brings forth a cheer from both Mater and Debbie:

CONGRATULATIONS. YOUR PUTATIVE SON'S LOCI RANKINGS ON YEAR SEVEN PSYCHOMETRIC TESTS ARE SUFFICIENTLY HIGH TO ELEVATE YOUR FAMILIAL PERCENTILE TO NINETY-TWO. YOU ARE THEREBY ASSIGNED TO BINGHAMTON VILLAGE, NEW YORK TERRITORIAL JURISDICTION, FOR RECREATIONAL SABBATICAL, CONSUMER REPROGRAMMING, AND ONE-HALF TIME LEISURE CASTE PRIVILEGES. DETAILED LOGISTICS WILL FOLLOW. THE CONTINENTAL SYNOD EXTENDS PERSONAL RECOGNITION TO YOUNG BRADLEY NINE AS WELL AS TO THE BASIC FAMILY UNIT.

"Yay, Brad, you did it!" Debbie cheers.

"Goodbye, Newark, hello, Binghamton!" Mater crows out. Then she does a fat muffled somersault on the rug, and damned if she doesn't hug me again. "Just wait till Daddy hears about this," she says. "He'll be so happy."

I feel happy too. Apparently I have plenty of brain cells, they're all in their places (with sunshiny faces), and they're all getting zapped with optimal oxygenates. So I score high on the psychos. I can't take any special motivational bows, or say I deserve any medals, but what the hell, here's my seven-tier-old chest if they want to pin a medallion on it—a big fat merit badge for smartness.

And would you believe it, Debbie is hugging me from starboard, Mater's got me in a portside quarter nelson, and they're chortling at me like I'm their harem master. Debbie's cat is purring in my lap, and here comes my Afghan hound, smiling and wagging his tail, and subvoking BRAD, BABY! I feel important. Even though I'm just seven. Just a young boy. Gee, I hope Binghamton is a keen place.

CONTENTMENT, SATISFACTION, CHEER, WELL-BEING, GLADNESS, JOY, COMFORT, AND NOT HAVING TO GET UP EARLY ANY MORE

George Alec Effinger

George Alec Effinger, a refugee from Ohio, at present "moves around a lot." He recently moved from New Orleans, where he had been working hard to acquire Southern decadence. His opening gambit was to play tennis every morning at eight o'clock, "one of the most ludicrous sights since the beginning of the Industrial Revolution." Now he wakes up to the fumes and blue mists of New Jersey mornings.

Here, Effinger gives us hope of real progress, after the political bunglings and fiascos of the last few years, by showing us how much better these things will be done in the future.

And we won't even have to get up to change the channel.

EDITORS' NOTE: THIS IS AN ORIGINAL STORY, PUBLISHED HERE FOR THE FIRST TIME.

FOR centuries the world had been run by the Representatives. This must sound wonderful. You know, an organization of devoted men, chosen by the population of the entire world on the basis of individual merit, working together for the betterment of mankind as a whole, rather than national interests. Well, it does sound wonderful. It *wasn't* wonderful, though. Still, at times, it was pretty good despite itself.

In the early days, there were six Representatives: the Representative of North America, one from South America, and Representatives of Europe, Asia, Africa, and the Pacific. In the beginning, it seemed a very logical and reasonable way of running things. There were the advantages of several different political systems, each of which had enjoyed popularity at one time or another: despotism, democracy, the benevolent monarchy, and so on. Eclecticism was the mood of the people, and the Representatives didn't see any reason to oppose the trend.

After some centuries of Representative rule, the then-current Representative of North America phoned the Representative of Asia, on the pretext of returning a friendly call. Sooner or later, though, their talk got around to the administrative problems of running continents.

"You know," said Tom, the Representative of North America, "sometimes it gets to be a pain in the neck, handling all these 'minority group members.' I'll bet they're worse than the original minorities ever were."

"I know just what you mean," said Denny, the Representative of Asia. "Only last month I had some guy dressed up like a monk or something who set himself on fire in downtown Kowloon. Now, we haven't had real Buddhist monks in five hundred years. This guy was a regular Fiver Dash Jerry civil service man, probably from Trenton, New Jersey, or somewhere. But he really got into his job. He was supposed to give speeches, pray a lot, burn incense, chant, that kind of thing. There was nothing in the personnel specs about setting himself on fire."

"You just never know," said Tom. "The job gets to them sometimes. I have the same trouble every day with my people. And not just the ones you'd expect. I have to have a famous melting pot over here. All the slag rises to the top."

The Representative of Asia laughed. "Maybe we ought to get rid of these pretend minorities altogether. They're too much trouble."

"No," said Tom. "They serve a purpose. But it might help to kind of consolidate our efforts a little."

The Representative of Asia sounded suspicious. "What do you mean?" he asked.

Tom spoke in an unnaturally light tone. "Well," he said, "look at it this way. The more Representatives there are, the more our decisions get diluted, and the weaker our power is. It's like the old days, with a million rulers and a billion legislators. It's better now, but it's not perfect yet."

Denny's voice became a whisper. "I'll bet you've got some terrific idea to improve things."

"There's the whole area of the Pacific," said Tom. "Stan's running that show. But I keep finding myself beating my head against his stupid plans. I'll bet you do, too. Now, if there were someone else in his place, someone who understood me better—"

"You want to have Stan replaced, before the election."

"Yes," said Tom.

"Who? You wouldn't just say that if you didn't already have ideas."

"I don't want to put someone else in Stan's job," said the Representative of North America. "That would just prolong the trouble. I think we could do a better job ourselves."

"Squeeze him out, and move in ourselves."

"Now you got it," said Tom cheerfully. And that's how the six Representatives who ruled the world became five.

It was very easy to set a precedent in those days. There weren't dozens upon dozens of nations any more, each with its own peculiar ways. There was a loud cry of alarm and anger from the people of the Pacific territories when they learned that Stan had been retired to a nice ranch in California, and that Tom and Denny had divided his former domain. But the alarm and the anger did not last very long; most people in the Pacific territories couldn't tell the difference between Stan and either Tom or Denny in the first place. Things settled down, just as Tom knew they would, and everything got back to normal in a matter of weeks.

Several years later, the Representative of North America made a phone call to Chuck, the Representative of Europe. It was, in many respects, very similar to the phone call Tom had made to Denny, except that his new ideas were even more daring. "Listen," said

Tom, "and I'm speaking frankly, honestly, and with a high regard for our constituents."

"Of course," said Chuck. "Aren't you always worrying about the voters? Don't you just stay up nights wondering if they still like you?"

"Shut up. I was thinking about what makes our continents run as smoothly as they do."

"Your continent, maybe," said Chuck. "My continent won't shut up long enough for me to tell it what to do."

"You're too kind," said Tom. "You have to be tough with the people."

"Easy for you to say," said Chuck. "You've got Americans. Just Americans. And Canadians. Even Stan could have dealt with them. Me, I've got Polish, German, Italian, French, Spanish, those damn inscrutable Finns, and God knows what all. And don't tell me about the withering of national identities, because you don't know what you're talking about. The countries may be gone, but the tempers aren't."

"All right, all right," said Tom. "Forget it. I was just thinking of a way that we could make things run a lot better, on a world-wide scale."

There was a short pause and a quiet laugh from Chuck. "We could turn the whole thing over to the prairie dogs, and let them have their shot at it."

"No," said Tom. "Not quite."

"Then I'll bet it's something really exciting and fun," said Chuck cynically. "If you give me a moment, I think I can get in the right ball park."

"Take all the time you want," said Tom.

"Does it have to do with, say, Ed or Nelson?"

Now Tom laughed. "Amazing," he said. "Now guess which one."

"Nelson in South America."

"No," said Tom. "How could you oversee anything in South America when you're sitting in Ponta do Sol?"

"All right," said Chuck. "Ed in Africa, and the same thing applies to you, sitting in your shuffleboard palace in Florida."

"Yes—Ed. Africa isn't a difficult place to govern any longer. Everything's the same, just the same as it is here, just the same as it is where you are. They have things in Africa that we need, we have things they need. The one thing that nobody needs is Ed."

"I've been saying that for years," said Chuck. "Now, are we just going to campaign for his removal or what?"

"Well, I've got a plan. I remember how well the operation against Stan went. I mean, not even Stan minded terribly much. He's very happy. He's playing shuffleboard, too, out in California. I visit him sometimes. He's getting good. I never saw anybody get topspin on one of those disks before. Anyway, I just thought he could use some company, and Ed doesn't seem to be doing much."

"That's his charm," said Chuck. "How do we do it? The same way you and Denny squeezed out Stan?"

"Pretty much," said Tom, pleased that Chuck was reacting so favorably.

So, in about six months, after a carefully drawn-up scheme of rumor, innuendo, planned dissatisfaction, false news leaks, skillfully aimed gossip, and character assassination, Tom and Chuck took over the governing of Africa, and Ed was retired to a nice ranch only a few miles from Stan. Denny didn't say anything; he was in no position to complain. But it was obvious that Nelson in South America was watching Tom with some nervousness.

The people of Africa were also a little more distraught than the citizens of the Pacific had been. Africa had long since lost its distinctive personality as a continent. There were no more desert nomadic tribes. There were no more vast savannahs, populated by fierce and beautiful beasts. There were few animals of any kind, in this once-rich continent overflowing with life. The Sahara had been made into a huge area virtually indistinguishable from Brooklyn or Queens; indeed, if you blindfolded someone from New York City and set him down anywhere in Africa, he would have a difficult time telling you where he was. The only giveaway might be the climate; a New Yorker would suspect that it was cooler in Africa in the summertime.

The government—meaning, of course, the Representatives—had hired a number of people to be Arabs, and a number of people to be goat or cow-herding tribesmen. But they never went so far as to maintain anything like the old society and culture. Music, sculpture, art, and the oral literary tradition were dead and gratefully lost. These things just got in the way of making one's living.

The removal of Ed as Representative made the African people think that this, too, would cause a major disturbance in their lives. That was the reason for their outcry; they didn't have the time, the energy, or the interest for a major disturbance. But Tom and Chuck moved in quickly, splitting the continent between them, taking over the government immediately and suppressing any reactions that looked potentially dangerous. Like the people of the Pacific, the Africans were astonished at how little their private lives were changed. Once this fact was accepted, so were Tom and Chuck, and Ed was easily forgotten. The six Representatives were now four. Three confident Representatives, and one very, very fearful one.

The frightened Representative was Nelson, in South America, and he had every reason in the world to be afraid. After making two unprecedented power grabs in less than ten years, Tom was casting his eye around for more, and the logical choice was Nelson. One of the chief advantages to supplanting Nelson was that Tom needed the help of nobody. He didn't have to go to Chuck or Denny with his ideas. He had gained enough experience to plan the entire operation himself; in fact, the maneuver had been thought up, at least in some rough form, from the time of the first takeover in the Pacific. Tom had only waited until his own position of power was sufficiently well-grounded. According to population figures, Tom now governed as many people as Chuck, possibly even more; Tom had graciously allowed Chuck the majority of Africa. Tom did not rule as many people as Denny, but his territory was richer in natural resources and all of that kind of thing, about which he knew little but about which his advisers were always very happy. Tom, Chuck, and Denny were about equal in power; Nelson was far, far behind. It hadn't yet occurred to Chuck and Denny that, should Tom replace Nelson single-handedly, the Representative of North America (and South America, and parts of Africa and the Pacific) would undeniably take a commanding lead.

Nelson tried to hint at this, in order to get help from Chuck and Denny. Neither Representative paid much attention. They always had problems of their own, and South America did not seem very important, even if Tom did succeed in grabbing it. After all, what would he get? A couple of dozen cities that could not be distinguished from Houston, Baltimore, Duluth, Vienna, Lisbon, Bratislava, Istanbul . . .

Tom had larger ideas. In only eight weeks, Nelson was living on a rather nice ranch-style home completely furnished with built-ins and two-and-a-half-car garage, not far from schools and shopping centers, between Ed's house and Stan's. And Tom had gotten himself some sunny new vacation homes in Brazil, a very pretty canal in Central America, and a staging point for future operations. Certainly *he* had no doubts that there would be future operations, even though Chuck and Denny thought that he had come to the end of his amusing games.

Now, before the discussion of the rest of Tom's affairs begins, it's time to talk about the other great influence in the lives of the people and the actions of the Representatives. This was TECT, the largest, most comprehensive, most versatile mechanical calculating device ever built. It had been in existence in one form or another for many years. Sometimes the electronic storage system was increased and made more efficient. Sometimes a technician would devise completely new techniques which would expand the powers of the gigantic computer beyond even what the Representatives could understand. TECT started off as a relatively small installation beneath the island of Malta. Other satellite units were added from time to time. After nearly a century, TECT was virtually autonomous, needing a minimum of human maintenance. Soon that minimum was reduced to zero. Meanwhile, TECT had become the repository and synthesizer of all human knowledge. Any book, newspaper, magazine, film, or sound recording that was in existence could be obtained from TECT. The computer—although "computer" is as poor a term for TECT as "star" is for Rigel, as far as conveying size is concerned—was provided with capabilities that allowed it to answer purely philosophical questions, using the vast resources at its command. By the time of Tom, Chuck, and Denny, there was no single human alive who comprehended all that TECT meant or all that TECT could do.

But there were a few folks around who had an idea.

Someone once came up with what he considered to be a cure for inflation. At least, he reasoned, inflation could be slowed down if everyone did away with money. The Representatives thought this over for a few years and decided to try it. No more currency was printed, only a small quantity of coins of small denominations, for use in minor transactions. All other transfers of goods was controlled and remembered by TECT; if one bought an item, TECT would deduct the value of the property from the buyer's credit account, and add it to the seller's. Everyone had an official government ID card, and this was used to record every business transaction in the world; the card was placed in a small bookkeeping machine and the amount of the sale was registered. There were millions of these machines in the world, in every store, restaurant, official church, newsstand on every continent, and every machine was tied directly to TECT. TECT could handle it all easily; the shifting of credit happened instantaneously, and a good deal of fraud was ended by TECT's sure knowledge of everyone's current financial situation. The Representatives were very fond of the plan, and it worked very well indeed. The research team that put it into operation were rewarded with luxurious gifts and appliances, and generous gift certificates from the Representatives' own large chain of department stores.

Long before Tom first got the idea of removing Stan, almost every household in the world had its own tect, its own external terminal of the huge TECT buried beneath the ground. Now everyone had access to any information that they might want, except, of course, that information which had been classified for security reasons or which TECT might deem an infringement on another person's privacy. Books could be printed out on microfiche cards in a matter of seconds, and read on a built-in screen. Any music or film could be requested.

At the same time, the Representatives had an accurate and relatively inconspicuous way of keeping tabs on everyone on the planet; TECT remembered every request that was made of it, and sometimes this information could be very useful, too. It was impossible to purchase anything without TECT learning where one was, so fugitives from justice had a much more difficult time. The official ID cards became the most valuable possession a person had: without it, he could not eat, he could not clothe himself, he could not rent lodgings, he would find it nearly impossible to find sexual gratification.

One of the reasons that the Representatives liked TECT so much was that the computer did much to make their own jobs easier. If everyone had a tect in his home, then there was a simple way of communicating with each constituent. An election could be held, with billions of individual voting machines; the vote would be made on the tect, and TECT would count the world-wide tally.

One of the reasons that Tom, Chuck, Denny, Nelson, Stan, and Ed had been Representatives for so long was that they controlled the computer technicians who wrote the programs that governed the counting of the votes. The Representatives lied.

Naturally, there were those who suspected, but they were powerless. TECT's records of past elections were altered to fit the Representatives' designs. And very little interest could be stirred among the populations to investigate; the angry few who demanded a recount found very few listeners.

Another great step forward was made when the discovery of matter teleportation was made. TECT could be used to move objects or people safely from one place to another—again, instantaneously. TECT had always been able to do this, from the days since it had ceased being just another huge computer; it was just that no one had realized the potential of the machine. It isn't necessary to go into what matter transmission did to the politics and economy of the world. Ordinarily, it might be assumed that the effect would be tremendous. But everything was already the same, so very few people noticed the difference. It speeded up the mail delivery, and you could get back and forth to the moon faster, but teletrans units were too expensive to install in the home. It was still cheaper to take the plane.

So, against this background, Tom found himself master of quite a bit of the world. He ruled over more territory than anyone since Charles V of Spain and a lot of other places. But, naturally enough, Tom was not satisfied. One morning Denny awoke to find both Tom and Chuck in his bedroom, each holding a glass of water and a pill. Denny shrugged and accepted the pills, and when he awoke again, he was inside a lovely four-bedroom house from which he could hear the shuffleboard disks clacking at Stan's.

Of course, Chuck realized that he was in pretty unstable circumstances himself. What had happened to Stan, Ed, Nelson, and Denny could very well happen to him—could, ha. *Would*. There wasn't any doubt about it. The only question was when Tom would move. From the day that Chuck helped Tom retire Denny, Chuck had hired a guard to watch while he slept. In Chuck's retinue, the Representative had an eccentric reputation, but he was just being careful. He ruled the world with Tom for many years. They used TECT and they used television, they used sports and popular entertainment media, they used sex and they used drugs, all to their benefit, all to keep their people happy. They became identified as a team—the Representatives, Tom and Chuck. The others were forgotten. Tom and Chuck, the Representatives. They were doing a good job. Nobody was bothered. It seemed that they might go on like that forever.

They might well have, except that after about twelve years Chuck let his guard down. Tom moved quickly; he had been watchful all during that time. Chuck excused himself to go to the lavatory, and the young woman he was dining with never saw him again. Chuck took up collecting shells in California, and Nelson paid him back a decades-old sock on the jaw that Chuck had completely forgotten about. Except for that, the five Representatives-in-exile spent the rest of their days in friendly community activities, watched over by Tom and his associates.

Now, at last, Tom alone ruled the world. It was the first time that anyone had ever done that. It was certainly a noteworthy occasion, and to be sure, Tom received a great number of congratulatory telegrams and flowers subceived to his personal teletrans unit. In Europe, everyone missed Chuck. "What happened to old Chuck?" asked the Danish fishermen, the German industrialists, the Italian tenors, the British working stiffs, the Spanish dancers, the French chefs. No one seemed to know. There were plenty of people in Europe who squinted one eye, shook one finger, and said, "I'll bet he's gone the same place as those others." Life went on, and by lunchtime Chuck had ceased to be a cause for concern.

In the United States and Canada, there was a certain pride involved in living under the Representative who seemed to have come out on top. No one had even been aware that there was any sort of power struggle, but if there was—and now it surely seemed that way—well, it was better to be in on the winning side. There wasn't anyone who could explain why, or how having been governed by Tom before anyone else had been would work to their benefit; and so by lunchtime Tom had ceased to be a topic of conversation.

During that time, Tom, the Representative of the world, was kept informed of how his coup had affected the voters. He was surprised and gratified that the transition was easy; he didn't have any need for the massive public relations job that he had planned. That was just as well. He could put the time and resources into other things; it seemed that the people loved him, or if not, they kept their mouths shut. Maybe they had him mixed up with someone else. In any event, it didn't make any difference. The regime replaced the old twelve-year Tom-and-Chuck routine without the slightest rough moment. Tom wondered in private: did those people, those ten billion people, did they ever wonder what happened to Chuck (let alone Denny, Nelson, and so on)? Did they have any idea what would happen if something accidental happened to Tom?

In the most private of these moments, Tom wondered what would happen if something accidental happened to Tom.

So, in Asia, in little islands in the ocean, in the frozen Greenland stations, in Cleveland, everyone accepted Tom as the boss. It wasn't much different than having a bunch of Representatives, after all; the only adjustment that people could make (although few did) was to realize that everyone else in the world had the same Representative. Was that so terrible?

About this time, Tom turned from the petty cares of his office to benevolence. It was a sudden and wonderful thing. One day he called in his secretary. "Miss Brant," he said, "today I am going to do these benevolent things. Take a memo." And he listed over two dozen charitable, praiseworthy acts which he, through the resources of his office, was easily able to accomplish. Nuns—that is, civil servants hired as nuns—in Africa were given clean linens. Sons of pseudo-Chicanos were given softballs and bats. A hospital in Lima, Peru, was begun and another in Lima, Ohio, torn down. Many other things happened that first day, and people all over the world were surprised and gratified.

The next morning, Tom anxiously waited for word to come into the Representative headquarters. He kept asking TECT, "How am I doing?" TECT kept responding, "Fine. Just fine." That wasn't what Tom was looking for. He called in Miss Brant. "How do you think I'm doing?" he asked.

"Fine," she said. Tom gave her another list of kindly deeds for that day. An hour later, Tom asked TECT, "How am I doing? Break it down statistically. Print it out as a comparison with one year ago today."

TECT complied. The answer read:

23:48:13 30August 1 YT   OffRepl

OffNot/OffRep

***RepNA:*
   Popularity at highest level in twelve months. As of this date, one year ago, popularity of the Representative of

*North America was 8.37483+. Data received as of
23:47:54 30August 1 YT indicates popularity has risen to
8.84747+.*

Tom looked at the figures silently. He had certainly worked hard
at being liked. Apparently he was succeeding. Well, that was fine.
Miss Brant was right. It was just fine. He stared at the figures on
the tect's screen: 8.84747+. That meant that out of ten people there
were 1.15253 who *didn't* like him. Tom ignored the percentage in
the larger, positive figure who had been counted merely as "no
opinion." He didn't ask TECT about that; it was a side to the question he didn't want to know more about. Instead, he gave the
money to begin a subway system in Ljubljana, Yugoslavia.

Five hours later, the popularity index stood at 8.84751+. Tom
was making progress.

There was a newspaper article the next morning, wondering why
Tom was doing all of this. Had he been involved in some unspeak-
able horror, was he trying to channel the people's attention away
from his evil nature? TECT reported all of this without interest,
only because everything that directly mentioned the Representative
was sorted, coded, and abridged for his benefit. Tom was very
unhappy. He decided to take tect time and speak to the world
again.

"My fellow humans," he said, wondering if that were any better
than "Earthlings." His face was wan and lined, a testimonial to the
skills of his wardrobe and make-up staff. He chewed on a thumb-
nail while he stood, uncomfortably, in front of a large globe. The
room looked like some important office, but it was just a stage-set
near his bathroom. "My fellow humans," he said, "I haven't done
anything wrong. Look at me. It's Tom, you remember. I've been
with you a long time. We've done a lot of things together, you and
I, we've seen a lot of changes. Can it be that the people of the
world, *my* people, *my* world, your world, too, are so starved for
novelty that they have to attack me in this way?" In the hand that
wasn't being bitten he waved the article. It was printed on a
microfiche card, and impossible to see clearly. "I sure hate to think
that. And I won't, because I know my people better. My staff keeps
me posted."

Tom looked out at the audience, all the people in the world, all
ten billion of them, and smiled sincerely. "I'm doing the best I
can," he said. Then he walked out of the room.

The next morning the newspaper printed an article that defended Tom, but suggested that his henchmen and underlings were using their greater power to further their own ends. Tom shrugged; well, sure they were. His popularity index had held fast; he asked TECT about the trustworthy quotient of his henchmen and underlings, in the eyes of the constituents. This was quoted as 3.28537+. The juniors had messed up again; in a little while they would begin to affect Tom adversely as well. He went back on the air and explained that, *if* anything wrong happened, anywhere in the world, it could likely be traced to an honest mistake by one of the underlings and henchmen. "I have to admit that I am limited by the skills of these good men," he said. "I have to be dependent on somebody. Everybody has to be dependent on somebody." This time he didn't even smile. He just walked away.

"What is Tom going to do?" asked many millions of people. "It's true that the quality of our lives is higher than ever before, but he's prevented from raising it even further by those underlings and henchmen upon whom he depends." Millions of people were saying these very words, all over the world; millions of other people only shrugged. In California, five ex-Representatives were uneasy about their friend's predicament.

Everyone had made the reckoning without taking into account Tom's superior foresight. He called a meeting of technicians, technologists, scientists, researchers, savants, and stenographers to hear his views. His views were roundly applauded; then Tom asked for the views of the other people present. Some of these ideas were rejected, others incorporated. Things moved along at an excellent pace, in a comfortable atmosphere of democratic fellowship, until the decision was made to build even more sophisticated capabilities into TECT.

Among Tom's own associates, his underlings and henchmen, there was a great amount of celebration. One might have thought that another habitable planet had been discovered, an event that occurred only once or twice a year. The underlings and the henchmen were sure that they would be given positions of greater responsibility, although those positions hadn't been in existence for many, many years. And along with those positions, they reasoned, must go greater privileges. But no one wanted to bring the matter up; certainly it was too early to approach Tom. He had earned a period of adjustment. So, by lunchtime, all of Tom's underlings and henchmen were trying to act naturally. They all sweated a lot and laughed nervously, but they pretended that it was natural. They never gave any thought to the possibility that the sole ruler of the world might not want a bunch of sweating, giggling apes as his subordinates. That kind of junior executive never consider the broad perspective; Tom was well aware of the situation.

"I am well aware of the situation," he said as he headed up his first staff meeting that afternoon. "I know what you must be thinking. That's how I got to be where I am today. And, first off, I'd like to thank each and every one of you." The henchmen and the underlings looked at each other and tried to hide their smirks behind their hands. They waited to hear what Tom had planned for them.

Tom looked around the large, polished metal table. The men who sat listening to him had served him for a long time, relieving him of many irritating duties. Some of the men had been with him so long he had forgotten who they were and what they did. He glanced from face to face, and he couldn't suppress a shudder. "Who is responsible for this report?" he asked, holding up a thick notebook. "Number 18192-J-495?"

One of the men coughed softly and raised a hand. "My group," he said timidly.

"Fine," said Tom. "Fine work."

The man gave his Representative a short, tight smile.

"Have you read the report?" asked Tom.

"No, sir," said the man. "A résumé was due to be put on my desk this morning, but, well, with all the commotion and everything—"

Tom interrupted the underling with a gesture. "Just as well," he said. "You're out of a job. You saved yourself a lot of depressing reading. TECT has your job now. The report estimated that I didn't need any of you any more. TECT estimated that, too. I figured it out for myself, a while ago. So now you can go out and enjoy life. I alone will worry and cry over the pain of government. I, and TECT. You may go. Go out now; there's always a job for a henchman."

When Tom ordered the next day that the island of Java be cleared of its inhabitants, he received no opposition. The new adjunct to TECT was constructed there. It was completed within the year, and TECT took on even more of Tom's troublesome duties.

Tom could go anywhere in the known universe, just by stepping through the portals of a TECT teletrans unit. He could summon up any fact or thought that had ever been recorded in human history.

He could ask TECT, "Can we ever really 'know' anything?" and the answer would come back instantaneously, in about three medium-sized paragraphs of colloquial language. But Tom suspected, he *planned*, that TECT could do more.

Meanwhile, all through Tom's domain, things were looking up. In the Pacific, Stan's old constituency, people moved over to make room for the former residents of Java. There wasn't a single relocation that caused any problems, either for the Javanese or their new hosts; this was because every place in the Pacific looked like every other place. The language was the same, the clothing was the same, the food was the same, the attitudes were the same. It made moving a lot easier and a lot less traumatic.

About this time a team of specialists compiled a report that stated that the settled worlds around the nearby stars were advanced enough to begin legitimate commerce with the mother world. They had products at last, things that Earth could use, and for which they could be given earth-made goods; the economy was stimulated, and some megalomaniac thinkers began dreaming in terms of commercial domination of the stars. Not many, though.

In Africa, times were so good that the civil servants who lived their lives as poor nomadic tribespeople were given promotions. Now they wore suits and ties and dresses shipped from New York, all five years behind the current style. The younger members of this civil service group were directed to complain about the loss of their national identity and their cultural heritage. But only on Monday through Friday, from nine until five.

The basic unit used in dwellings, the modular apartment, was standardized, so that a family could move their boxlike home to any continent, to any planet, and find a skeletal building that would accept it, barring the usual difficulties in finding vacancies. The manufacturers were informed by TECT that agreements had to be reached so that all products likely to be taken from one continent to another could be used in either place with equal facility. This was TECT's first major independent decision, and no one was more surprised than Tom himself; everyone in the world cheered the wisdom and good sense apparent in TECT's judgment.

Naturally, TECT could not be affected by praise or by threats. Therefore, it was unsound reasoning to think that TECT was encouraged by its first success. It was illogical to assume that TECT's next flurry of announcements were at all connected with the universal approbation which greeted the first one. Nevertheless, when

TECT ordered the disbanding of the CAS police force, as the group had outlasted its usefulness, many people around the world were secretly pleased. TECT had won a great victory again, and many more supporters. Even the former CAS police were happy, because they never had anything to do, anyway. They were all relocated and retrained, and many became productive members of society thereafter.

In Europe, people had begun to identify TECT with the memory of Chuck. It had been Tom and Chuck for so long; now, with prosperity growing, the Europeans wanted another team of leaders to look toward. Tom and TECT. The machine assumed a personality in the minds of the people, a personality that Tom had given up trying to explain away. There was no personality to TECT; there were only the effects caused by TECT's decisions. But if the people wanted to believe—well, whatever the people wanted was all right with Tom. Mostly.

On the moon, in plastic domes that tinted the sun green, the settlers and scientists were governed almost entirely by TECT, although they never realized it. All of their directives came through Tom's office, but originated with TECT; Tom had given the moon to the computer at an early stage. That colony had always been a headache for him.

And in the United States and Canada, where the citizens had known Tom longer than anyone else in the world, there was a growing feeling that the Western Hemisphere had displayed some kind of natural superiority; Tom's assumption of leadership was looked on as an odd kind of victory for North America. Tom told TECT to find some way of eliminating that attitude.

After several months of this, the strain was beginning to show on Tom. He made a public speech, and it was clear that this was not the same Tom who had broadcast baseball games with Chuck, had done kids' shows in the mornings, had provided housewives over half the world with recipes for dinner each afternoon. He talked about how burdensome it was, to be the only Representative, but said that he was willing to accept the load. He knew it was best for mankind; he'd take the worry and the sorrow—after all, that was his job. And if no one ever showed any sign of appreciation—well, Tom could live without that. So what? he said. It was always like that at the top.

The responsibilities *were* tremendous. Everyone watching the speech on their tects could understand that. They felt a little guilty about not giving Tom the respect he was due. They didn't know exactly how to go about doing it; after all, they didn't even know where he *was*. They couldn't send him a card or a funny birthday note. But when the guilt passed, as it always did, rather quickly, the feeling remained that Tom was losing some of his sharpness.

A year later, Tom made another public address. "My fellow earthlings (he had tried to find a better word, but he had been unable to; also, he hadn't tried all that hard)," he said slowly, in a voice that filled his audience with surprise and concern, "I don't really have much to say to you. I mean, if you were doing anything important, go back to it. This isn't a major announcement or anything. I just wanted to talk to you. You know, it's a real headache keeping your lives in order for you. I hope you appreciate that. I have to admit that there are rough times. There sure are. I have to admit that.

"But being the Representative has its rewards, too. So in case you were worrying about me, you can just stop. I'm fine, really. There are problems every morning that I have to wade into, but I knew that before I took the job. Somebody had to do it. Sometimes I hate getting up out of bed. Sometimes I can't sleep.

"So I just wanted you to know. It isn't all a bed of roses, but I think that together we'll all struggle through. Things aren't so bad for you, are they? That just shows that I'm doing my level best. So try to keep from hurting each other, and we'll all be happy. I'm as happy as I can be, under the circumstances. But don't worry about me. I'm fine. Good night."

Tom sighed softly and walked out of the room. He went to his bedroom, took two large blue capsules, and fell quickly asleep. He didn't communicate with another human being for months.

"Things would really be terrific," people said to each other after this speech, "if we had the old Tom back." TECT reported these conversations to Tom whenever he requested them, and he couldn't understand them. After all, he was getting older all the time.

Tom told TECT a lot of things now, because he was very lonely. Sometimes, he went on tect time to tell his people that they shouldn't worry about him, that although the responsibilities weighed heavily and all that, he was strong. But he would walk around his house complaining all the time. Miss Brant, his secretary, used to get tired of hearing about it.

"It's very lonely here," said Tom.

Miss Brant sighed. "So go out. Meet people."

Tom laughed softly. "I wish I could. Me? The Representative? I can't just go out. I have things to do."

"Then stay in," said Miss Brant. "You can have people brought in. You remember those parties Denny used to throw."

"I can't do that either."

"Then it's just too bad," said Miss Brant. She picked up her notebook and left Tom alone. He turned to TECT for consolation.

"Good old TECT," he whispered. "What do you think of me, huh? After all these years?"

The answer came across Tom's tect, flashing in green letters on the darker green screen.

09:25:42 16May 3 YT   OffRepl

OffNot/OffRep

***RepNA:*
You're all right, I suppose.

"You've seen worse, right?" said Tom, pressing the glowing button that switched off the tect.

Tom had been the solitary ruler of the world for nearly two and a half years; he thought that it was about time that he started to give some thought to his future. After all, he couldn't depend on anyone when he got old; he had no family, no friends. It was beyond the realm of possibility that one of the henchmen or underlings would be so loyal; Tom pictured his feeble, helpless old age, nothing left but his scrapbook of microfiche cards. He wondered why he had forsaken love.

Well, he answered himself, somebody had to. Somebody had to make the sacrifices. He was actually very proud of himself, but he had no illusions about what the people of the world would think of him ten, twenty years after he turned the governmental control over. They would remember him in much the way they remembered Stan, Ed, Nelson, Denny, and Chuck: on stamps every once in a while, in little plastic figures collected by the nostalgic, and very often by the wrong names.

"I've got a great deal for you," he said to TECT. The computer made no reply. It had heard the same thing from many, many people over the years. "How would you like to speed things up? Let's take a look at Operation Knee. I want the specs printed out, please. I also want an analysis of how things have changed since we first worked out the operation, and a projection of what the effects would be of activating the operation now instead of in seventeen years."

TECT produced everything that Tom asked for in a few moments. The Representative read through the original report, in which the eventual handling of all facets of government would be turned over to TECT. So much progress had been made during Tom's administration that TECT's analysis and projection showed that the public would be little disrupted by the changeover. Tom had mixed feelings about that.

"How do you feel about the moral implications of Operation Knee?" asked Tom.

RepNA:
There aren't any.

"There must be," said Tom. "I can't understand you. There certainly were moral implications a few years ago. I find it hard to believe that they've disappeared."

RepNA:
Twelve cc. of phosphoric colioate administered intramuscularly will make it much easier to believe.

"All right, all right," said Tom. He sighed. What was he but an extension of TECT already? What was he but an obstacle for TECT? He felt sorry for himself. He had an impulse to call in Miss Brant. He would explain what he contemplated doing, and get her reaction. *Then* TECT would see that there definitely were unfavorable moral connections, at least in the minds of the people at large; but TECT had made a careful analysis, and Tom realized that if Miss Brant came in and voiced her opinion, she might give Tom an unpleasant surprise. "Okay," he said to his tect. "Do it." He tossed the reports into a wastebasket.

The red *Advise* light flashed on the tect.

"What is it?" asked Tom irritably.

09:57:32 16May 3 YT   ReplReq**

RepNA:
Operating coded key phrase is needed.

"I don't remember what it is," said Tom.

RepNA:
"Get thee hence."

"Sure," said Tom sourly. "'Get thee hence.'"

**RepNA:*
Thank you. Operation Knee has begun.

"Fine," said Tom. Then he called in Miss Brant, after all.

Clearing out his desk the next morning, Tom recalled all the wonderful times he had spent during his career. Many times he stopped his work and asked TECT to produce a printed record of some exploit or other, which already had faded from the ex-Representative's mind. Then Tom would return to his labor, packing shopping bags and liquor cartons with the junk that had accumulated since his first election.

Just before lunch, he was interrupted by Miss Brant. "What is it?" he asked.

"Well," said his former secretary, "the office staff wanted to present you with this." She handed him a small package, wrapped in brightly colored foil.

Tom was startled. "Did TECT tell you to do this?" he asked.

Miss Brant looked hurt. "Of course not," she said. "We just thought it would be nice. To thank you and all."

"Of course," said Tom absently, wondering how he could have grown to be so out of touch with people's feelings. He accepted the present with as much grace as he could summon. "I hope it isn't a tie," he said. "I won't be needing a tie where I'm going."

Both he and Miss Brant laughed. "No, it isn't a tie. Open it. We all chipped in."

Tom opened the package. Inside was a pen and pencil stand, with a little metal plaque glued on it that said *To our Representative forever, from his gang down at the shop.* Tom felt nothing as he looked at it. When he glanced back up at Miss Brant, he faked a choked voice and a slight sniff. "Thank them all," he said. "Do that for me." Then he waved and turned around, as though to hide a tear. He was relieved to hear the sound of his door closing again.

TECT had already reassigned Miss Brant and the others to new jobs. Tom wondered where his secretary would go, but he didn't wonder enough to ask her.

That afternoon he stepped through his teletrans unit and emerged into the harsh glare of the California sunlight. He carried a couple of suitcases with him; the rest of his belongings had already been sent ahead. There was a pleasant road through a grove of strange flowering trees. Tom walked slowly along the road toward the house that TECT had prepared for him. The house was pleasant enough from the outside. Tom leaned against his white wooden fence for some time, thinking. Then he went inside.

The house smelled freshly painted and sounded empty. There were odd, uncomfortable echoes wherever he walked. He put his suitcases down in the largest of the three bedrooms. Then he went back to the living room. On the back of the front door, there was a piece of paper taped to the small diamond-shaped window. Tom shrugged and went to see what it was. It was a note from Nelson. It said:

> *Hey, Tom!*
> *Glad you're here finally. When you're all settled in,*
> *come on over. We're eating here tonight. Denny and*
> *Ed are cooking (Ed's gotten a whole lot better). Don't*
> *worry about bringing anything.*
> *We'll work on your mood if you're depressed. Things*
> *aren't so unpleasant here.*
> *After dark, the game starts. Hundred credit minimums.*
> *You ought to clean up—you're a bluffer from 'way back,*
> *ha-ha. No hard feelings. See you soon.*
>
> > *Best,*
> > *Nelson*

Tom tore the note off the door and crumpled it, but he couldn't find a place to throw it. He stuffed it into a pocket and went outside. He had forgotten about the time difference; it was still a couple of hours before dinnertime. He began walking slowly toward Nelson's house. As he walked, he imagined that he could feel the throbbing, buzzing, rumbling of TECT beneath his feet.

COMING-OF-AGE DAY

A. K. Jorgensson

Although sex is still "dirty," it has crept out of shuttered bridal suites to blip on and off on movie marquees from Queens to Tuscaloosa—the blue movie has come of age, along with singles' mixers, married swingers' parties, the pill, legalized abortion, long hair for men, miniskirts, women's rights, living together, and the "youth generation." But there have been small setbacks in the cultural race to freedom—the recent Supreme Court rulings on pornography, the cultural preoccupation with the thirties and forties. Young people have given up social protest, have again become ready to swallow goldfish and pack themselves into telephone booths rather than risk their security. Our "youth generation" is now looking toward a time when we can forget dirty politics, the oil crisis, the cold war, the Manson style of freedom: a time when everything will be ordered and clean and safe. And the pendulum swings inexorably, slowly, cutting down the prophets who have "proven" that the past cannot repeat itself, that technology and progress have forever banished the cyclic nature of morality.

So the future might not be the freaky, psychedelic, incomprehensible world that we might expect—perhaps, instead, a new Victorian age? An age when the ugly, sordid, sexual preoccupations of the past have been taken care of aseptically. Maybe the converse of the pill with be Jorgensson's idea of the consex. Surely sex without sweat and heavy breathing is preferable to "primitive sex." So we might be rushing toward another age of repression, for "all the right reasons." Tomorrow's technology might take care of the misery of adolescence and the "unnatural" natural expression of sex. Perhaps the pendulum is already making its return swing.

A. K. Jorgensson here examines a future in which it has already swung.

I was ten and I still had not seen them! You didn't expect to see a woman's unless you were lucky, which a very few boys at my school professed to be. But nearly everyone my age knew what a man's looked like.

But you got some funny answers.

"You're too young," said a squirt about half my size, and another very big boy nodded agreement.

"We don't want to do any harm," the big one said, wisely as it turned out. His voice was already breaking, and I think he was on the change.

"We're not going to tell you." There were a number of small knots in the playground that took a secretive line, and whispered with their backs to everybody. I belonged to a loose group of boys who, looking back, I would say were intelligent and sensitive and from better homes. Their interests were academic, or real hobbies. But I was a little contemptuous of their ignorance and softness. And I ended up hanging about behind a group led by a capable boy, or breaking roughly into a fighting gang, having a punch-up and then going to skip with the girls. I tried everything. I was nobody's buddy. But a few groups could expect to rely on me if they needed an extra hand to defend themselves against a rough bunch or to try a good game. "Go and get Rich Andrews," someone would say. "He'll play."

They got me one day after school for a very secret meeting on the waste plot between the churchyard and the playing fields. Guards were out at the edge of the bushes. We had to enter over the churchyard wall. And we had to crouch to approach the spot, crawling along the bottoms of crater left between bulldozed heaps and tips of earth.

It was a good hide-out behind a solid screen of leaves, deep in the bushes. Churchill was there; so was Edwards and my friend Pete Loss. They had started something, and I saw it was a bit dubious, because Churchill and Gimble were in a little arbor away from the others, and though I could not see much, they had their trousers down.

"What's up?" I asked Pete.

"Oh, they're playing sexy-lovers," said Pete.

"Why? What's the idea?"

"D'you know all about it?" he asked. "I don't s'pose you do. Oh, I did it once. It's not much. Old Churchill thinks he's got a better way. It gives him a thrill."

"I don't like it," I said. I was curious and afraid, but hoped I sounded like you should when someone's trying to get one up on you and you're not having any.

"Come on," I urged Pete. "Let's go."

"They want to show you," he said.

"Oh, I know all about that," I lied. "I'm not going to play pansy for that dirty beast Churchill."

It took more urging, but when I made a move Pete came too. The guards tried to stop us, as though they had designs on me. I shouted, "Stop it! I shall shout! Aw, come on; play the game," and they let me go. But they persuaded Pete to stay.

I got away and of course kept quiet. And lost another chance to know all about sex. It was the time for sex education, of course, and this gave me a fair technical knowhow, but I didn't have the practical experience. I hesitated to muck about and the teachers didn't exactly encourage it: also, my parents were a bit strict. So I left it.

It was after that party in the bushes that controversy arose. Someone said to Churchill: "You nit. You don't just play about with it. And you don't just get hairy all round. You get something put there at the right age. It's the operation!"

"I don't care about the operation," he said. "You can do this—" and he described masturbation openly enough to make me feel hot.

Miss Darlington was getting close and I was afraid she'd overhear. She had an A-1 pot on her front.

They silenced as she approached, but I heard Elkes say under his breath to Churchill, "Look at their pots! That's where they keep their sex organs. You get outside ones put on your inside ones. Darlie's got a big male thing on hers, it sticks out a mile."

Quite frankly, this horrified me. I had always wondered whether all the hairiness of men came up from the private place and how large the organs grew. But separate adult bathing had come a few years before my first swim, and if they did wear these things on the beach, you couldn't tell them from pot bellies. It sounded like a book I had read which said how pot bellies grew on adolescents now whereas it used to be only old men and middle-aged women. I wondered what lay behind that expression "pot belly." It made me feel funny even to think of it. But it also made me feel sad, just as a fuller sexual awareness did later. You never know which gives more satisfaction—the relief of the sexual act, or the retention of that inner virile feeling when you have refrained for a good while. And there is a sort of dimension that is all power and mind and strength, that the physical conditions don't seem to improve or improve upon.

In the old days, I am told, there used to be more explicit sexual bits in the films. But on television these days, as in the theater, they are very cagey. I heard one master from the upper school, who is reputed to be a wild unrestrained type, call this a second Victorian Age. According to him, every time we get a queen reigning to a ripe old age, it's nearing the end of the century: and people are afraid the millennium will come at the end of 1999. So what with one thing and another, they are fearfully prudish.

Which is ridiculous, because when the naked torso was the fashion they could not have hidden the pot-bellied things they wear these days.

I asked my father one day what happened when people got pot-bellied.

"You know all about that from school, surely, son."

"Well, no, it's the one thing they've never taught us."

"Why did you want to know? It's not always good to know these things."

"Well, I didn't—I mean, well, the boys at school talk about it in the playground. I'm getting pretty big now, dad, nearly eleven. I ought to know what they mean by now."

"I see. I shall have to talk to your head teacher, Rich, I can see that. Anyway, pot bellies are just when people get fat around the lower part of the abdomen. People eat too much these days."

"Oh . . . Only they said at school it wasn't that. Gluttony is frowned on now, and drinking too much. But people still have—"

"That is enough, Rich. In a year or two you will be grown up enough to be able to understand. In the meantime you have had at least two years of education in biology, and you know all about the primitive sex processes."

I knew when to be quiet. Parents were not so strict in the middle of the twentieth century, so the history books say, and it was a bad thing. I wonder if that is why people are ashamed and hide their sexual excesses now. Do as I say and not as I do, etcetera—unwilling hypocrisy, but they can't help it. But that mention of "primitive" sex, it foxed me, because Edwards asked at school what "primitive" meant, and was told that it referred to an early form before it developed. Well, there are two sorts of development, natural maturation and scientific application, and I do not believe the scientific part has been explained to us yet.

Before I peeped and saw, I had just about worked it out. It was a diffident sort of guess, but I reckon it proves what Socrates said. People may not believe me, but I was on the right lines. It was more than those funny ideas I had as a small boy—that people grew their tails long, or that they carried a little hairy monkey about inside their trousers. I tied it up with the artificial creation of living tissue over twenty years ago. These days they are always coming up with new forms of living tissue: they can give you a new body for an old one in bits or *in toto* nowadays. And they have perfected their methods so much that the so-called artificial one is better than the natural one. After all, they have eliminated all these subtle differences between the chemical product and the equivalent natural one, which was one major advance in many.

Now if you see people lose a leg, as I did once (rather, it had to be removed later) and a few months later they've grown a new one, why not improve on the natural, or primitive, sexual organs? I am beginning to agree with an aunt of mine who, in an episode I won't relate, told me there was no pleasure in sex; the sensation of pleasure was in the mind, not the organ or nerve. Well, what if you did get a better organ? If you're not much of a chap anyway, it would do you no good unless it had a psychological improvement on your confidence.

I have more evidence of this point. The only other clue I had before I was thirteen and registered as an adolescent was hearing a conversation between two old men: all they did was complain that the new pot bellies had not solved people's sexual problems after all.

Except the time when I peeped. It was on the beach one day when the sun was very hot and a lot of people sat perspiring in their many light clothes. All of a sudden a woman began to scream and clutch at the lower part of her body, as if to pull something off. After a while women started gathering round and trying to help. But she was desperate and tore her costume, an enveloping thing, until this sort of huge fleshy roll could be seen clinging to her. It could have been a flabby woman's breast, or a fantastic roll of fat, but this would be a bit too unlikely, I reckon. The woman pulled at it, and it gave and stretched out like a tentacle and—"Get away! You nasty little boy. How dare you peep? Go away." After a screech like that I crawled away.

Going to the sexiatrist was the call-up day for coming-of-age even more than one's initiation into the forces came through the medical examination. It was with mixed feelings that I faced the ceremony, having had an enjoyable childhood with no great attraction urging me into manhood. I reported at the Center, and a nurse took my particulars. I signed an agreement that I was prepared to undertake the responsibilities of adulthood; all rather vague, as it was a matter of contracting out to avoid the consequences rather than contracting in. Had I refused, I should have had twenty forms to sign and dozens of conditions written in fine print. Either that, I had heard, or I ended up in a harsh institution for the backward.

First a doctor checked my family doctor's assessment of my sexual age. He examined me with that frankness and propriety that scientific control over sexual phenomena demanded, took blood samples and a tiny piece of my skin, looked into my eyes and checked my height, coloring and so on. Most of the time I was modestly allowed to keep my pants on, even though I was stripped of all else, including my watch.

After going through the mass radiography room, the cancer-heat-test room and other places, and receiving various boosters against the various plagues, I was sent home, walking out with a curious sense of illness-at-ease, ordinariness and anticlimax.

It took me by surprise to get another Ministry postcard two weeks later, requesting my presence once more at the Sexual

Health Center. This time it was in the afternoon, and the nurse ushered me into the doctor's other surgery with a little more respect. There was a tiny holding of the breath and it made me more expectant.

"Good afternoon, Andrews. Nice to see you again. Still feeling in good health?"

"Yes, sir, thank you." One never admits that one has never felt quite the same since being pumped with inoculatives.

"Ready to have a consex fitted! Now, Andrews, this is a most private matter which I think will explain itself. We are not afraid to be scientific about sex as a subject, but I trust you will keep this to yourself. If you are not completely satisfied—*for any reason whatsoever*—tell no one but come and see me. Is that understood?"

"Yes, Doctor."

"I am a sexiatrist, actually, not a doctor. Now come and look in this glass container."

I looked. As I believe it usually does to others, it struck me with a sort of horror to see this thing alive, a collapsed sort of dumpling with ordinary human skin, sitting in its case like a part of a corpse that had been cut off.

"Get used to it," he said. "It's only ordinary flesh. It has a tiny pulse with a primitive sort of heart, and blood and muscle. And fat. It's just flesh. Alive, of course, but perfectly harmless."

He lifted the lid and touched it. It gave, then formed round his finger. He moulded it like dough or plasticine and it gave way, though it tended to roll back to a certain shapelessness.

"Touch it."

"I couldn't."

"Go on."

He was firm and I obeyed. It had a touch like skin and was warm. It might have been part of someone's fat stomach. I pushed my finger in, and the thing squeezed the finger gently with muscular contractions.

"It's yours," he announced.

I nearly fainted with horror. It strikes everyone that way until they realize how simple, harmless and useful free living tissue can be, and its many healing purposes. It embarrassed me to guess where the "consex" was to be located on my body, and my intuition was uncertain with equally embarrassing ignorance. But one only has to wear a consex a short while to realize how utterly natural it is, and how delightfully pleasant when in active use. It is a boon to lone explorers, astronauts, occupants of remote weather and defense stations, and so on.

"Don't worry," said the specialist as I drew back in disgust. "It's no more horrible than the way you came into the world, or the parts each of your parents played in starting the process. In fact, it's cleaner, more foolproof, and efficient, and far more satisfying than a woman. Thank heaven, without them we'd be overrun."

I feared to do anything. He said, "I'll show you how it works. Don't take it off for at least a week, not for any reason. See me at once if there is any discomfort. Later on, you may remove it for athletics, though you can do most things with it on—swimming, for instance. In the toilet it rolls up easily enough. But don't disturb the suction or play around. It clings well if you leave it alone, and it's very comfortable."

He took me into a private cubicle, where I undressed and lay under a soft blanket. Then he brought the thing in on his hand and pulled the blanket back.

I held my breath. It was the worst moment of my life for fear, though not for pain.

"I've stimulated it a bit," he said. "It'll take over for you this time, but every time after that it's up to you to make the first move, or nothing will happen. It's very responsive. Now you must lie here half an hour until I let you go."

He let it rest between my thighs, and it covered all those parts you never see on pictures of nudes except those in classical religious paintings. It was comfortable. It felt pleasant. This first time when the sexiatrist goes out and leaves one alone with one's body and one's consex and one's private thoughts is the crucial one.

It was only pleasant sensation; I had not been given any warning. So I tolerated it. But at the same time I was disgusted at the smallness of sophisticated adult behavior. Hell, I thought, they take a lot for granted. But my curiosity overcame my dignity, and I did not rebel.

It was hardly over when I heard a conversation which startled me.

"Do you have a letter from your parents?" the sexiatrist was asking someone.

"No."

"But you still refuse to have an appliance fitted?"

"Yes."

"Well, I agree it is not compulsory. But you'll have to give a very good reason for refusing. And without a letter from a doctor or parent or guardian we may not accept your reasons."

"I'm a conscientious objector."

"On what grounds? Do you realize what you're letting yourself in for by refusing to wear a consex?"

"I don't believe all the claims made for it," he said, but feebly.

"You don't even know them," said the sexiatrist, condescendingly. "I'm quite sure of that. But surely you want to know what it's all about first? Surely the subject fascinates you so that you are interested enough to desire the experience for a while?"

"No, sir. In principle."

"In principle! What do *you* know about it? Tell me. What *do* you know about so vast a subject?"

"I don't believe in the principles the welfare authorities base it on."

"You don't believe in them! You don't believe them despite the fact that the government authorizes me to fit every boy and girl with an appropriate consex as soon as he or she reaches puberty. Every boy and girl in this population of over eighty million wears one—"

"Not *every* boy and girl."

"All but one or two in a million, and those are mostly for health or mixed-sex reasons. They are approved by the R. M. A. and every major health, legal and educational authority in the country. Virtually all religious denominations have welcomed them. But you refuse."

"Welcomed, sir? I don't believe any of them."

"I see. You don't believe that this country is heavily overpopulated? You don't believe that before consexes came out the years of adolescence were years of miserable misfits trying to adjust to a half-baked situation? And that boys slept promiscuously in spurious natural sexual relations, that girls had illegitimate babies sometimes from the earliest years it is possible to conceive, and that mere children contracted serious venereal diseases from these methods.

"You think you can do without all this. And what sort of substitute will you have? Tearing about on a rocket-scooter or getting drunk! Raping a woman or just stealing her handbag! And if and when you grow up . . .

"Did you know that there are ten million bachelors and the same number of spinsters in this country who have never been married nor had a so-called love affair but are sexually wholly satisfied and consummated? Did you?"

"It may have been in the papers, sir."

"Tell me." He spoke kindly and coaxingly for a moment. "Is it because you've picked up some little bad habit? It's very common, nothing to be ashamed of. This thing will help you."

"No, sir."

"Come on now, man of principles. Square with me. Haven't you? Are you sure you've never committed . . . well, self-abuse?"

"What, sir? I—I haven't done anything wrong."

"Come off it, lad. No one has ever never done anything wrong."

"But I haven't, sir."

"Do your parents approve of your attitude?"

"I think so, sir."

"You think so? That's not good enough. Now come on. Be a good chap and let us fit you a consex. It's much nicer than natural sex or any of that. You don't want to be the odd man out, do you?"

"No, sir—"

"Good. All right, then. Nurse, he's accepted after all. Get it out, will you."

"No, I haven't, sir. No!"

"I am an authority on this, lad. You mean to say you still haven't accepted that the government knows what is best for the nation after all I've told you?"

"I haven't, sir, no. It's not the government—"

"You haven't? But I thought just now you said you had."

"I didn't want to be the odd man out; but I can't wear one of these."

"Then you will be the odd man out, won't you? What d'you mean, you can't? Come into the laboratory and let me show you."

There was silence then for nearly half an hour. Now I know what one of those laboratories looks like, I can imagine the sexiatrist taking him round, telling him to peer into a microscope and see tiny microbes swiveling about in plasma, showing him charts of the amino acids, the blood-types, the cell-types, the skin-types, etcetera, pulling out samples for quick-fire experiments, and showing him a few easily digested examples of living tissues artificially made for various purposes. Then the door opened and in they came.

"Well, what did you think of it?"

"Very interesting, sir."

"Impressive, wasn't it? Wasn't it?"

"Yes, sir."

"Now what do you say? It's up to you. You have some idea how it works now, and you're not afraid any longer, I hope."

"No, sir."

"You'll consider it."

"I am considering it, sir."

"Oh, good. Do you think you'll be able to decide now?"

"Oh, yes."

"Good. I'll call the nurse then, shall I?"

No answer. He rang the desk bell.

"You won't refuse us after all that, now, will you?"

"Well . . . Please, sir . . ."

"I'm going to ring your parents."

The nurse came in, dropped my clothes on the bed, and shut the door. I heard the phone click as I slid out of bed, then click again.

"I'll give you one more chance," said the sexiatrist. "In case you're ashamed or anything. Nurse, tell me, do you wear a consex?"

"Yes, doctor, I do."

"A male consex?"

"Yes."

"And you like it? It's comfortable, not unhealthy? You can do what you like? You don't feel guilty about it?"

"I love it," she said. "I've never had difficulty with it. It always responds to my lead and never disobeys."

"Thank you. Now, boy, are you satisfied?"

"What happened the first time?" the boy asked the nurse with a mixture of sheepishness and daring.

The nurse said nothing. I wondered if she blushed. The boy said: "My father called it an artificial prostitute."

"Nonsense, lad. You don't know what you're talking about. They say worse things about holy matrimony, so-called."

"I have religious objections," said the boy. "I can control myself without all this."

"All what? Without all what?" the doctor asked sharply.

"This . . . appliance."

"It's only living flesh," he said. "Look, here's one. See? I touch it. If God hadn't meant this stuff to exist, it wouldn't exist, would it? Now you touch it. Don't your parents wear one?"

"No, sir, they don't."

"Ah! Well, you're quite free to do as *you* please. Don't be afraid to go against them. As I told you, the authorities have called you up for the purpose of giving you one, and you are protected by the law. We shall support you to the hilt. Your parents don't object to fluoridation, do they? Or antismog in the air?"

"Yes, sir, they do."

"Hmmm."

I heard a muttered "Nut cases" outside my door, and the nurse opened it for the sexiatrist. He strode through, booming.

"Andrews, ah, Andrews, you're a sensible lad. Now you've just become a man and learned all about it. How d'you like it?"

"All right, sir."

"Feels okay, doesn't it?"

"Yes, sir," I said, "very nice," though sneakingly I sympathized with the boy out there. I knew the voice of all the temporal powers was speaking through the sexiatrist, and all the pressures were being brought to bear, but I admired him for resisting.

The sexiatrist knelt and held me.

"Now, sir," he said, "now, Mr. Andrews, would you mind very much if we showed our friend here how nicely the little consex fits? We have to show you how it feeds, too, because it's going to grow and mature right along with you. That's why it's important this lad Topolski has his fitted now."

I detected the tiny note of disdain at the boy's foreign name, and half inclined to retort at the sexiatrist for the one he had used all along.

"He doesn't have to, does he?"

"Now don't you start," said the doctor, and he drew me forward, levering off my pants at the same time.

"What's wrong with that?" asked the sexiatrist, showing the consex fitting like a fig leaf and looking as innocuous as a fold of skin. "I've even thought," he went on, half to himself, half to the young nurse, "that they're far more aesthetic than the bare uni-sex, and this return to clothing oneself at all times and in all places is quite unnecessary. The time will come when things will turn full circle, and we shan't be afraid to go completely nude again."

I saw the point. I began almost to like my consex, even though the sensation it could give was disturbingly overwhelming. But the boy turned away after a cursory examination. He said nothing.

"Well?" asked the big man, and I realized all of a sudden the mental pressure, the semi-mesmeric force of it that I had allowed to ride me, and that this small dark twelve-year-old was bucking. "You don't want a black mark on your book, do you?"

I wondered, What book? I did not know, then, that the State's records kept its finger on this one more aspect of a man's "suitability."

"I do a lot of sport," he said weakly, almost visibly wilting, and looking for somewhere to hide. He must have felt awful, foolish and mixed-up.

"Ah, so that's what it is! Well now. Dearson, the world champion marathon runner, actually wears his running! And all the other athletes have them. They simply take them off and wrap them in a little blanket—like this one—while they're participating. No trouble at all. Now come on, be a good chap. We'll just take your measurements—most of them are compulsory—and leave it to you to come back later and collect your consex. How about that?"

"All right," he said. I saw him stiffening his resistance again to the paternal air, and felt fairly sure the internalized authority would not be strong enough in him to bring him to accepting the consex. But he would have to submit to the tests as required. The sexiatrist would ring his parents later, then he would have to return and sign the many forms, by one of which he would delegate to the Minister of Health responsibility for his sexual welfare—a condition mentally as unacceptable to him and his parents as the consex was physically unacceptable.

I was dressed and dismissed, yet I lingered at the specialist's door waiting vaguely for something. Then the boy gave his address. It was just round the corner from mine.

The fact that we were neighbors does not seem important, perhaps. But it's going to be. I am going round when I have a chance, to ask Topolski the real reason why he refused to put on the "appliance."

THANATOS

Vonda N. McIntyre

Western technological nations are often seduced by the idea that you can fix something after the fact, that you can turn omelets back into eggs. This is a comforting, visceral concept—especially when we are faced with problems that seem nearly insolvable. It lets us sit still and do nothing, and yet not feel guilty about it; in fact, we are likely to experience that smug technological complacency known as "breadth of vision"—and that is one hell of a lot better than having to face an August night on the Lower East Side of Manhattan when the air conditioner has just browned out.

The "fix-it-later" philosophy takes our problems comfortably out of our hands, out of sight, out of mind. All is solved by the simple expedient of passing the responsibility for today's problems on to future generations, putting the onus on people who might not even *exist because of our own abnegation, let alone be capable of alleviating situations better dealt with fifty years before.*

This is the logic of the child who breaks the cookie jar, but keeps on playing anyway, serenely confident that the shattered pieces of crockery can somehow be pressed back together long before Mommy gets home.

In this fashion, it becomes acceptable to strip-mine—you fill in the pits with water when you're done, and turn them into children's swimming holes. You don't have to worry about pollution, because someday we'll be able to vacuum it right out of the air. You don't have to worry about the race problem, because in the future, intermarriage will have turned everybody gray. You don't have to worry about the way we're wiping out whole species of animals and birds, because in the future we'll always be able to clone more. You don't have to worry about making this planet an unfit place to live, because we can always go out and find another one.

Nebula winner Vonda N. McIntyre here examines the ultimate consequences of this kind of buck-passing, cookie-jar logic: a shattered future world no glue will ever be strong enough to put together, a society too drained to be able to afford anything other than the brutal black-and-white logic of survival, a life in which you must perpetually run merely to stay in place. Along the way, she also makes some pertinent comments as to the nature of the Enemy, and the processes which turn revolutionaries into reactionaries, radicals into bank executives, and young idealists into scarred and weary oldsters. Walt Kelly once said that "We have met the enemy and he is us."

Who else did we expect him to be?

EDITORS' NOTE: THIS IS AN ORIGINAL STORY, PUBLISHED HERE FOR THE FIRST TIME.

SECURITY took Allin to the factory in chains: she had tried to escape twice, and almost succeeded once. On this kind of assignment, they could not use the anesthetic they carried, for it lingered in the blood.

The duocar slid out of heavy traffic and stopped on the parking rail. It had run electric all the way from court, slowly, without the use of the gas engine that was only legal in security cars. Allin was glad of any delay, anything that gave her a few more minutes.

The factory was a low, innocuous gray building among other low gray buildings. Most of it was safely underground. The two security men took Allin out of the mesh cage in the back of the car. She stopped on the dirty sidewalk despite the press of other people, despite the city smells nauseating her, despite the city noises roaring around them. She looked up.

Wide stairs led half a flight to a featureless door. The windows of the next two floors were covered with riveted metal plates. Above the building, above the whole city, yet seeming very close, the cloudy-gray-brown sky threatened snow. Involuntarily Allin shivered, but she could not pretend she was cold. The security people expected her to try again to bolt for freedom and concealment in the crowds. She could feel their fingers, nervously tight on her arms, and the thin steel chain cutting into her palms where she gripped it. Beneath the cuffs her wrists were scraped raw.

"Come on." They half lifted her. She held up her head and would not let them hurry her off-balance. The manacles should have been around her throat, to explain the tightness there.

They reached the top of the stairs. In fumbling for the pass, one let go of her arm. Without thinking she jerked around, half away from the other, already running.

He was too well trained; he had been ready for her. He yanked her back hard; her boot slipped on the concrete step. She fell backwards, unable to catch herself. Cement scraped cloth and bruised her hip; she heard a single quick gruff word, "Don't," a corner of the stair slammed into her side, just below her ribs. It took her a moment to regain her breath. She looked up and saw the two men glaring at each other. The one who had let her go had his pass in one hand and his partner's club in the other, holding it back.

"I'm sick and tired—"

"It won't matter in a little while. Maybe—" But he did not finish what had begun in sadness and ended in disgust. He turned away, slapping the car onto the sensor next to the door. The other man looked down at Allin, scowling. He met her gaze for a moment, then looked away. Allin took a deep breath and climbed to her feet. Neither of them helped her. She had not expected them to. "Suck," she muttered, and got the satisfaction of seeing his knuckles whiten around the club at her use of the slang.

The door opened. They led her down a long hall painted pale gray-green, lined with closed doors, stretching away to an elevator.

They did not speak during the long drop. Allin could feel the tension, in them and in herself. It peaked with the deceleration of the slowing cage.

A technician was waiting for them at the bottom. It was the first time Allin really had to believe that she was here and that there was no way out.

"You're late."

"We had some trouble."

The technician shrugged. "Doesn't matter. Doctor won't be here for a while."

"Where do you want her?" The gentler security man seemed to have withdrawn inside himself. His eyes could not stay still.

"You're anxious to get out." The technician sounded at the same time defensive and contemptuous.

"That's right."

"We've probably saved your life more than once."

"Yeah." Even the agreement was accusation. "You've probably saved everybody in the world at least once." He looked at Allin. She could see hurt in his pale eyes; she did not think he had done this job before. She wondered if he would talk about duty if she asked him why he could not have turned his head and let her go. "Probably even her." He was not speaking to the technician any more.

"Sit her down over there and you can sign and get out."

"She'll kill you," the suck told him. "I said we had trouble."

Allin scowled: she had broken laws, but she had never killed. She remained silent.

"Chain her, then, I don't care." He went back to his desk and pressed buttons on a console.

The security men took her to a bench, unchained one of her hands, and relocked the manacle around the armrest. Walking away, neither agent looked back at her.

At his desk, the technician brought out a light-pen so they could sign the screen. Allin wondered what the printing said. "Brought on this day into involuntary servitude, one human being, having been deprived of life, liberty, consciousness, and humanity, as punishment for acts against society, and for the good of mankind . . ." The technician made out a receipt for her. He watched the two agents in silence with an ugly half-smile until they were almost inside the elevator. "Hey, sucks, how about the key?"

The gentler one flushed, pulled it out of his pocket, and threw it into the room just as the doors closed. The technician sauntered over and picked it up, tossed it and caught it and laughed when he saw Allin watching. His eyes measured her, as if for a scalpel or a shroud. Contemptuous of herself for it, she felt blood rise in her face.

"You ought to last a long time," the tech said. His face held the child's innocence of a psychopath. He turned back to his desk and called up another form. "Name," he said. He knew it: it must be on the screen before him.

"Press the right button and your machine will tell you." She regretted the words as soon as she spoke; he was taunting her for his own amusement, and a response would only make his game more pleasurable.

"Listen," he said, very patiently, "don't make trouble." She did not answer. "Christ." He looked at the ceiling in mock supplication. "A stubborn one." He glanced back at her, but his expression held no mercy. "This can be as easy or as hard as you want." He gave her a moment to think that over; it was not necessary. "Things happen to people in the wards . . . did you know that some of them can feel pain through the drugs we use? They go crazy from it, and then" He pointed his finger at her and cocked his thumb. "Bang! We shoot them." He laughed and caressed the control panel of the console. The green fluorescence of the printing gave his face an eerie cast. "No offspring, no dependents, no contracts . . ." He raised an eyebrow. "Ah, you're one of the guerrillas. What a stupid way to waste your life."

She forced herself to sit silently through it. Her nails, despite their shortness, dug into her palms. Her life *was* a waste; even in the idealistic enthusiasm of her adolescence, she had known that a bunch of kids and aging revolutionaries could have none but a gadfly effect on the institutions they had sworn to change. The planet's living system was battered to homogeneity before Allin was even born. Her guerrilla team was a sad, lost conscience, never strong enough to halt the progression and turn it around. Every one of her friends knew they would end up dead in the sea, decomposing in a dying forest, or . . . here.

The technician tried again. "Some of the orderlies . . . they come pretty close to being necrophiles. Long hours. Boredom. You know. I can't watch them all the time. Not much to do here but feed the animals and milk them." He smiled, and his teeth showed. He sickened her. She turned away, and he laughed. A shallow, bloody crescent in her palm cut across the lifeline.

"The animals sometimes end up looking pretty awful," he said. "Scars and things . . . one of them got pregnant once. We let her have it even after we used a genetic virus on her—"

"It won't matter to me," Allin said. "I'll have no mind."

"Sometimes they get pardoned," he said. "We bring them back almost as good as new . . . unless something's happened—"

"You're a liar."

He stood up, smiling again. "You're right." He moved toward her, wearing a deceptively engaging expression. "So how about one last little bit of fun?" He reached to touch her.

In the final minutes of her life, Allin might have been able to accept a gift of a few moments of pleasure, a gift of human contact, but this would be no gift. It was an expression of power. She kicked the technician in the groin with all the thrust in her long legs. He cried out in agony, falling, writhing. Allin sat back on the bench, as the technician curled in fetal position as though to avoid further blows. Regaining his breath, he crawled away from her. After a few minutes he was able to use the desk corner to pull himself up. "What'd you do that for?" His voice was that of a child wrongly punished.

She looked past him, silent.

He laughed, but the sound was shaky. He made work for himself.

The elevator door slid open, and the doctor entered. She glanced from the tech, still pale, to Allin, but said nothing. She picked up the key, and stopped a meter out of Allin's reach. "There's no way out and I'm very good at judo."

Silence kept Allin's pride more than a direct acquiescence. The doctor freed her from the bench but kept the chains locked around her wrists. Taking her arm, she led Allin through another door, to a sterile white room with an examining table and glass cases of drugs and instruments. The room smelled of astringent antiseptics and sick-sweet anesthetic. Allin stopped in the doorway, against the pressure of the doctor's hand.

"It's really not bad. Just sleep . . ."

"We're all asleep," Allin said.

"Did you think you could wake people up?" The doctor's voice was tense, intense. "All that energy, all that vision—"

"—wasted," Allin finished for her, harshly.

"Come along." The doctor spoke coldly and professionally again; Allin had a quick vision of the future: the flashes of anger and pain would slowly seep from the doctor's soul, and she would survive.

She would survive, while Allin was approaching the end of her conscious life.

"I want to see where I'll be," she whispered.

Allin startled her: the doctor did not speak for what seemed a very long time.

". . . All right."

She led Allin through a labyrinth of corridors, deeper into the earth. The air grew cooler. When they reached wide double doors the doctor took her arm again. The doors swung open, allowing an incongruous breeze to escape. The room beyond was kept at positive pressure, to exclude unapproved germs. The doctor led Allin onto the ward.

No mammals remained on earth, except a few rodents in laboratories and slums, and perhaps the potential of wildlife, stored as frozen ova and sperm or cell clones in universities or museums, for some unlikely future. No birds lived but a few garbage scavengers. Complete food protein came from fish, cell cultures, improved grains, but the world had discovered that only the intricate biochemistry of a living animal sufficed for some endeavors. Horses, for decades, produced antibodies against human disease: infected, the animals lived and produced serum, vaccines for people.

All the horses, all the mammals larger and smaller than a rat, were extinct. Except for human beings.

Allin hardly saw the orderlies staring at her. Before her stretched long rows of frame beds, their circular supports echoing each other across a vast distance. A still and silent body hung suspended in each. Nakedness and sex were incidentally concealed by torso supports. No pressure sores would develop on these valuable animals.

The ceiling was a transparent plastic web of pipes carrying nutrient fluid to tubes, to needles, to permanent inlets sewn in veins. Catheters carried wastes to outlets in the floor. Allin took one more step inside the room. She could hear quiet breathing, like sounds in a cemetery. The anesthetic smell was very strong. All the eyelids were dark and sunken and all the heads and bodies shaved bald. Needle scars and the scars of viral lesions covered projecting arms and legs and sexless faces, and halfway down the nearest row, orderlies were drawing blood, cleanly, sterilely, to extract antibodies with the serum.

Milking the animals.

The sound in Allin's throat was half a moan, half sob. The doctor heard her, sensed the danger, held her tighter, but Allin caught her in the sternum with her elbow and ran. Behind her, she could hear gasping, and the footsteps and voices of the orderlies. She knew she could not escape the ward or the building, that any action she could take would be foolish and futile. She climbed a shining arc of frame between hanging tubes like snakes. She was only slightly hampered by the chains. She hesitated at the apex of a frame, then leaped for the largest nutrient pipe within her reach. It was never meant for extra strain. Her momentum pulled it loose and as she hit the floor the sticky warm wet stuff splashed across her, the tile, the zombies in the beds. She sprinted for another place to climb where the network burbled on.

"Stop!"

She was ready to jump again when she heard the warning. The fumes of anesthetic mixed with nutrients dizzied her, but she saw the doctor, and she saw the gun, as though through heat waves rising from a desert. She gauged her distance to the next tube and jumped.

The bullet shattered the prisoner's skull, tore through her brain, and threw her crumpled to the floor.

An orderly rushed out to turn off the nutrient flow. The doctor stood silently as a pool of the stuff reached her feet. The gun was warm in her hand, smoking. She heard the other orderly pick up the phone. "We need the heart-lung machine," he said.

If not for this place, the doctor thought, *millions of people would die. If not for this place . . .* The gun fell heavily to the floor.

"Never mind," she said abruptly.

"What, ma'am?"

"Never mind."

"The body's still usable—"

"Call the morgue," the doctor said. No one ever argued with her when she used that tone. "Have her cremated."

The orderly hesitated, then cut the connection. "Yes, ma'am." He keyed out a different number.

THE EYEFLASH MIRACLES

Gene Wolfe

In a recent Vector *article, Gene Wolfe says: "Oz was a place you could go to: this was the great and striking fact about it. I spent a good deal of time for twenty years or so in trying to figure out how to do it, and found the answer at last."*

Similarly, a good story is like a map of life—not the humdrum, everyday, nonresolution life that we trundle through daily from nine to five, but the life that we tenderly piece together out of what we love best. We throw away the dross, polish the rare moments of wonder, and turn the gray muddle of mundane life into meaningful emotional experience. Fiction can be a guidebook to the brighter, more intense countries that exist alongside our own, solid as concrete, insubstantial as a feather. It can sketch out walking tours through the wonderful gardens and the haunted forests, point out interesting places to visit and comfortable—or exciting—places to stay, bring us safely through the sulfur swamps and guide us up to high places overlooking vistas of shattering ugliness and dangerous beauty. More importantly, it can enable us to meet the people who live in that other place, and to look out through their eyes—the monsters, the angels, the gods, the aliens, the glittering creatures, the clayfolk, a marvelous and terrible populace speaking in strange tongues that are your own. As R. A. Lafferty says in The Devil Is Dead: *"the monstrous and wonderful archetypes are not inside you, not in your own unconscious; you are inside them, trapped, and howling to get out."*

For the far countries have a life of their own—they can impinge on everyday reality at any time, settling down like snow and covering our world with theirs, turning our cold, hard-edged world into a chip of flint englobed in amber. Swallowing the reality of school and state, life and death, cause and effect, all the things from which we can't escape.

Or can we?

Here Nebula winner Gene Wolfe—considered by many to be one of the best SF writers of the decade—offers us a tour of just such an alien country, one contiguous with our own. It's a country that will be familiar to those of us who are secretly Dorothy or the Scarecrow or the Wizard or even the Witch of the West, no matter whom we tell outsiders we are, or what lying name we have on our mailboxes; to those who look at Birmingham or Tallahassee or Philadelphia and see through them to the hidden reality of Oz.

EDITORS' NOTE: THIS IS AN ORIGINAL STORY, PUBLISHED HERE FOR THE FIRST TIME.

> *"I cannot call him to mind."*
>
> —ANATOLE FRANCE, *The Procurator of Judea*

LITTLE TIB heard the train coming while it was still a long way away, and he felt it in his feet. He stepped off the track onto a prestressed concrete tie, listening. Then he put one ear to the endless steel and listened to that sing, louder and louder. Only when he began to feel the ground shake under him did he lift his head at last and make his way down the embankment through the tall, prickly weeds, probing the slope with his stick.

The stick splashed water. He could not hear it because of the noise the train made roaring by; but he knew the feel of it, the kind of drag it made when he tried to move the end of the stick. He laid it down and felt with his hands where his knees would be when he knelt, and it felt all right. A little soft, but no broken glass. He knelt then and sniffed the water, and it smelled good and was cool to his fingers, so he drank, bending down and sucking up the water with his mouth, then splashing it on his face and the back of his neck.

"Say!" an authoritative voice called. "Say, you boy!"

Little Tib straightened up, picking up his stick again. He thought, This could be Sugarland. He said, "Are you a policeman, sir?"

"I am the superintendent."

That was almost as good. Little Tib tilted his head back so the voice could see his eyes. He had often imagined coming to Sugarland and how it would be there; but he had never considered just what it was he should say when he arrived. He said, "My card . . ." The train was still rumbling away, not too far off.

Another voice said: "Now don't you hurt that child." It was not authoritative. There was the sound of responsibility in it.

"You ought to be in school, young man," the first voice said. "Do you know who I am?"

Little Tib nodded. "The superintendent."

"That's right, I'm the superintendent. I'm Mr. Parker himself. Your teacher has told you about me, I'm sure."

"Now don't hurt that child," the second voice said again. "He never did hurt you."

"Playing hooky. I understand that's what the children call it. We never use such a term ourselves, of course. You will be referred to as an absentee. What's your name?"

"George Tibbs."

"I see. I am Mr. Parker, the superintendent. This is my valet; his name is Nitty."

"Hello," Little Tib said.

"Mr. Parker, maybe this absentee boy would like to have something to eat. He look to me like he has been absentee a long while."

"Fishing," Mr. Parker said. "I believe that's what most of them do."

"You can't see, can you?" A hand closed on Little Tib's arm. The hand was large and hard, but it did not bear down. "You can cross right here. There's a rock in the middle—step on that."

Little Tib found the rock with his stick and put one foot there. The hand on his arm seemed to lift him across. He stood on the rock for a moment with his stick in the water, touching bottom to steady himself. "Now a great big step." His shoe touched the soft bank on the other side. "We got a camp right over here. Mr. Parker, don't you think this absentee boy would like a sweet roll?"

Little Tib said, "Yes, I would."

"I would too," Nitty told him.

"Now, young man, why aren't you in school?"

"How is he going to see the board?"

"We have special facilities for the blind, Nitty. At Grovehurst there is a class tailored to make allowance for their disability. I can't at this moment recall the name of the teacher, but she is an exceedingly capable young woman."

Little Tib asked, "Is Grovehurst in Sugarland?"

"Grovehurst is in Martinsburg," Mr. Parker told him. "I am superintendent of the Martinsburg Public School System. How far are we from Martinsburg now, Nitty?"

"Two, three hundred kilometers, I guess."

"We will enter you in that class as soon as we reach Martinsburg, young man."

Nitty said, "We're going to Macon—I keep on tellin' you."

"Your papers are all in order, I suppose? Your grade and attendance records from your previous school? Your withdrawal permit, birth certificate, and your retinal pattern card from the Federal Reserve?"

Little Tib sat mute. Someone pushed a sticky pastry into his hands, but he did not raise it to his mouth.

"Mr. Parker, I don't think he's got papers."

"That is a serious—"

"Why he got to have papers? He ain't no dog!"

Little Tib was weeping. "I see!" Mr. Parker said. "He's blind; Nitty, I think his retinas have been destroyed. Why, he's not really here at all."

"'Course he's here."

"A ghost. We're seeing a ghost, Nitty. Sociologically he's not real —he's been deprived of existence."

"I never in my whole life seen a ghost."

"You dumb bastard," Mr. Parker exploded.

"You don't have to talk to me like that, Mr. Parker."

"You dumb bastard. All my life there's been nobody around but dumb bastards like you." Mr. Parker was weeping too. Little Tib felt one of his tears, large and hot, fall on his hand. His own sobbing slowed, then faded away. It was outside his experience to hear grown people—men—cry. He took a bite from the roll he had been given, tasting the sweet, sticky icing and hoping for a raisin.

"Mr. Parker," Nitty said softly. "Mr. Parker."

After a time, Mr. Parker said, "Yes."

"He—this boy George—might be able to get them, Mr. Parker. You recall how you and me went to the building that time? We looked all around it a long while. And there was that window, that old window with the iron over it and the latch broken. I pushed on it and you could see the glass move in a little. But couldn't either of us get between those bars."

"This boy is blind, Nitty," Mr. Parker said.

"Sure he is, Mr. Parker. But you know how dark it was in there. What is a man going to do? Turn on the lights? No, he's goin' to take a little bit of a flashlight and put tape or something over the end till it don't make no more light than a lightnin' bug. A blind person could do better with no light than a seeing one with just a little speck like that. I guess he's used to bein' blind by now. I guess he knows how to find his way around without eyes."

A hand touched Little Tib's shoulder. It seemed smaller and softer than the hand that had helped him across the creek. "He's crazy," Mr. Parker's voice said. "That Nitty. He's crazy. I'm crazy, I'm the one. But he's crazier than I am."

"He could do it, Mr. Parker. See how thin he is."

"Would you do it?" Mr. Parker asked.

Little Tib swallowed a wad of roll. "Do what?"

"Get something for us."

"I guess so."

"Nitty, build a fire," Mr. Parker said. "We won't be going any farther tonight."

"Won't be goin' this way at *all*," Nitty said.

"You see, George," Mr. Parker said. "My authority has been temporarily abrogated. Sometimes I forget that."

Nitty chuckled somewhere farther away than Little Tib had thought he was. He must have left very silently.

"But when it is restored, I can do all the things I said I would do for you: get you into a special class for the blind, for example. You'd like that, wouldn't you, George?"

"Yes." A whippoorwill called far off to Little Tib's left, and he could hear Nitty breaking sticks.

"Have you run away from home, George?"

"Yes," Little Tib said again.

"Why?"

Little Tib shrugged. He was ready to cry again. Something was thickening and tightening in his throat, and his eyes had begun to water.

"I think I know why," Mr. Parker said. "We might even be able to do something about that."

"*Here* we are," Nitty called. He dumped his load of sticks, rattling, more or less in front of Little Tib.

Later that night Little Tib lay on the ground with half of Nitty's blanket over him, and half under him. The fire was crackling not too far away. Nitty said the smoke would help to drive the mosquitoes off. Little Tib pushed the heels of his hands against his eyes and saw red and yellow flashes like a real fire. He did it again, and there was a gold nugget against a field of blue. Those were the last things he had been able to see for a long time, and he was afraid, each time he summoned them up, that they would not come. On the other side of the fire Mr. Parker breathed the heavy breath of sleep.

Nitty bent over Little Tib, smoothing his blanket, then pressing it in against his sides. "It's okay," Little Tib said.

"You're goin' back to Martinsburg with us," Nitty said.

"I'm going to Sugarland."

"After. What you want to go there for?"

Little Tib tried to explain about Sugarland, but could not find words. At last he said, "In Sugarland they know who you are."

"Guess it's too late then for me. Even if I found somebody knew who I was I wouldn't be them no more."

"You're Nitty," Little Tib said.

"That's right. You know I used to go out with those gals a lot. Know what they said? Said, 'You're the custodian over at the school, aren't you?' Or, 'You're the one that did for Buster Johnson.' Didn't none of them know who I was. Only ones that did was the little children."

Little Tib heard Nitty's clothes rustle as he stood up, then the sound his feet made walking softly away. He wondered if Nitty was going to stay awake all night; then he heard him lie down.

His father had him by the hand. They had left the hanging-down train, and were walking along one of the big streets. He could see. He knew he should not have been noticing that particularly, but he did, and far behind it somewhere was knowing that if he woke up he would not see. He looked into store windows, and he could see big dolls like girls' dolls wearing fur coats. Every hair on every coat stood out drenched with light. He looked at the street and could see all the cars like big, bright-colored bugs. "Here," Big Tib said; they went into a glass thing that spun them around and dumped them out inside a building, then into an elevator all made of glass that climbed the inside wall almost like an ant, starting and stopping like an ant did. "We should buy one of these," Little Tib said. "Then we wouldn't have to climb the steps."

He looked up and saw that his father was crying. He took out his, Little Tib's, own card and put it in the machine, then made Little Tib sit down in the seat and look at the bright light. The machine was a man in a white coat who took off his glasses and said, "We don't know who this child is, but he certainly isn't anyone." "Look at the bright light again, Little Tib," his father said, and something in the way he said it told Little Tib that the man in the white coat was much stronger than he was. He looked at the bright light and tried to catch himself from falling.

And woke up. It was so dark that he wondered for a minute where the bright light went. Then he remembered. He rolled over a little and put his hand out toward the fire until he could feel some heat. He could hear it too when he listened. It crackled and snapped, but not very much. He lay the way he had been before, then turned over on his back. A train went past, and after a while an owl hooted.

He could see here too. Something inside him told him how lucky he was, seeing twice in one night. Then he forgot about it, looking at the flowers. They were big and round, growing on long stalks, and had yellow petals and dark brown centers, and when he was not looking at them, they whirled around and around. They could see him, because they all turned their faces toward him, and when he looked at them they stopped.

For a long way he walked through them. They came a little higher than his shoulder.

Then the city came down like a cloud and settled on a hill in front of him. As soon as it was there it pretended that it had been there all the time, but Little Tib could feel it laughing underneath. It had high, green walls that sloped in as they went up. Over the top of them were towers, much taller, that belonged to the city. Those were green too, and looked like glass.

Little Tib began to run, and was immediately in front of the gates. These were very high, but there was a window in them, just over his head, that the gate-man talked through. "I want to see the king," Little Tib said, and the gate-man reached down with a long, strong arm and picked him up and pulled him through the little window and set him down again inside. "You have to wear these," he said, and took out a pair of toy glasses like the ones Little Tib had once had in his doctor set. But when he put them on Little Tib, they were not glasses at all, only lines painted on his face, circles around his eyes joined over his nose. The gate-man held up a mirror to show him, and he had the sudden, dizzying sensation of looking at his own face.

A moment later he was walking through the city. The houses had their gardens sidewise—running up the walls so that the trees thrust out like flagpoles. The water in the birdbaths never ran out until a bird landed in it. Then a fine spray of drops fell to the street like rain.

The palace had a wall too, but it was made by trees holding hands. Little Tib went through a gate of bowing elephants and saw a long, long stairway. It was so long and so high that it seemed that there was no palace at all, only the steps going up and up forever into the clouds, and then he remembered that the whole city had come down out of the clouds. The king was coming down those stairs, walking very slowly. She was a beautiful woman, and although she did not look at all like her, Little Tib knew that she was his mother.

He had been seeing so much while he was asleep that when he woke up he had to remember why it was so dark. Somewhere in the back of his mind there was still the idea that waking should be light and sleep dark, and not the other way around. Nitty said: "You ought to wash your face. Can you find the water all right?"

Little Tib was still thinking of the king, with her dress all made of Christmas-tree stuff; but he could. He splashed water on his face and arms while he thought about how to tell Nitty about his dream. By the time he had finished, everything in the dream was gone except for the king's face.

Most of the time Mr. Parker sounded like he was important and Nitty was not, but when he said, "Are we going to eat this morning, Nitty?" it was the other way around.

"We eat on the train," Nitty told him.

"We are going to catch a train, George, to Martinsburg," Mr. Parker told Little Tib.

Little Tib thought that the trains went too fast to be caught, but he did not say that.

"Should be one by here pretty soon," Nitty said. "They got to be going slow because there's a road crosses the tracks down there a way. They won't have no time to get the speed up again before they get here. You won't have to run—I'll just pick you up an' carry you."

A rooster crowed way off somewhere.

Mr. Parker said: "When I was a young man, George, everyone thought all the trains would be gone soon. They never said what would replace them, however. Later it was believed that it would be all right to have trains, provided they were extremely modern in appearance. That was accomplished, as I suppose you learned last year, by substituting aluminum, fiberglass, and magnesium for much of the steel employed previously. That not only changed the image of the trains to something acceptable, but saved a great deal of energy by reducing weight—the ostensible purpose of the cosmetic redesign." Mr. Parker paused, and Little Tib could hear the water running past the place where they were sitting, and the sound the wind made blowing the trees.

"There only remained the awkward business of the crews," Mr. Parker continued. "Fortunately it was found that mechanisms of the same type that had already displaced educators and others could be substituted for railway engineers and brakemen. Who would have believed that running a train was as routine and mechanical a business as teaching a class? Yet it proved to be so."

"Wish they would do away with those railroad police," Nitty said.

"You, George, are a victim of the same system," Mr. Parker continued. "It was the wholesale displacement of labor, and the consequent nomadism, that resulted in the present reliance on retinal patterns as means of identification. Take Nitty and me, for example. We are going to Macon—"

"We're goin' to Martinsburg, Mr. Parker," Nitty said. "This train we'll be catching will be going the *other* way. We're goin' to get into that building and let you program, you remember?"

"I was hypothesizing," Mr. Parker said. "We are going—say—to Macon. There we can enter a store, register our retinal patterns, and receive goods to be charged to the funds which will by then have accumulated in our social relief accounts. No other method of identification is so certain, or so adaptable to data processing techniques."

"Used to have money you just handed around," Nitty said.

"The emperors of China used lumps of silver stamped with an imperial seal," Mr. Parker told him. "But by restricting money solely—in the final analysis—to entries kept by the Federal Reserve Bank, the entire cost of printing and coining is eliminated; and of course control for tax purposes is complete. While for identification, retinal patterns are unsurpassed in every—"

Little Tib stopped listening. A train was coming. He could hear it far away, hear it go over a bridge somewhere, hear it coming closer. He felt around for his stick and got a good hold on it.

Then the train was louder, but the noise did not come as fast. He heard the whistle blow. Then Nitty was picking him up with one strong arm. There was a swoop and a jump and a swing, swing, swing, and they were on the train and Nitty set him down. "If you want to," Nitty said, "you can sit here at the edge and hang your feet over. But you be careful."

Little Tib was careful. "Where's Mr. Parker?"

"Laying down in the back. He's going to sleep—he sleeps a lot."

"Can he hear us?"

"You like sitting like this? This is one of my most favorite of all things to do. I know you can't see everything go by like I can, but I could tell you about it. You take right now. We are going up a long grade, with nothing but pinewoods on this side of the train. I bet you there is all kinds of animals in there. You like animals, George? Bears and big old cats."

"Can he hear us?" Little Tib asked again.

"I don't think so, because he usually goes to sleep right away. But it might be better to wait a little while, if you've got something you don't want him to hear."

"All right."

"Now there's one thing we've got to worry about. Sometimes there are railroad policemen on these trains. If someone is riding on

them, they throw him off. I don't think they'd throw a little boy like
you off, but they would throw Mr. Parker and me off. You they
would probably take back with them and give over to the real
police in the next town."

"They wouldn't want me," Little Tib said.

"How's that?"

"Sometimes they take me, but they don't know who I am. They
always let me go again."

"I guess maybe you've been gone from home longer than what I
thought. How long since you left your Mom and Dad?"

"I don't know."

"Must be some way of telling blind people. There's lots of blind
people."

"The machine usually knows who blind people are. That's what
they say. But it doesn't know me."

"They take pictures of your retinas—you know about that?"

Little Tib said nothing.

"That's the part inside your eye that sees the picture. If you
think about your eye like it was a camera, you got a lens in the
front, and then the film. Well, your retinas is the film. That's what
they take a picture of. I guess yours is gone. You know what it is
you got wrong with your eyes?"

"I'm blind."

"Yes, but you don't know what it is, do you, baby. Wish you
could look out there now—we're going over a deep place; lots of
trees, and rocks and water way down below."

"Can Mr. Parker hear us?" Little Tib asked again.

"Guess not. Looks like he's asleep by now."

"Who is he?"

"Like he told you. He's the superintendent; only they don't want
him any more."

"Is he really crazy?"

"Sure. He's a dangerous man, too, when the fit comes on him. He
got this little thing put into his head when he was superintendent
to make him a better one—extra remembering and arithmetic, and
things that would make him want to work more and do a good job.
The school district paid for most of it; I don't know what you call
them, but there's a lot of teenie little circuits in them."

"Didn't they take it out when he wasn't superintendent
anymore?"

"Sure, but his head was used to it by then, I guess. Child, do you feel well?"

"I'm fine."

"You don't look so good. Kind of pale. I suppose it might just be that you washed off a lot of the dirt when I told you to wash that face. You think it could be that?"

"I feel all right."

"Here, let me see if you're hot." Little Tib felt Nitty's big, rough hand against his forehead. "You feel a bit hot to me."

"I'm not sick."

"Look there! You see that? There was a bear out there. A big old bear, black as could be."

"Probably it was a dog."

"You think I don't know a bear? It stood up and waved at us."

"Really, Nitty?"

"Well, not like a person would. It didn't say *bye-bye*, or *hi there*. But it held up one big old arm." Nitty's hands lifted Little Tib's right arm.

A strange voice, a lady's voice, Little Tib thought, said, "Hello there yourself." He heard the thump as somebody's feet hit the floor of the boxcar; then another thump as somebody else's did.

"Now wait a minute," Nitty said. "Now you look here."

"Don't get excited," another lady's voice told him.

"Don't you try to throw us off of this train. I got a little boy here, a little blind boy. He can't jump off no train."

Mr. Parker said, "What's going on here, Nitty?"

"Railroad police, Mr. Parker. They're going to make us jump off of this train."

Little Tib could hear the scraping sounds Mr. Parker made when he stood up, and wondered whether Mr. Parker was a big man or a little man, and how old he was. He had a pretty good idea about Nitty; but he was not sure of Mr. Parker, though he thought Mr. Parker was pretty young. He decided he was also medium-sized.

"Let me introduce myself," Mr. Parker said. "As superintendent, I am in charge of the three schools in the Martinsburg area."

"Hi," one of the ladies said.

"You will begin with the lower grades, as all of our new teachers do. As you gain seniority, you may move up if you wish. What are your specialties?"

"Are you playing a game?"

Nitty said: "He don't quite understand—he just woke up. You woke him up."

"Sure."

"You going to throw us off the train?"

"How far are you going?"

"Just to Howard. Only that far. Now you listen, this little boy is blind, and sick too. We want to take him to the doctor at Howard—he ran away from home."

Mr. Parker said, "I will not leave this school until I am ready. I am in charge of the entire district."

"Mr. Parker isn't exactly altogether well either," Nitty told the women.

"What has he been using?"

"He's just like that sometimes."

"He sounds like he's been shooting up on chalk."

Little Tib asked, "What's your name?"

"Say," Nitty said, "that's right. You know, I never did ask that. This little boy here is telling me I'm not polite."

"I'm Alice," one of the ladies said.

"Mickie," said the other.

"But we don't want to know your names," Alice continued. "See, suppose someway they heard you were on the train—we'd have to say who you were."

"And where you were going," Mickie put in.

"Nice people like you—why do you want to be railroad police?"

Alice laughed. "What's a nice girl like you doing in a place like this? I've heard that one before."

"Watch yourself, Alice," Mickie said. "He's trying to make out."

Alice said, "What'd you three want to be 'boes for?"

"We didn't. 'Cept maybe for this little boy here. He run away from home because the part of his eyes that they take pictures of is gone, and his momma and daddy couldn't get benefits. At least, that's what I think. Is that right, George?"

Mr. Parker said, "I'll introduce you to your classes in a moment."

"Him and me used to be in the school," Nitty continued. "Had good jobs there, or so we believed. Then one day that big computer downtown says, 'Don't need you no more,' and out we goes."

"You don't have to talk funny for us," Mickie said.

"Well, that's a relief. I always do it a little, though, for Mr. Parker. It makes him feel better."

"What was your job?"

"Buildings maintenance. I took care of the heating plant, and serviced the teaching and cleaning machines, and did the electrical repair work generally."

"Nitty!" Little Tib called.

"I'm here, li'l boy. I won't go way."

"Well, we have to go," Mickie said. "They'll miss us pretty soon if we don't get back to patrolling this train. You fellows remember you promised you'd get off at Howard. And try not to let anyone see you."

Mr. Parker said, "You may rely on our cooperation."

Little Tib could hear the sound of the women's boots on the box-car floor, and the little grunt Alice gave as she took hold of the ladder outside the door and swung herself out. Then there was a popping noise, as though someone had opened a bottle of soda, and a bang and clatter when something struck the back of the car.

His lungs and nose and mouth all burned. He felt a rush of saliva too great to contain. It spilled out of his lips and down his shirt; he wanted to run, and he thought of the old place, where the creek cut (cold as ice) under banks of milkweed and goldenrod. Nitty was yelling: "Throw it out! Throw it out!" And somebody, he thought it was Mr. Parker, ran full tilt into the side of the car. Little Tib was on the hill above the creek again, looking down across the bluebonnets toward the surging, glass-dark water, and a kite-flying west wind was blowing.

He sat down again on the floor of the boxcar. Mr. Parker must not have been hurt too badly, because he could hear him moving around, as well as Nitty.

"You kick it out, Mr. Parker?" Nitty said. "That was good."

"Must have been the boy. Nitty—"

"Yes, Mr. Parker."

"We're on a train . . . The railroad police threw a gas bomb to get us off. Is that correct?"

"That's true sure enough, Mr. Parker."

"I had the strangest dream. I was standing in the center corridor of the Grovehurst school, with my back leaning against the lockers. I could feel them."

"Yeah."

"I was speaking to two new teachers—"

"I know." Little Tib could feel Nitty's fingers on his face, and Nitty's voice whispered, "You all right?"

"—giving them the usual orientation talk. I heard something make a loud noise, like a rocket. I looked up then, and saw that one of the children had thrown a stink bomb—it was flying over my head, laying a trail of smoke. I went after it like I used to go after a ball when I was an outfielder in college, and I ran right into the wall."

"You sure did. Your face looks pretty bad, Mr. Parker."

"Hurts too. Look, there it is."

"Sure enough. Nobody kick it out after all."

"No. Here, feel it; it's still warm. I suppose a chemical burns to generate the gas."

"You want to feel, George? Here, you can hold it."

Little Tib felt the warm metal cylinder pressed into his hands. There was a seam down the side, like a Coca-Cola can, and a funny-shaped thing on top.

Nitty said, "I wonder what happened to all the gas."

"It blew out," Mr. Parker told him.

"It shouldn't of done that. They threw it good—got it right back in the back of the car. It shouldn't blow out that fast, and those things go on making gas for a long time."

"It must have been defective," Mr. Parker said.

"Must have been." There was no expression in Nitty's voice.

Little Tib asked, "Did those ladies throw it?"

"Sure did. Came down here and talked to us real nice first, then to get up on top of the car and do something like that."

"Nitty, I'm thirsty."

"Sure you are. Feel of him, Mr. Parker. He's hot."

Mr. Parker's hand was softer and smaller than Nitty's. "Perhaps it was the gas."

"He was hot before."

"There's no nurse's office on this train, I'm afraid."

"There's a doctor in Howard. I thought to get him to Howard . . ."

"We haven't anything in our accounts now."

Little Tib was tired. He lay down on the floor of the car, and heard the empty gas canister roll away, too tired to care.

". . . a sick child . . ." Nitty said. The boxcar rocked under him, and the wheels made a rhythmic roar like the rushing of blood in the heart of a giantess.

He was walking down a narrow dirt path. All the trees, on both sides of the path, had red leaves, and red grass grew around their roots. They had faces, too, in their trunks, and talked to one another as he passed. Apples and cherries hung from their boughs.

The path twisted around little hills, all covered with the red trees. Cardinals hopped in the branches, and one fluttered to his shoulder. Little Tib was very happy; he told the cardinal, "I don't want to go away—ever. I want to stay here, forever. Walking down this path."

"You will, my son," the cardinal said. It made the sign of the cross with one wing.

They went around a bend, and there was a tiny little house ahead, no bigger than the box a refrigerator comes in. It was painted with red and white stripes, and had a pointed roof. Little Tib did not like the look of it, but he took a step nearer.

A full-sized man came out of the little house. He was made all of copper, so he was coppery-red all over, like a new pipe for the bathroom. His body was round, and his head was round too, and they were joined by a real piece of bathroom pipe. He had a big mustache stamped right into the copper, and he was polishing himself with a rag. "Who are you?" he said.

Little Tib told him.

"I don't know you," the copper man said. "Come closer so I can recognize you."

Little Tib came closer. Something was hammering, *bam, bam, bam,* in the hills behind the red and white house. He tried to see what it was, but there was a mist over them, as though it were early morning. "What is that noise?" he asked the copper man.

"That is the giant," the copper man said. "Can't . . . you . . . see . . . her?"

Little Tib said that he could not.

"Then . . . wind . . . my . . . talking key . . . I'll . . . tell . . . you . . ."

The copper man turned around, and Little Tib saw that there were three keyholes in his back. The middle one had a neat copper label beside it printed with the words "TALKING ACTION."

". . . about . . . her."

There was a key with a beautiful handle hanging on a hook beside the hole. He took it and began to wind the copper man.

"That's better," the copper man said. "My words—thanks to your fine winding—will blow away the mists, and you'll be able to see her. I can stop her; but if I don't, you'llbekilledthatsenough."

As the copper man had said, the mists were lifting. Some, however, did not seem to blow away—they were not mists at all, but a mountain. The mountain moved, and was not a mountain at all, but a big woman wreathed in mist, twice as high as the hills around her. She was holding a broom, and while Little Tib watched, a rat as big as a railroad train ran out of a cave in one of the hills. *Bam,* the woman struck at it with her broom; but it ran into another cave. In a moment it ran out again. *Bam!* The woman was his mother, but he sensed that she would not know him—that she was cut off from him in some way by the mists, and the need to strike at the rat.

"That's my mother," he told the copper man. "And that rat was in our kitchen in the new place. But she didn't keep hitting at it and hitting at it like that."

"She is only hitting at it once," the copper man said, "but that once is over and over again. That's why she always misses it. But if you try to go any farther down this path, her broom will kill you and sweep you away. Unless I stop it."

"I could run between the swings," Little Tib said. He could have, too.

"The broom is bigger than you think," the copper man told him. "And you can't see it as well as you think you can."

"I want you to stop her," Little Tib said. He was sure he could run between the blows of the broom, but he was sorry for his mother, who had to hit at the rat all the time, and never rest.

"Then you must let me look at you."

"Go ahead," Little Tib said.

"You have to wind my motion key."

The lowest keyhole was labeled "MOVING ACTION." It was the largest of all. There was a big key hanging beside it, and Little Tib used it to wind the moving action, hearing a heavy pawl clack inside the copper man each time he turned the key. "That's enough," the copper man said. Little Tib replaced the key, and the copper man turned around.

"Now I must look into your eyes," he said. His own eyes were stampings in the copper, but Little Tib knew that he could see out of them. He put his hands on Little Tib's face, one on each side. They were harder even than Nitty's, but smaller too, and very cold. Little Tib saw his eyes coming closer and closer.

He saw his own eyes reflected in the copper man's face as if they were in a mirror, and they had little flames in them like the flames of two candles in church; and the flames were going out. The copper man moved his face closer and closer to his own. It got darker and darker. Little Tib said, "Don't you know me?"

"You have to wind my thinking key," the copper man said.

Little Tib reached behind him, stretching his arms as far as they would go around the copper body. His fingers found the smallest hole of all, and a little hook beside it; but there was no key.

A baby was crying. There were medicine smells, and a strange woman's voice said, "There, there." Her hands touched his cheeks, the hard, cold hands of the copper man. Little Tib remembered that he could not really see at all, not any more.

"He *is* sick, isn't he," the woman said. "He's hot as fire. And screaming like that."

"Yes, ma'am," Nitty said. "He's sick sure enough."

A little girl's voice said, "What's wrong with him, Mamma?"

"He's running a fever, dear, and of course he's blind."

Little Tib said, "I'm all right."

Mr. Parker's voice told him, "You will be when the doctor sees you, George."

"I can stand up," Little Tib said. He had discovered that he was sitting on Nitty's lap, and it embarrassed him.

"You awake now?" Nitty asked.

Little Tib slid off his lap and felt around for his stick, but it was gone.

"You been sleepin' ever since we were on the train. Never did wake up more than halfway, even when we got off."

"Hello," the little girl said. *Bam. Bam. Bam.*

"Hello," Little Tib said back to her.

"Don't let him touch your face, dear. His hands are dirty."

Little Tib could hear Mr. Parker talking to Nitty, but he did not pay any attention to them.

"I have a baby," the girl told him, "and a dog. His name is Muggly. My baby's name is Virginia Jane." *Bam.*

"You walk funny," Little Tib said.

"I have to."

He bent down and touched her leg. Bending down made his head peculiar. There was a ringing sound he knew was not real, and it seemed to have fallen off him, and to be floating around in front of him somewhere. His fingers felt the edge of the little girl's skirt, then her leg, warm and dry, then a rubber thing with metal under it, and metal strips like the copper man's neck going down at the sides. He reached inside them and found her leg again, but it was smaller than his own arm.

"Don't let him hurt her," the woman said.

Nitty said, "Why, he won't hurt her. What are you afraid of? A little boy like that."

He thought of his own legs walking down the path, walking through the spinning flowers toward the green city. The little girl's leg was like them. It was bigger than he had thought, growing bigger under his fingers.

"Come on," the little girl said. "Mamma's got Virginia Jane. Want to see her?" *Bam.* "Momma, can I take my brace off?"

"No, dear."

"I take it off at home."

"That's when you're going to lie down, dear, or have a bath."

"I don't need it, Momma. I really don't. See?"

The woman screamed. Little Tib covered his ears. When they had still lived in the old place and his mother and father had talked too loudly, he had covered his ears like that, and they had seen him and become more quiet. It did not work with the woman. She kept on screaming.

A lady who worked for the doctor tried to quiet her, and at last the doctor herself came out and gave her something. Little Tib could not see what it was, but he heard her say over and over, "Take this, take this." And finally the woman took it.

Then they made the little girl and the woman go into the doctor's office. There were more people waiting than Little Tib had known about, and they were all talking now. Nitty took him by the arm. "I don't want to sit in your lap," Little Tib said. "I don't like sitting in laps."

"You can sit here," Nitty said. He was almost whispering. "We'll move Virginia Jane over."

Little Tib climbed up into a padded plastic seat. Nitty was on one side of him, and Mr. Parker on the other.

"It's too bad," Nitty said, "you couldn't see that little girl's leg. I saw it. It was just a little matchstick-sized thing when we set down here. When they carried her in, it looked just like the other one."

"That's nice," Little Tib said.

"We were wondering—did you have something to do with that?"

Little Tib did not know, and so he sat silent.

"Don't push him, Nitty," Mr. Parker said.

"I'm not pushing him. I just asked. It's important."

"Yes, it is," Mr. Parker said. "You think about it, George, and if you have anything to tell us, let us know. We'll listen."

Little Tib sat there for a long time, and at last the lady who worked for the doctor came and said, "Is it the boy?"

"He has a fever," Mr. Parker told her.

"We have to get his pattern. Bring him over here."

Nitty said, "No use." And Mr. Parker said, "You won't be able to take his pattern—his retinas are gone."

The lady who worked for the doctor said nothing for a little while; then she said, "We'll try anyway," and took Little Tib's hand and led him to where a bright light machine was. He knew it was a bright light machine from the feel and smell of it, and the way it fitted around his face. After a while she let him pull his eyes away from the machine.

"He needs to see the doctor," Nitty said. "I know without a pattern you can't charge the government for it. But he is a sick child."

The lady said, "If I start a card on him, they'll want to know who he is."

"Feel his head. He's burning up."

"They'll think he might be in the country illegally. Once an investigation like that starts, you can never stop it."

Mr. Parker asked, "Can we talk to the doctor?"

"That's what I've been telling you. You can't see the doctor."

"What about me. I'm ill."

"I thought it was the boy."

"I'm ill too. Here." Mr. Parker's hands on his shoulders guided Little Tib out of the chair in front of the bright light machine, so that Mr. Parker could sit down himself instead. Mr. Parker leaned forward, and the machine hummed. "Of course," Mr. Parker said, "I'll have to take him in with me. He's too small to leave alone in the waiting room."

"This man could watch him."

"He has to go."

"Yes, ma'am," Nitty said, "I sure do. I shouldn't have stayed around this long, except this was all so interesting."

Little Tib took Mr. Parker's hand, and they went through narrow, twisty corridors into a little room to see the doctor.

"There's no complaint on this," the doctor said. "What's the trouble with you?"

Mr. Parker told her about Little Tib, and said that she could put down anything on his own card that she wanted.

"This is irregular," the doctor said. "I shouldn't be doing this. What's wrong with his eyes?"

"I don't know. Apparently he has no retinas."

"There are such things as retinal transplants. They aren't always effective."

"Would they permit him to be identified? The seeing's not really that important."

"I suppose so."

"Could you get him into a hospital?"

"No."

"Not without a pattern, you mean."

"That's right. I'd like to tell you otherwise, but it wouldn't be the truth. They'd never take him."

"I understand."

"I've got a lot of patients to see. I'm putting you down for influenza. Give him these, they ought to reduce his fever. If he's not better tomorrow, come again."

Later, when things were cooling off, and the day-birds were all quiet, and the night-birds had not begun yet, and Nitty had made a fire and was cooking something, he said, "I don't understand why she wouldn't help the child."

"She gave him something for his fever."

"More than that. She should have done more than that."

"There are so many people—"

"I know that. I've heard all that. Not really that many at all. More in China and some other places. You think that medicine is helping him?"

Mr. Parker put his hand on Little Tib's head. "I think so."

"We goin' to stay here so we can take him, or keep on goin' back to Martinsburg?"

"We'll see how he is in the morning."

"You know, the way you are now, Mr. Parker, I think you might do it."

"I'm a good programmer, Nitty. I really am."

"I know you are. You work that program right, and that machine will find out they need a man running it again. Need a maintenance man too. Why does a man feel so bad if he don't have real payin' work to do—tell me that. Did I let them put something in my head like you?"

"You know as well as I," Mr. Parker said.

Little Tib was no longer listening to them. He was thinking about the little girl and her leg. I dreamed it, he thought. Nobody can do that. I dreamed that I only had to touch her, and it was all right. That means what is real is the other one, the copper man and the big woman with the broom.

An owl called, and he remembered the little buzzy clock that stood beside his mother's bed in the new place. Early in the morning the clock would ring, and then his father had to get up. When they had lived in the old place, and his father had a lot of work to do, he had not needed a clock. Owls must be the real clocks; they made their noise so he would wake up to the real place.

He slept. Then he was awake again, but he could not see. "You best eat something," Nitty said. "You didn't eat nothing last night. You went to sleep, and I didn't want to rouse you." He gave Little Tib a scrap of cornbread, pressing it into his hands. "It's just left-overs now," he said, "but it's good."

"Are we going to get on another train?"

"Train doesn't go to Martinsburg. Now, we don't have a plate, so I'm putting this on a piece of newspaper for you. You get your lap smoothed out so it doesn't fall off."

Little Tib straightened his legs. He was hungry, and he decided it was the first time he had been hungry in a long while. He asked, "Will we walk?"

"Too far. Going to hitchhike. All ready now? It's right in the middle." Little Tib felt the thick paper, still cool from the night before, laid upon his thighs. There was weight in the center; he moved his fingers to it and found a yam. The skin was still on it, but it had been cut in two. "Baked that in the fire last night," Nitty said. "There's a piece of ham there too that we saved for you. Don't miss that."

Little Tib held the half yam like an ice cream cone in one hand, and peeled back the skin with the other. It was loose from having been in the coals, and crackly and hard. It broke away in flakes and chips like the bark of an old sycamore. He bit into the yam and it was soft but stringy, and its goodness made him want a drink of water.

"Went to a poor woman's house," Nitty said. "That's where you go if you want something to eat for sure. A rich person is afraid of you. Mr. Parker and I, we can't buy anything. We haven't got credit for September yet—we were figuring we'd have that in Macon."

"They won't give anything for me," Little Tib said. "Mama had to feed me out of hers."

"That's only because they can't get no pattern. Anyway, what difference does it make? That credit's so little-bitty that you almost might not have anything. Mr. Parker gets a better draw than I do because he was making more when we were working, but that's not very much, and you wouldn't get but the minimum."

"Where is Mr. Parker?"

"Down a way, washing. See, hitchhiking is hard if you don't look clean. Nobody will pick you up. We got one of those disposable razor things last night, and he's using it now."

"Should I wash?"

"It couldn't hurt," Nitty said. "You got tear-streaks on your face from cryin' last night." He took Little Tib's hand and led him along a cool, winding path with high weeds on the sides. The weeds were wet with dew, and the dew was icy cold. They met Mr. Parker at the edge of the water. Little Tib took off his shoes and clothes and waded in. It was cold, but not as cold as the dew had been. Nitty waded in after him and splashed him, and poured water from his cupped hands over his head, and at last ducked him under—telling him first—to get his hair clean. Then the two of them washed their clothes in the water and hung them on bushes to dry.

"Going to be hard, hitchhiking this morning," Nitty said.

Little Tib asked why.

"Too many of us. The more there is, the harder to get rides."

"We could separate," Mr. Parker suggested. "I'll draw straws with you to see who gets George."

"No."

"I'm all right. I'm fine."

"You're fine now."

Mr. Parker leaned forward. Little Tib knew because he could hear his clothes rustle, and his voice got closer as well as louder. "Nitty, who's the boss here?"

"You are, Mr. Parker. Only if you went off by yourself like that, I'd worry so I'd about go crazy. What have I ever done to you that you would want to worry me like that?"

Mr. Parker laughed. "All right, I'll tell you what we'll do. We'll try until ten o'clock together. If we haven't gotten a ride by then,

I'll walk half a mile down the road and give the two of you the first shot at anything that comes along." Little Tib heard him get to his feet. "You think George's clothes are dry by now?"

"Still a little damp."

"I can wear them," Little Tib said. He had worn wet clothing before, when he had been drenched by rain.

"That's a good boy. Help him put them on, Nitty."

When they were walking out to the road, and he could tell that Mr. Parker was some distance ahead of them, Little Tib asked Nitty if he thought they would get a ride before ten.

"I know we will," Nitty said.

"How do you know?"

"Because I've been praying for it hard, and what I pray hard for I always get."

Little Tib thought about that. "You could pray for a job," he said. He remembered that Nitty had told him he wanted a job.

"I did that, right after I lost my old one. Then I saw Mr. Parker again and how he had got to be, and I started going around with him to look after him. So then I had a job—I've got it now. Mr. Parker's the one that doesn't have a job."

"You don't get paid," Little Tib said practically.

"We get our draws, and I use that—both of them together—for whatever we need; and if he kept his and I kept mine, he would have more than me. You be quiet now—we're coming to the road."

They stood there a long time. Occasionally a car or a truck went by. Little Tib began to wonder if Mr. Parker and Nitty were holding out their thumbs. He remembered seeing people holding out their thumbs when he and his parents were moving from the old place. He thought of what Nitty had said about praying and began to pray himself, thinking about God and asking that the next car stop.

For a long time more no cars stopped. Little Tib thought about a cattle truck stopping and told God he would ride with the cattle. He thought about a garbage truck stopping, and told God he would ride on top of the garbage. Then he heard something old coming down the road. It rattled, and the engine made a strange, high-pitched noise an engine should not make. "Looks like a old school bus," Nitty said. "But look at those pictures on the side."

"It's stopping," Mr. Parker said, and then Little Tib could hear the sound the doors made opening.

A new voice, high for a man's voice and talking fast, said, "You seek to go this way? You may come in. All are welcome in the temple of Deva."

Mr. Parker got in, and Nitty lifted Little Tib up the steps. The doors closed behind them. There was a peculiar smell in the air.

"You have a small boy. That is well. The god is most fond of small children and the aged. Small boys and girls have innocence. Old persons have tranquillity and wisdom. These are the things that are pleasing to the god. We should strive without effort to retain innocence, and to attain tranquillity and wisdom as soon as we can."

Nitty said, "Right on."

"He is a handsome boy." Little Tib felt the driver's breath, warm and sweet, on his face, and something dangling struck him lightly on the chest. He caught it, and found that it was a piece of wood with three crossbars, suspended from a thong. "Ah," the new voice said, "you have discovered my amulet."

"George can't see," Mr. Parker explained. "You'll have to excuse him."

"I am aware of this, having observed it earlier; but perhaps it is painful for him to hear it spoken of. And now I must go forward again before the police come to inquire why I have stopped. There are no seats—I have removed all the seats but this one. It is better that people take seats on the floor before Deva. But you may stand behind me if you wish. Is that agreeable?"

"We'll be happy to stand," Mr. Parker said.

The bus lurched into motion. Little Tib held onto Nitty with one hand and onto a pole he found with the other. "We are in motion again. That is fitting. It would be most fitting if we might move always, never stopping. I had thought to build my temple on a boat—a boat moves always because of the rocking of the waves. I may still do this."

"Are you going through Martinsburg?"

"Yes, yes, yes," the driver said. "Allow me to introduce myself: I am Dr. Prithivi."

Mr. Parker shook hands with Dr. Prithivi, and Little Tib felt the bus swerve from its lane. Mr. Parker yelled, and when the bus was straight again, he introduced Nitty and Little Tib.

"If you're a doctor," Nitty said, "you could maybe look at George sometime. He hasn't been well."

"I am not this sort of doctor," Dr. Prithivi explained. "Rather instead I am a doctor for the soul. I am a Doctor of Divinity of the University of Bombay. If someone is sick a physician should be summoned. Should they be evil they should summon me."

Nitty said, "Usually the family don't do that because they're so glad to see them finally making some money."

Dr. Prithivi laughed, a little high laugh like music. It seemed to Little Tib that it went skipping around the roof of the old bus, playing on a whistle. "But we are all evil," Dr. Prithivi said, "and so few of us make money. How do you explain that? That is the joke. I am a doctor for evil, and everyone in the world should be calling me even myself all the time. But I cannot come. Office hours nine to five, that is what my sign should say. No house calls. But instead I bring my house, the house of the god, to everyone. Here I collect my fares, and I tell all who come to step to the back of my bus."

"We didn't know you had to pay," Little Tib said. He was worried because Nitty had told him that he and Mr. Parker had no money in their accounts.

"No one must pay—that is the beauty. Those who desire to buy near-diesel for the god may imprint their cards here, but all is voluntary and other things we accept too."

"Sure is dark back there," Nitty said.

"Let me show you. You see we are approaching a roadside park? So well is the universe regulated. There we will stop and recreate ourselves, and I will show you the god before proceeding again."

Little Tib felt the bus swerve with breathtaking suddenness. During the last year that they had lived at the old place, he had ridden a bus to school. He remembered how hot it had been, and how ordinary it had seemed after the first week; now he was dreaming of riding this strange-smelling old bus in the dark, but soon he would wake and be on that other bus again; then, when the doors opened, he would run through the hot, bright sunshine to the school.

The doors opened, clattering and grinding. "Let us go out," Dr. Prithivi said. "Let us recreate ourselves and see what is to be seen here."

"It's a lookout point," Mr. Parker told him. "You can see parts of seven counties from here." Little Tib felt himself lifted down the steps. There were other people around; he could hear their voices, though they were not close.

"It is so very beautiful," Dr. Prithivi said. "We have also beautiful mountains in India—the Himalayas, they are called. This fine view makes me think of them. When I was just a little boy, my father rented a house for summer in the Himalayas. Rhododendrons grew wild there, and once I saw a leopard in our garden."

A strange voice said: "You see mountain lions here. Early in the morning is the time for it—look up on the big rocks as you drive along."

"Exactly so!" Dr. Prithivi sounded excited. "It was very early when I saw the leopard."

Little Tib tried to remember what a leopard looked like, and found that he could not. Then he tried a cat, but it was not a very good cat. He felt hot and tired, and reminded himself that it had only been a little while ago that Nitty had washed his clothes. The seam at the front of his shirt, where the buttons went, was still damp. When he had been able to see, he had known precisely what a cat looked like. He felt now that if only he could hold a cat in his arms he would know again. He imagined such a cat, large and long-haired. It was there, unexpectedly, standing in front of him. Not a cat, but a lion, standing on its hind feet. It had a long tail with a tuft at the end, and a red ribbon knotted in its mane. Its face was a kindly blur and it was dancing—dancing to the remembered flute-music of Dr. Prithivi's laughter—just out of reach.

Little Tib took a step toward it and found his way barred by two metal pipes. He slipped between them. The lion danced, hopping and skipping, striking poses without stopping; it bowed and jigged away, and Little Tib danced too, after it. It would be cheating to run or walk—he would lose the game, even if he caught the lion. It high-stepped, far away then back again almost close enough to touch, and he followed it.

Behind him he heard the gasp of the people, but it seemed dim and distant compared to the piping to which he danced. The lion jigged nearer and he caught its paws and the two of them romped up and down, its face growing clearer and clearer as they whirled and turned—it was a funny, friendly, frightening face.

It was as though he had backed into a bush whose leaves were hands. They clasped him everywhere, drawing him backward against hard metal bars. He could hear Nitty's voice, but Nitty was crying so that he could not tell what he said. A woman was crying too—no, several women; and a man whose voice he did not know was shouting: "We've got him! We've got him!" Little Tib was not sure who he was shouting to; perhaps to nobody.

A voice he did recognize, it was Dr. Prithivi's, was saying: "I have him. You must let go of him so that I may lift him over."

Little Tib's left foot reached out as if it were moving itself and felt in front of him. There was nothing there, nothing at all. The lion was gone, and he knew, now, where he was, on the edge of a mountain, and it went down and down for a long way. Fear came.

"Let go and I will lift him over," Dr. Prithivi told someone else. Little Tib thought of how small and boneless Dr. Prithivi's hands had felt. Then Nitty's big ones took him on one side, an arm and a leg, and the medium-sized hands of Mr. Parker (or someone like him) on the other. Then he was lifted up and back, and put down on the ground.

"He walked . . ." a woman said. "Danced."

"This boy must come with me," Dr. Prithivi piped. "Get out of the way, please." He had Little Tib's left hand. Nitty was lifting him up again, and he felt Nitty's big head come up between his legs and he settled on his shoulders. He plunged his hands into Nitty's thick hair and held on. Other hands were reaching for him; when they found him, they only touched, as though they did not want to do anything more.

"Got to set you down," Nitty said, "or you'll hit your head." The steps of the bus were under his feet, and Dr. Prithivi was helping him up.

"You must be presented to the god," said Dr. Prithivi. The inside of the bus was stuffy and hot, with a strange, spicy, oppressive smell. "Here. Now you must pray. Have you anything with which to make an offering?"

"No," Little Tib said. People had followed them into the bus.

"Then only pray." Dr. Prithivi must have had a cigarette lighter—Little Tib heard the scratching sound it made. There was a soft, "oooah" sound from the people.

"Now you see Deva," Dr. Prithivi told them. "Because you are not accustomed to such things, the first thing you have noticed is that he has six arms. It is for that reason that I wear this cross, which has six arms also. You see I wish to relate Deva to Christianity here. You will note that one of Deva's hands holds a two-armed cross. The others—I will begin here and go around—hold the crescent of Islam, the star of David, a figure of the Buddha, a phallus, and a *katana* sword, which I have chosen to represent the faith of Shintoism."

Little Tib tried to pray, as Dr. Prithivi had directed. In one way he knew what he had been doing when he had been dancing with the lion, and in another he did not. Why hadn't he fallen? He thought of how the stones at the bottom would feel when they hit his face, and shivered.

Stones he remembered very well. Potato-shaped but much larger, hard and gray. He was lost in a rocky land where frowning walls of stone were everywhere, and no plant grew. He stood in the shadow of one of these walls to escape the heat; he could see the opposite wall, and the rubble of jumbled stones between, but this time the knowledge that he could see again gave him no pleasure. He was thirsty, and pressed farther back into the shadow, and found that there was no wall there. The shadow went back and back, farther and farther into the mountain. He followed it and, turning, saw the little wedge of daylight disappear behind him, and was blind again.

The cave—for he knew it was a cave now—went on and on into the rock. Despite the lack of sunlight, it seemed to Little Tib that it grew hotter and hotter. Then from somewhere far ahead he heard a tapping and rapping, as though an entire bag of marbles had been poured onto a stone floor and were bouncing up and down. The noise was so odd, and Little Tib was so tired, that he sat down to listen to it.

As if his sitting had been a signal, torches kindled—first one on one side of the cave, then another on the opposite side. Behind him a gate of close-set bars banged down, and toward him, like spiders, came two grotesque figures. Their bodies were small, yet fat; their arms and legs were long and thin; their faces were the faces of mad old men, popeyed and choleric and adorned with towering peaks of fantastic hair, and spreading mustaches like the feelers of night-crawling insects, and curling three-pointed beards that seemed to have a life of their own so that they twisted and twined like snakes. These men carried long-handled axes, and wore red clothes and the widest leather belts Little Tib had ever seen. "Halt," they cried. "Cease, hold, stop, and arrest yourself. You are trespassing in the realm of the Gnome King!"

"I have stopped," Little Tib said. "And I can't arrest myself because I'm not a policeman."

"That wasn't why we asked you to do it," one of the angry-faced men pointed out.

"But it *is* an offense," added the other. "We're a Police State, you know, and it's up to you to join the force."

"In your case," continued the first gnome, "it will be the labor force."

"Come with us," both of them exclaimed, and they seized him by the arms and began to drag him across the pile of rocks.

"Stop," Little Tib demanded, "you don't know who I am."

"We don't *care* who you am, either."

"If Nitty were here, he'd fix you. Or Mr. Parker."

"Then he'd better fix Mr. Parker, because we're not broken, and we're taking you to see the Gnome King."

They went down twisted sidewise caves with no lights but the eyes of the gnomes. And through big, echoing caves with mud floors, and streams of steaming water in the middle. Little Tib thought, at first, that it was rather fun, but it became realer and realer as they went along, as though the gnomes drew strength and realness from the heat, and at last he forgot that there had ever been anyplace else, and the things the gnomes said were no longer funny.

The Gnome King's throne-cavern was brilliantly lit, and crammed with gold and jewels. The curtains were gold—not gold-colored cloth, but real gold—and the king sat on a bed covered with a spread of linked diamonds, crosslegged. "You have trespassed my dominions," he said. "How do you plead?" He looked like the other gnomes, but thinner and meaner.

"For mercy," Little Tib said.

"Then you are guilty?"

Little Tib shook his head.

"You have to be. Only the guilty can plead for mercy."

"You are supposed to forgive trespasses," Little Tib said, and as soon as he had said that, all the bright lamps in the throne room went out. His guards began to curse, and he could hear the whistle of their axes as they swung them in the dark, looking for him.

He ran, thinking he could hide behind one of the gold curtains; but his outstretched arms never found it. He ran on and on until at last he felt sure that he was no longer in the throne room. He was about to stop and rest then, when he saw a faint light—so faint a light that for a long time he was afraid it might be no more than a trick of his eyes, like the lights he saw when he ground his hands against them. This is my dream, he thought, and I can make the light to be whatever I want it to be. All right, it will be sunlight;

and when I get out into it, it will be Nitty and Mr. Parker and me camped someplace—a pretty place next to a creek of cold water—and I'll be able to see.

The light grew brighter and brighter; it was gold-colored, like sunlight.

Then Little Tib saw trees, and he began to run. He was actually running among the trees before he realized that they were not real trees, and that the light he had seen came from them—the sky overhead was a vault of cold stone. He stopped, then. The trunks and branches of the trees were silver; the leaves were gold; the grass under his feet was not grass but a carpet of green gems, and birds with real rubies in their breasts twittered and flew among the trees —but they were not real birds, only toys. There was no Nitty and no Mr. Parker and no water.

He was about to cry when he noticed the fruit. It hung under the leaves, and was gold, as they were; but for fruit that did not look so unnatural. Each was about the size of a grapefruit. Little Tib wondered if he could pull them from the trees, and the first he touched fell into his hands. It was not heavy enough to be solid. After a moment he saw that it unscrewed in the center. He sat down on the grass (which had become real grass in some way, or perhaps a carpet or a bedspread) and opened it. There was a meal inside, but all the food was too hot to eat. He looked and looked, hoping for a salad that would be wet and cool; but there was nothing but hot meat and gravy, and smoking hot cornmeal muffins, and boiled greens so hot and dry he did not even try to put them in his mouth.

At last he found a small cup with a lid on it. It held hot tea—tea so hot it seemed to blister his lips—but he managed to drink a little of it. He put down the cup and stood up to go on through the forest of gold and silver trees, and perhaps find a better place. But all the trees had vanished, and he was in the dark again. My eyes are gone, he thought, I'm waking up. Then he saw a circle of light ahead and heard the pounding; and he knew that it was not marbles dropped on a floor he heard, but the noise of hundreds and hundreds of picks, digging gold in the mines of the gnomes.

The light grew larger—but dimmed at the same time, as a star-shaped shadow grew in it. Then it was not a star at all, but a gnome coming after him. And then it was a whole army of gnomes, one behind the other, with their arms sticking out at every angle; so that it looked like one gnome with a hundred arms, all reaching for him.

Then he woke, and everything was dark.

He sat up. "You're awake now," Nitty said.

"Yes."

"How you feel?"

Little Tib did not answer. He was trying to find out where he was. It was a bed. There was a pillow behind him, and there were clean, starched sheets. He remembered what the doctor had said about the hospital, and asked, "Am I in the hospital?"

"No, we're in a motel. How do you feel?"

"All right, I guess."

"You remember about dancing out there on the air?"

"I thought I dreamed it."

"Well, I thought I dreamed it too—but you were really out there. Everybody saw it, everybody who was around there when you did it. And then when we got you to come in close enough that we could grab hold of you and pull you in, Dr. Prithivi got you to come back to his bus."

"I remember that," Little Tib said.

"And he explained about his work and all that, and he took up a collection for it and you went to sleep. You were running that fever again, and Mr. Parker and me couldn't wake you up much."

"I had a dream," Little Tib said, and then he told Nitty all about his dream.

"When you thought you were drinking that tea, that was me giving you your medicine, is what I think. Only it wasn't hot tea, it was ice water. And that wasn't a dream you had, it was a nightmare."

"I thought it was kind of nice," Little Tib said. "The king was right there, and you could talk to him and explain what had happened." His hands found a little table next to the bed. There was a lamp on it. He knew he could not see when the bulb lit, but he made the switch go click with his fingers anyway. "How did we get here?" he asked.

"Well, after the collection, when everybody had left, that Dr. Prithivi was hot to talk to you. But me and Mr. Parker said you were with us, and we wouldn't let him unless you had a place to sleep. We told him how you were sick, and all that. So he transferred some money to Mr. Parker's account, and we rented this room. He says he always sleeps in his bus to look after that Deva."

"Is that where he is now?"

"No, he's downtown talking to the people. Probably I should have told you, but it's the day after you did that, now. You slept a whole day full, and a little more."

"Where's Mr. Parker?"

"He's looking around."

"He wants to see if that latch on that window is still broken, doesn't he? And if I'm really little enough to get between those bars."

"That's one thing, yes."

"It was nice of you to stay with me."

"I'm supposed to tell Dr. Prithivi when you're awake. That was part of our deal."

"Would you have stayed anyway?" Little Tib was climbing out of bed. He had never been in a motel before, though he did not want to say so, and he was eager to explore this one.

"*Somebody* would have had to stay with you." Little Tib could hear the faint whistles of the numbers on the telephone.

Later, when Dr. Prithivi came, he made Little Tib sit in a big chair with puffy arms. Little Tib told him about the dancing and how it had felt.

"You can see a bit, I think. You are not entirely blind."

Little Tib said, "No," and Nitty said, "The doctor in Howard told us he didn't have any retinas. How is anybody going to see if they don't have retinas?"

"Ah, I understand, then. Someone told you, I think, about my bus—the pictures I have made on the sides of it. Yes, that must be it. Did they tell you?"

"Tell me about what?" Little Tib asked.

Talking to Nitty, Dr. Prithivi said, "You have described the paintings on the side of my bus to this child?"

"No," Nitty said. "I looked at them when I got in, but I never talked about them."

"Yes, indeed, I did not think so. It was not likely I think that you had seen it before I stopped for you on the road, and you were in my presence after that. Nevertheless, there is a picture on the left side of my bus that is a picture of a man with a lion's head. It is Vishnu destroying the demon Hiranyakasipu. Is it not interesting that this boy, arriving in a vehicle with such a picture should be led to dance on air by a lion-headed figure? It was Vishnu also who circled the universe in two strides; this is a kind of dancing on air, perhaps."

"Uh-huh," Nitty said. "But George here couldn't have seen that picture."

"But perhaps the picture saw him—that is the point you are missing. Still, the lion has many significations. Among the Jews, it is the emblem of the tribe of Judah. For this reason the Emperor of Ethiopia is styled Lion of Judah. Also the son-in-law of Mohammed, whose name I cannot recall now when I need it, was styled Lion of God. Christianity too is very rich in lions. You noticed perhaps that I asked the boy particularly if the lion he saw had wings. I did that because a winged lion is the badge of Saint Mark. But a lion without wings indicates the Christ—this is because of the old belief that the cubs of the lion are dead at birth, and are licked to life afterward by the lioness. In the writings of Sir C. S. Lewis a lion is used in that way; and in the prayers revealed to Saint Bridget of Sweden, the Christ is styled, 'Strong Lion, immortal and invincible King.'"

"And it is the lion that will lay down with the lamb when the time comes," Nitty said. "I don't know much, maybe, about all this, but I know that. And the lamb is about the commonest symbol for Jesus. A little boy—that's a sign for Jesus too."

Mr. Parker's voice said, "How do either of you know God had anything to do with it?" Little Tib could tell that it was a new voice to Nitty and Dr. Prithivi—besides, Mr. Parker was talking from farther away, and after he said that he came over and sat on the bed, so that he was closest of all.

"The hand of the god is in all, Mr. Parker," Dr. Prithivi told him. "Should you prove that it is not to be found, it would be the not-finding. And the not-found, also."

"All right, that's a philosophical position that cannot be attacked, since it already contains the refutation of any attack. But because it can't be attacked, it can't be demonstrated either—it's simply your private belief. My point is that that wasn't what you were talking about. You were trying to find a real, visible, apparent Hand of God—to take His fingerprints. I'm saying they may not be there. The dancing lion may be nothing more than a figment of George's imagination—a dancing lion. Levitation—which is what that was—has often been reported in connection with other paranormal abilities."

"This may be so," Dr. Prithivi said, "but possibly we should ask him. George, when you were dancing with the lion man, did you perhaps feel him to be the god?"

"No," Little Tib said, "an angel."

A long time later, after Dr. Prithivi had asked him a great many questions and left, Little Tib asked Nitty what they were going to do that night. He had not understood Dr. Prithivi.

Mr. Parker said, "You have to appear. You're going to be the boy Krishna."

"Just play like," Nitty added.

"It's supposed to be a masquerade, more or less. Dr. Prithivi has talked some people who are interested in his religion into playing the parts of various mythic figures. Everyone wants to see you, so the high spot will be when you appear as Krishna. He brought a costume for you."

"Where is it?" Little Tib asked.

"It might be better if you don't put it on yet. The important thing is that while everybody is watching you and Nitty and Dr. Prithivi and the other masquers, I'll have an opportunity to get into the County Administration Building and perform the reprogramming I have in mind."

"Sounds good," Nitty said. "You think you can do it all right?"

"It's just a matter of getting a print-out of the program, and adding a patch. It's set up now to eliminate personnel whenever the figures indicate that their functions can be performed more economically by automation. The patch will exempt the school superintendent's job from the rule."

"And mine," Nitty said.

"Yes, of course. Anyway, it's highly unlikely that it will ever be noticed in that mass of assembler-language statements—certainly it won't be for many years, and then, when it is found, whoever comes across it will think that it reflects an administrative decision."

"Uh-huh."

"Then I'll add a once-through and erase subroutine that will rehire us and put George here in the blind program at Grovehurst. The whole thing ought not to take more than two hours at the outside."

"You know what I've been thinking?" Nitty said.

"What's that?"

"This little boy here—he's what you call a wonder-worker."

"You mean the little girl's leg. There wasn't any dancing lion then."

"Before that. You remember when those railroad police ladies threw the gas-bomb at us?"

"I'm pretty vague on it, to tell the truth."

(Little Tib had gotten up. He had learned by this time that there was a kitchen in the motel, and he knew that Nitty had bought cola to put in the refrigerator. He wondered if they were looking at him.)

"Yeah," Nitty said. "Well, back before that happened—with the gas-bomb—you were feelin' bad a lot. You know what I mean? You would think that you were still superintendent, and sometimes you got real upset when somebody said something."

"I had emotional problems as a result of losing my position—maybe a little worse than most people would. But I got over it."

"Took you a long time."

"A few weeks, sure."

(Little Tib opened the door of the refrigerator as quietly as he could, hearing the light switch click on. He wondered if he should offer to get something for Nitty and Mr. Parker, but he decided it would be best if they did not notice him.)

"'Bout three years."

(Little Tib's fingers found the cold cans on the top shelf. He took one out and pulled the ring, opening it with a tiny pop. It smelled funny, and after a moment he knew that it was beer and put it back. A can from the next shelf down was cola. He closed the refrigerator.)

"Three years."

"Nearly that, yes."

There was a pause. Little Tib wondered why the men were not talking.

"You must be right. I can't remember what year it is. I could tell you the year I was born, and the year I graduated from college. But I don't know what year it is now. They're just numbers."

Nitty told him. Then for a long time, again, nobody said anything. Little Tib drank his cola, feeling it fizz on his tongue.

"I remember traveling around with you a lot, but it doesn't seem like . . ."

Nitty did not say anything.

"When I remember, it's always summer. How could it always be summer, if it's three years?"

"Winters we used to go down on the Gulf Coast. Biloxi, Mobile, Pascagoula. Sometimes we might go over to Panama City or Tallahassee. We did that one year."

"Well, I'm all right now."

"I know you are. I can see you are. What I'm talking about is that you weren't—not for a long time. Then those railroad police ladies threw that gas, and the gas disappeared and you were all right again. Both together."

"I got myself a pretty good knock on the head, running into the wall of that freight car."

"I don't think that was it."

"You mean you think George did it? Why don't you ask him?"

"He's been too sick; besides, I'm not sure he knows. He didn't know much about that little girl's leg, and I know he did that."

"George, did you make me feel better when we were on the train? Were you the one that made the gas go away?"

"Is it all right if I have this soda pop?"

"Yes. Did you do those things on the train?"

"I don't know," Little Tib said. He wondered if he should tell them about the beer.

Nitty asked, "How did you feel on the train?" His voice, which was always gentle, seemed gentler than ever.

"Funny."

"Naturally he felt funny," Mr. Parker said. "He was running a fever."

"Jesus didn't always know. 'Who touched me?' he said. He said, 'I felt power go out from me.'"

"Matthew fourteen: five—Luke eighteen: two. In overtime."

"You don't have to believe he was God. He was a real man, and he did those things. He cured all those people, and he walked on that water."

"I wonder if he saw the lion."

"Saint Peter walked on it too. Saint Peter saw Him. But what I'm wondering about is, if it is the boy, what would happen to you if he was to go away?"

"Nothing would happen to me. If I'm all right, I'm all right. You think maybe he's Jesus or something. Nothing happened to those people Jesus cured when he died, did it?"

"I don't know," Nitty said. "It doesn't say."

"Anyway, why should he go away? We're going to take care of him, aren't we?"

"Sure we are."

"There you are, then. Are you going to put his costume on him before we go?"

"I'll wait until you're inside. Then when he comes out, I'll take him back here and get him dressed up and take him over to the meeting."

Little Tib heard the noise the blinds made when Mr. Parker pulled them up—a creaky, clattery little sound. Mr. Parker said, "Do you think it would be dark enough by the time we got over there?"

"No."

"I guess you're right. That window is still loose, and I think he can get through—get between the bars. How long ago was it we looked? Was that three years?"

"Last year," Nitty said. "Last summer."

"It still looks the same. George, all you really have to do is to let me in the building, but it would be better if I didn't come through the front door where people could see me. Do you understand?"

Little Tib said that he did.

"Now it's an old building, and all the windows on the first floor have bars on them; even if you unlocked some of the other windows from inside, I couldn't get through. But there is a side door that's only used for carrying in supplies. It's locked on the outside with a padlock. What I want you to do is to get the key to the padlock for me, and hand it to me through the window."

"Where is the computer?" Little Tib asked.

"That doesn't matter—I'll deal with the computer. All you have to do is let me in."

"I want to know where it is," Little Tib insisted.

Nitty said, "Why is that?"

"I'm scared of it."

"It can't hurt you," Nitty said. "It's just a big number-grinder. It will be turned off at night anyway, won't it, Mr. Parker?"

"Unless they're running an overnight job."

"Well, anyway you don't have to worry about it," Nitty said.

Then Mr. Parker told Little Tib where he thought the keys to the side door would be; and told him that if he could not find them, he was to unlock the front door from inside. Nitty asked if he would like to listen to the television, and he said yes, and they listened to a show that had country and western music, and then it was time to go. Nitty held Little Tib's hand as the three of them walked up the street. Little Tib could feel the tightness in Nitty. He knew that Nitty was thinking about what would happen if someone found them. He heard music—not country and western music like they had heard on the television—and to make Nitty talk so he would not worry so much, he asked what it was.

"That's Dr. Prithivi," Nitty told him. "He's playing that music so that people will come and hear his sermon, and see the people in the costumes."

"Is he playing it himself?"

"No, he's got it taped. There's a loudspeaker on the top of the bus."

Little Tib listened. The music was a long way away, but it sounded as if it were even farther away than it was. As if it did not belong here in Martinsburg at all. He asked Nitty about that.

Mr. Parker said, "What you sense is remoteness in time, George. That Indian flute music belongs, perhaps, to the fifth century A.D. Or possibly the fifth century B.C., or the fifteenth. It's like an old, old thing that never knew when to die, that's still wandering over the earth."

"It never was here before, was it?" Little Tib asked. Mr. Parker said that that was correct, and then Little Tib said, "Then maybe it isn't an old thing at all." Mr. Parker laughed, but Little Tib thought of the time when the lady down the road had had her new baby. It had been weak and small and toothless, like his own grandmother; and he had thought that it was old until everyone told him it was very new, and it would be alive, probably, when its mother was an old woman and dead. He wondered who would be alive a long time from now—Mr. Parker, or Dr. Prithivi.

They turned a corner. "Just a little way farther," Nitty said.

"Is anybody here to watch us?"

"Don't you worry. We won't do anything if anybody's here."

Quite suddenly, Mr. Parker's hands were moving up and down his body. "He'll be able to get through," Mr. Parker said. "Feel how thin he is."

They turned another corner, and there were dead leaves and old newspapers under Little Tib's feet. "Sure is dark in here," Nitty whispered.

"You see," Mr. Parker said, "no one can see us. It's right here, George." He took one of Little Tib's hands and moved it until it touched an iron bar. "Now, remember, through the storeroom, out to the main hall, turn right, past six doors—I think it is—and down half a flight of stairs. That will be the boiler room, and the janitor's desk is against the wall to your right. The keys should be hanging on a hook near the desk. Bring them back here and give them to me. If you can't find them, come back here and I'll tell you how to get to the front door and open it."

"Will you put the keys back?" Little Tib asked. He was getting his left leg between two of the bars, which was easy. His hips slid in after it. He felt the heavy, rusty window swing in as he pushed against it.

"Yes, the first thing I'll do after you let me in is go back to the boiler room and hang the keys back up."

"That's good," Little Tib said. His mother had told him that you must never steal, though he had taken things since he had run away.

For a little while he was afraid he was going to scrape his ears off. Then the wide part of his head was through, and everything was easy. The window pushed back, and he let his legs down onto the floor. He wanted to ask Mr. Parker where the door to this room was, but that would look as if he were afraid. He put one hand on the wall, and the other one out in front of him, and began to feel his way along. He wished he had his stick, but he could not even remember, now, where he had left it.

"Let me go ahead of you."

It was the funniest-looking man Little Tib had ever seen.

"I'm soft. If I bump into anything, I won't be hurt."

Not a man at all, Little Tib thought. Just clothes padded out, with a painted face at the top. "Why can I see you?" Little Tib said.

"You're in the dark, aren't you?"

"I guess so," Little Tib admitted. "I can't tell."

"Exactly. Now, when people who can see are in the light, they can see things that *are* there. And when they're in the dark, why, they *can't* see them. Isn't that correct?"

"I suppose so."

"But when *you're* in the light you can't see things. So naturally when you're in the dark, you see things that *aren't* there. You see how simple it is?"

"Yes," Little Tib said, not understanding.

"There. That proves it. You *can* see it, and it *isn't* really simple at all." The Clothes Man had his hand—it was an old glove, Little Tib noticed—on the knob of a big metal door now. When he touched it, Little Tib could see that too. "It's locked," the Clothes Man said.

Little Tib was still thinking about what he had said before. "You're smart," he told the Clothes Man.

"That's because I have the best brain in the entire world. It was given to me by the great and powerful Wizard himself."

"Are you smarter than the computer?"

"Much, much smarter than the Computer. But I don't know how to open this door."

"Have you been trying?"

"Well, I've been shaking the knob—only it won't shake. And I've been feeling around for a catch. That's trying, I suppose."

"I think it is," Little Tib said.

"Ah, you're thinking—that's good." Little Tib had reached the door, and the Clothes Man moved to one side to let him feel it. "If you had the ruby slippers," the Clothes Man continued, "you could just click your heels three times and wish, and you'd be on the other side. Of course, you're on the other side now."

"No, I'm not," Little Tib told him.

"Yes, you are," the Clothes Man said. "Over *there* is where you want to be—that's on *that* side. So this is the *other* side."

"You're right," Little Tib admitted. "But I still can't get through the door."

"You don't have to, now," the Clothes Man told him. "You're already on the other side. Just don't trip over the steps."

"What steps?" Little Tib asked. As he did, he took a step backward. His heel bumped something he did not expect, and he sat down hard on something else that was higher up than the floor should have been.

"Those steps," the Clothes Man said mildly.

Little Tib was feeling them with his hands. They were sidewalk-stuff, with metal edges; and they felt almost as hard and real to his fingers as they had a moment ago when he sat down on them without wanting to. "I don't remember going down these," he said.

"You didn't. But now you have to go up them to get to the upper room."

"What upper room?"

"The one with the door that goes out into the corridor," the Clothes Man told him. "You go to the corridor, and turn *that* way, and—"

"I know," Little Tib said. "Mr. Parker told me. Over and over. But he didn't tell me about that door that was locked, or these steps."

"It may be that Mr. Parker doesn't remember the inside of this building quite as well as he thinks he does."

"He used to work here. He told me." Little Tib was going up the stairs. There was an iron rail on one side. He was afraid that if he did not talk to the Clothes Man, he would go away. But he could not think of anything to say, and nothing of the kind happened. Then he remembered that he had not talked to the lion at all.

"I could find the keys for you," the Clothes Man said. "I could bring them back to you."

"I don't want you to leave," Little Tib told him.

"It would just take a moment. I fall down a lot, but keys wouldn't break."

"No," Little Tib said. The Clothes Man looked so hurt that he added, "I'm afraid . . ."

"You can't be afraid of the dark. Are you afraid of being alone?"

"A little. But I'm afraid you couldn't really bring them to me. I'm afraid you're not real, and I want you to be real."

"I could bring them." The Clothes Man threw out his chest and struck a heroic pose, but the dry grass that was his stuffing made a small, sad, rustling sound. "I *am* real. Try me."

There was another door—Little Tib's fingers found it. This one was not locked, and when he went out it, the floor changed from sidewalk to smooth stone. "I, too, am real," a strange voice said. The Clothes Man was still there when the strange voice spoke, but he seemed dimmer.

"Who are you?" Little Tib asked, and there was a sound like thunder. He had hated the strange voice from the beginning, but until he heard the thunder-sound he had not really known how much. It was not really like thunder, he thought. He remembered his dream about the gnomes, though this was much worse. It seemed to him that it was like big stones grinding together at the bottom of the deepest hole in the world. It was worse than that, really.

"I wouldn't go in there if I were you," the Clothes Man said.

"If the keys are in there, I'll have to go in and get them," Little Tib replied.

"They're not in there at all. In fact, they're not even close to there—they're several doors down. All you have to do is walk past the door."

"Who is it?"

"It's the Computer," the Clothes Man told him.

"I didn't think they talked like that."

"Only to you. And not all of them talk at all. Just don't go in and it will be all right."

"Suppose it comes out here after me?"

"It won't do that. It is as frightened of you as you are of it."

"I won't go in," Little Tib promised.

When he was opposite the door where the thing was, he heard it groaning as if it were in torture; and he turned and went in. He was very frightened to find himself there; but he knew he was not in the wrong place—he had done the right thing, and not the wrong thing. Still, he was very frightened. The horrible voice said: "What have we to do with you? Have you come to torment us?"

"What is your name?" Little Tib asked.

The thundering, grinding noise came a second time, and this time Little Tib thought he heard in it the sound of many voices, perhaps hundreds or thousands, all speaking at once.

"Answer me," Little Tib said. He walked forward until he could put his hands on the cabinet of the machine. He felt frightened, but he knew the Clothes Man had been right—the Computer was as frightened of him as he was of it. He knew that the Clothes Man was standing behind him, and he wondered if he would have dared to do this if someone else had not been watching.

"We are legion," the horrible voice said. "Very many."

"Get out!" There was a moaning that might have come from deep inside the earth. Something made of glass that had been on furniture fell over and rolled and crashed to the floor.

"They are gone," the Clothes Man said. He sat on the cabinet of the computer so Little Tib could see it, and he looked brighter than ever.

"Where did they go?" Little Tib asked.

"I don't know. You will probably meet them again." As if he had just thought of it, he said, "You were very brave."

"I was scared. I'm still scared—the worst since I left the new place."

"I wish I could tell you that you didn't have to be afraid of them," the Clothes Man said, "or of anybody. But it wouldn't be true. Still, I can tell you something that is really better than that—

that it will all come out right in the end." He took off the big,
floppy black hat he wore, and Little Tib saw that his bald head was
really only a sack. "You wouldn't let me bring the keys before, but
how about now? Or would you be afraid with me away?"

"No," Little Tib said, "but I'll get the keys myself."

At once the Clothes Man was gone. Little Tib felt the smooth,
cool metal of the computer under his hands. In the blackness, it
was the only reality there was.

He did not bother to find the window again; instead, he unlocked
another, and called Nitty and Mr. Parker to it, smelling as he did
the cool, damp air of spring. At the opening, he thrust the keys
through first, then squeezed himself between the bars. By the time
he was outside, he could hear Mr. Parker unlocking the side
door.

"You were a long time," Nitty said. "Was it bad in there by yourself?"

"I wasn't by myself," Little Tib said.

"I'm not even goin' to ask you about that. I used to be a fool, but
I know better now. You still want to go to Dr. Prithivi's meetin'?"

"He wants us to come, doesn't he?"

"You are the big star, the main event. If you don't come, it's
going to be like no potato salad at a picnic."

They walked back to the motel in silence. The flute music they
had heard before was louder and faster now, with the clangs of
gongs interspersed in its shrill wailings. Little Tib stood on a foot-
stool while Nitty took his clothes away and wrapped a piece of
cloth around his waist, and another around his head, and hung his
neck with beads, and painted something on his forehead.

"There, you look just ever so fine," Nitty said.

"I feel silly," Little Tib told him.

Nitty said that that did not matter, and they left the motel again
and walked several blocks. Little Tib heard the crowd, and the
loud sounds of the music, and then smelled the familiar dark, sweet
smell of Dr. Prithivi's bus; he asked Nitty if the people had not seen
him, and Nitty said that they had not, that they were watching
something taking place on a stage outside.

"Ah," Dr. Prithivi said. "You are here, and you are just in
time."

Nitty asked him if Little Tib looked all right.

"His appearance is very fine indeed, but he must have his instrument." He put a long, light stick into Little Tib's hands. It had a

great many little holes in it. Little Tib was happy to have it, knowing that he could use it to feel his way if necessary.

"Now it is time you met your fellow performer," Dr. Prithivi said. "Boy Krishna, this is the god Indra. Indra, it has given me the greatest pleasure to introduce to you the god Krishna, most charming of the incarnations of Vishnu."

"Hello," a strange, deep voice said.

"You are doubtless familiar already with the story, but I will tell it to you again in order to refresh your memories before you must appear on my little stage. Krishna is the son of Queen Devaki, and this lady is the sister of the wicked King Kamsa who kills all her children when they are born. To save Krishna, the good Queen places him among villagers. There he offends Indra, who comes to destroy him. . . ."

Little Tib listened with only half his mind, certain that he could never remember the whole story. He had forgotten the Queen's name already. The wood of the flute was smooth and cool under his fingers, the air in the bus hot and heavy, freighted with strange, sleepy odors.

"I am King Kamsa," Dr. Prithivi was saying, "and when I am through being he, I will be a cowherd, so I can tell you what to do. Remember not to drop the mountain when you lift it."

"I'll be careful," Little Tib said. He had learned to say that in school.

"Now I must go forth and prepare for you. When you hear the great gong struck three times, come out. Your friend will be waiting there to take you to the stage."

Little Tib heard the door of the bus open and close. "Where's Nitty?" he asked.

The deep voice of Indra—a hard, dry voice, it seemed to Little Tib—said: "He has gone to help."

"I don't like being alone here."

"You are not alone," Indra said. "I'm with you."

"Yes."

"Did you like the story of Krishna and Indra? I will tell you another story. Once, in a village not too far away from here—"

"You aren't from around here, are you?" Little Tib asked. "Because you don't talk like it. Everybody here talks like Nitty or like Mr. Parker except Dr. Prithivi, and he's from India. Can I feel your face?"

"No, I'm not from around here," Indra said. "I am from Niagara. Do you know what that is?"

Little Tib said, "No."

"It is the capital of this nation—the seat of government. Here, you may feel my face."

Little Tib reached upward; but Indra's face was smooth, cool wood, like the flute. "You don't have a face," he said.

"That is because I am wearing the mask of Indra. Once, in a village not too far from here, there were a great many women who wanted to do something nice for the whole world. So they offered their bodies for certain experiments. Do you know what an experiment is?"

"No," said Little Tib.

"Biologists took parts of these women's bodies—parts that would later become boys and girls. And they reached down inside the tiniest places in those parts and made improvements."

"What kind of improvements?" Little Tib asked.

"Things that would make the girls and boys smarter and stronger and healthier—that kind of improvement. Now these good women were mostly teachers in a college, and the wives of college teachers."

"I understand," Little Tib said. Outside, the people were singing.

"However, when those girls and boys were born, the biologists decided that they needed more children to study—children who had not been improved, so that they could compare them to the ones who had."

"There must have been a lot of those," Little Tib ventured.

"The biologists offered money to people who would bring their children in to be studied, and a great many people did—farm and ranch and factory people, some of them from neighboring towns." Indra paused. Little Tib thought he smelled like cologne; but like oil and iron too. Just when he thought the story was finished, Indra began to speak again.

"Everything went smoothly until the boys and girls were six years old. Then at the center—the experiments were made at the medical center, in Houston—strange things started to happen. Dangerous things. Things that no one could explain." As though he expected Little Tib to ask what these inexplicable things were, Indra waited; but Little Tib said nothing.

At last Indra continued. "People and animals—sometimes even

monsters—were seen in the corridors and therapy rooms who had never entered the complex and were never observed to leave it. Experimental animals were freed—apparently without their cages having been opened. Furniture was rearranged, and on several different occasions large quantities of food that could not be accounted for was found in the common rooms.

"When it became apparent that these events were not isolated occurrences, but part of a recurring pattern, they were coded and fed to a computer—together with all the other events of the medical center schedule. It was immediately apparent that they coincided with the periodic examinations given the genetically improved children."

"I'm not one of those," Little Tib said.

"The children were examined carefully. Thousands of man-hours were spent in checking them for paranormal abilities; none were uncovered. It was decided that only half the group should be brought in each time. I'm sure you understand the principle behind that—if paranormal activity had occurred when one half was present, but not when the other half was, we would have isolated the disturbing individual to some extent. It didn't work. The phenomena occurred when each half-group was present."

"I understand."

The door of the bus opened, letting in fresh night air. Nitty's voice said, "You two ready? Going to have to come on pretty soon now."

"We're ready," Indra told him. The door closed again, and Indra said: "Our agency felt certain that the fact that the phenomena took place whenever either half of the group was present indicated that several individuals were involved. Which meant the problem was more critical than we supposed. Then one of the biologists who had been involved originally—by that time we had taken charge of the project, you understand—pointed out in the course of a casual conversation with one of our people that the genetic improvements they had made could occur spontaneously. I want you to listen carefully now. This is important."

"I'm listening," Little Tib told him dutifully.

"A certain group of us were very concerned about this. We—are you familiar with the central data processing unit that provides identification and administers social benefits to the unemployed?"

"You look in it, and it's supposed to tell who you are," Little Tib said.

"Yes. It already included a system for the detection of fugitives. We added a new routine that we hoped would be sensitive to potential paranormalities. The biologists indicated that a paranormal individual might possess certain retinal peculiarities, since such people notoriously see phenomena, like Kirlian auras, that are invisible to normal sight. The central data bank was given the capability of detecting such abnormalities through its remote terminals."

"It would look into his eyes and know what he was," Little Tib said. And after a moment, "You should have done that with the boys and girls."

"We did," Indra told him. "No abnormalities were detected, and the phenomena persisted." His voice grew deeper and more solemn than ever. "We reported this to the President. He was extremely concerned, feeling that under the present unsettled economic conditions, the appearance of such an individual might trigger domestic disorder. It was decided to terminate the experiment."

"Just forget about it?" Little Tib asked.

"The experimental material would be sacrificed to prevent the continuance and possible further development of the phenomena."

"I don't understand."

"The brains and spinal cords of the boys and girls involved would be turned over to the biologists for examination."

"Oh, I know this story," Little Tib said. "The three Wise Men come and warn Joseph and Mary, and they take baby Jesus to the Land of Egypt on a donkey."

"No," Indra told him, "that isn't this story at all. The experiment was ended, and the phenomena ceased. But a few weeks later the alert built into the central data system triggered. A paranormal individual had been identified, almost five hundred kilometers from the scene of the experiment. Several agents were dispatched to detain him; but he could not be found. It was at this point that we realized we had made a serious mistake. We had utilized the method of detention and identification already used in criminal cases—destruction of the retina. That meant the subject could not be so identified again."

"I see," Little Tib said.

"This method had proved to be quite practical with felons—the subject could be identified by other means, and the resulting blindness prevented escape and effective resistance. Of course, the real reason for adopting it was that it could be employed without

any substantial increase in the mechanical capabilities of the remote terminals—a brief overvoltage to the sodium vapor light normally used for retinal photography was all that was required.

"This time, however, the system seemed to have worked against
us. By the time the agents arrived, the subject was gone. There had
been no complaints, no shouting and stumbling. The people in
charge of the terminal facility didn't even know what had occurred.
It was possible, however, to examine the records of those who had
preceded and followed the person we wanted, however. Do you
know what we found?"

Little Tib, who knew that they had found that it was he, said,
"No."

"We found that it was one of the children who had been part of
the experiment." Indra smiled. Little Tib could not see his smile,
but he could feel it. "Isn't that odd? One of the boys who had been
part of the experiment."

"I thought they were all dead."

"So did we, until we understood what had happened. But you
see, the ones who were sacrificed were those who had undergone
genetic improvement before birth. The *controls* were not dead, and
this was one of them."

"The other children," Little Tib said.

"Yes. The poor children, whose mothers had brought them in for
the money. That was why dividing the group had not worked—the
controls were brought in with both halves. It could not be true, of
course."

Little Tib said, "What?"

"It could not be true—we all agreed on that. It could not be one
of the controls. It was too much of a coincidence. It had to be that
one of the mothers—possibly one of the fathers, but more likely one
of the mothers—saw it coming a long way off and exchanged infants
to save her own. It must have happened years before."

"Like Krishna's mother," Little Tib said, remembering Dr.
Prithivi's story.

"Yes. Gods aren't born in cowsheds."

"Are you going to kill this last boy too—when you find him?"

"I know that you are the last of the children."

There was no hope of escaping a seeing person in the enclosed
interior of the bus, but Little Tib bolted anyway. He had not taken
three steps before Indra had him by the shoulders and forced him
back into his seat.

"Are you going to kill me now?"

"No."

Thunder banged outside. Little Tib jumped, thinking for an instant that Indra had fired a gun. "Not now," Indra told him, "but soon."

The door opened again, and Nitty said: "Come on out. It's goin' to rain, and Dr. Prithivi wants to get the big show on before it does." With Indra close behind him, Little Tib let Nitty help him down the steps and out the door of the bus. There were hundreds of people outside—he could hear the shuffling of their feet, and the sound of their voices. Some were talking to each other and some were singing; but they became quiet as he, with Nitty and Indra, passed through them. The air was heavy with the coming storm, and there were gusts of wind.

"Here," Nitty said, "high step up. Watch out."

They were rough wooden stairs, seven steps. He climbed the last one, and . . .

He could see.

For a moment (though it was only a moment) he thought that he was no longer blind. He was in a village of mud houses, and there were people all around him, brown-skinned people with large, soft, brown eyes—men with red and yellow and blue cloths wrapped about their heads, women with beautiful black hair and colored dresses. There was a cow-smell and a dust-smell and a cooking-smell all at once; and just beyond the village a single mountain perfect and pure as an ice cream cone; and beyond the mountain a marvelous sky full of palaces and chariots and painted elephants; and beyond the sky, more faces than he could count.

Then he knew that it was only imagination, only a dream; not his dream this time, but Dr. Prithivi's dream. Perhaps Dr. Prithivi could dream the way he did, so strongly that the angels came to make the dreams true; perhaps it was only Dr. Prithivi's dream working through him. He thought of what Indra had said—that his mother was not his real mother, and knew that that could not be so.

A brown-skinned, brown-eyed woman with a pretty, heart-shaped face said, "Pipe for us," and he remembered that he still had the wooden flute. He raised it to his lips, not certain that he could play it, and wonderful music began. It was not his, but he fingered the flute pretending that it was his, and danced. The women danced with him, sometimes joining hands, sometimes ringing little bells.

It seemed to him that they had been dancing for only a moment when Indra came. He was bigger than Little Tib's father, and his face was a carved, hook-nosed mask. In his right hand he had a cruel sword that curved and recurved like a snake, and in his left a glittering eye. When Little Tib saw the eye, he knew why it was that Indra had not killed him while they were alone in the bus. Someone far away was watching through that eye, and until he had seen him do the things he was able, sometimes, to do, make things appear and disappear, bring the angels, Indra could not use his sword. I just won't do it, he thought; but he knew he could not always stop what happened—that the happenings sometimes carried him with them.

The thunder boomed then, and Dr. Prithivi's voice said: "Play up to it! Up to the storm. That is ideal for what we are trying to do!"

Indra stood in front of Little Tib and said something about bringing so much rain that it would drown the village; and Dr. Prithivi's voice told Little Tib to lift the mountain.

Little Tib looked and saw a real mountain, far off and perfect; he knew he could not lift it.

Then the rain came, and the lights went out, and they were standing on the stage in the dark, with icy water beating against their faces. The lightning flashed and Little Tib saw hundreds of people running for their cars; among them were a man with a monkey's head, and another with an elephant's, and a man with nine faces.

And then he was blind again, and there was nothing left but the rough feel of wood underfoot, and the beating of the rain, and the knowledge that Indra was still before him, holding his sword and the eye.

And then a man made all of metal (so that the rain drummed on him) stood there too. He held an ax, and wore a pointed hat; and by the light that shown from his polished surface, Little Tib could see Indra too, and the eye.

"Who are you?" Indra said. He was talking to the Metal Man.

"Who are *you?*" the Metal Man answered. "I can't see your face behind that wooden mask—but wood has never stood for long against me." He struck Indra's mask with his ax; a big chip flew from it, and the string that held it in place broke, and it went clattering down.

Little Tib saw his father's face, with the rain running from it. "Who are you?" his father said to the Metal Man again.

"Don't you know me, Georgie?" the Metal Man said. "Why we used to be old friends, once. I have—if I may say so—a very sympathetic heart, and when—"

"Daddy!" Little Tib yelled.

His father looked at him and said, "Hello, Little Tib."

"Daddy, if I had known you were Indra I wouldn't have been scared at all. That mask made your voice sound different."

"You don't have to be afraid any longer, son," his father said. He took two steps toward Little Tib, and then, almost too quickly to see, his sword blade came up and flashed down.

The Metal Man's ax was even quicker. It came up and stayed up; Indra's sword struck it with a crash.

"That won't help him," Little Tib's father said. "They've seen him, and they've seen you. I wanted to get it over with."

"They haven't seen me," the Metal Man said. "It's darker here than you think."

At once it *was* dark. The rain stopped—or if it continued, Little Tib was not conscious of it. He did not know why he knew, but he knew where he was: he was standing, still standing, in front of the computer, with the devils not yet driven out.

Then the rain was back and his father was there again, but the Metal Man was gone, and the dark came back with a rush until he was blind again. "Are you still going to kill me, Father?" he asked.

There was no reply, and he repeated his question.

"Not now," his father said.

"Later?"

"Come here." He felt his father's hand on his arm, the way it used to be. "Let's sit down." It drew him to the edge of the platform and helped him to seat himself with his legs dangling over.

"Are you all right?" Little Tib asked.

"Yes," his father told him.

"Then why do you want to kill me?"

"I don't *want* to." Suddenly his father sounded angry. "I never said I *wanted* to. I have to do it, that's all. Look at us, look at what we been. Moving from place to place, working construction, working the land, worshiping the Lord like it was a hundred years ago. You know what we are? We're jackrabbits. You recall jackrabbits, Little Tib?"

"No."

"That was before your day. Big old long-legg'd rabbits with long ears like a jackass's. Back before you were born they decided they weren't any good, and they all died. For about a year I'd find them on the place, dead, and then there wasn't any more. They waited to join until it was too late, you see. Or maybe they couldn't. That's what's going to happen to people like us. I mean our family. What do you suppose we've been?"

Little Tib, who did not understand the question, said nothing.

"When I was a boy and used to go to school I would hear about all these great men and kings and queens and Presidents, and I liked to think that maybe some were family. That isn't so, and I know it now. If you could go back to Bible times, you'd find our people living in the woods like Indians."

"I'd like that," Little Tib said.

"Well, they cut down those woods so we couldn't do that any more; and we began scratching a living out of the ground. We've been doing that ever since and paying taxes, do you understand me? That's all we've ever done. And pretty soon now there won't be any call at all for people to do that. We've got to join them before it's too late—do you see?"

"No," Little Tib said.

"You're the one. You're a prodigy and a healer, and so they want you dead. You're our ticket. Everybody was born for something, and that was what you were born for, son. Just because of you, the family is going to get in before it's too late."

"But if I'm dead . . ." Little Tib tried to get his thoughts in order. "You and Mama don't have any other children."

"You don't understand, do you?"

Little Tib's father had put his arm around Little Tib, and now he leaned down until their faces touched. But when they did, it seemed to Little Tib that his father's face did not feel as it should. He reached up and felt it with both hands, and it came off in his hands, feeling like the plastic vegetables came in at the new place; perhaps this was Big Tib's dream.

"You shouldn't have done that," his father said.

Little Tib reached up to find out who had been pretending to be his father. The new face was metal, hard and cold.

"I am the President's man now. I didn't want you to know that, because I thought that it might upset you. The President is handling the situation personally."

"Is Mama still at home?" Little Tib asked. He meant the new place.

"No. She's in a different division—gee-seven. But I still see her sometimes. I think she's in Atlanta now."

"Looking for me?"

"She wouldn't tell me."

Something inside Little Tib, just under the hard place in the middle of his chest where all the ribs came together, began to get tighter and tighter, like a balloon being blown up too far. He felt that when it burst, he would burst too. It made it impossible to take more than tiny breaths, and it pressed against the voice-thing in his neck so he could not speak. Inside himself he said forever that that was not his real mother, and this was not his real father; that his real mother and father were the mother and father he had had at the old place; he would keep them inside for always, his real mother and father. The rain beat against his face; his nose was full of mucus; he had to breathe through his mouth, but his mouth was filling with saliva, which ran down his chin and made him ashamed.

Then the tears came in a hot flood on his cold cheeks, and the metal face fell off Indra like an old pie pan from a shelf, and went rattling and clanging across the blacktop under the stage.

He reached up to his father's face again, and it was his father's face, but his father said: "Little Tib, can't you understand? It's the Federal Reserve Card. It's the goddamned card. It's having no money, and nothing to do, and spending your whole life like a goddamn whipped dog. I only got in because of you—saying I'd hunt for you. We had training and all that, Skinnerian conditioning and deep hypnosis, they saw to that—but in the end it's the damn card." And while he said that, Little Tib could hear Indra's sword, scraping and scraping, ever so slowly, across the boards of the stage. He jumped down and ran, not knowing or caring whether he was going to run into something.

In the end, he ran into Nitty. Nitty no longer had his sweat and woodsmoke smell, because of the rain; but he still had the same feel, and the same voice when he said: "*There* you are. I been lookin' just everyplace for you. I thought somebody had run off with you to get you out of the wet. Where you been?" He raised Little Tib on his shoulders.

Little Tib plunged his hands into the thick, wet hair and hung on. "On the stage," he said.

"On the stage still? Well, I swear." Nitty was walking fast, taking big, long strides. Little Tib's body rocked with the swing of them. "That was the one place I never thought to look for you. I thought you would have come off there fast, looking for me, or someplace dry. But I guess you were afraid of falling off."

"Yes," Little Tib said, "I was afraid of falling off." Running in the rain had let all the air out of the balloon; he felt empty inside, and like he had no bones at all. Twice he nearly slid from Nitty's shoulders, but each time Nitty's big hands reached up and caught him.

The next morning a good-smelling woman came from the school for him. Little Tib was still in bed when she knocked on the door; but he heard Nitty open it, and her say, "I believe you have a blind child here."

"Yes'm," Nitty said.

"Mr. Parker—the new acting superintendent?—asked me to come over and escort him myself the first day. I'm Ms. Munson. I teach the blind class."

"I'm not sure he's got clothes fit for school," Nitty told her.

"Oh, they come in just anything these days," Ms. Munson said, and then she saw Little Tib, who had gotten out of bed when he heard the door open, and said, "I see what you mean. Is he dressed for a play?"

"Last night," Nitty told her.

"Oh. I heard about it, but I wasn't there."

Then Little Tib knew he still had the skirt-thing on that they had given him—but it was not; it was a dry, woolly towel. But he still had beads on, and metal bracelets on his arm.

"His others are real ragged."

"I'm afraid he'll have to wear them anyway," Ms. Munson said. Nitty took him into the bathroom and took the beads and bracelets and towel off, and dressed him in his usual clothes. Then Ms. Munson led him out of the motel and opened the door of her little electric car for him.

"Did Mr. Parker get his job again?" Little Tib asked when the car bounced out of the motel lot and onto the street.

"I don't know about *again*," Ms. Munson said. "Did he have it before? But I understand he's extremely well qualified in educational programming; and when they found out this morning that the computer was inoperative, he presented his credentials and offered to help. He called me about ten o'clock and asked me to go for you, but I couldn't get away from the school until now."

"It's noon, isn't it," Little Tib said. "It's too hot for morning."

That afternoon he sat in Ms. Munson's room with eight other blind children while a machine moved his hand over little dots on paper and told him what they were. When school was over and he could hear the seeing children milling in the hall outside, a woman older and thicker than Ms. Munson came for him and took him to a house where other, seeing, children larger than he lived. He ate there; the thick woman was angry once because he pushed his beets, by accident, off his plate. That night he slept in a narrow bed.

The next three days were all the same. In the morning the thick woman took him to school. In the evening she came for him. There was a television at the thick woman's house—Little Tib could never remember her name afterward—and when supper was over, the children listened to television.

On the fifth day of school he heard his father's voice in the corridor outside, and then his father came into Ms. Munson's room with a man from the school, who sounded important.

"This is Mr. Jefferson," the man from the school told Ms. Munson. "He's from the Government. You are to release one of your students to his care. Do you have a George Tibbs here?"

Little Tib felt his father's hand close on his shoulder. "I have him," his father said. They went out the front door, and down the steps, and then along the side. "There's been a change in orders, son; I'm to bring you to Niagara for examination."

"All right."

"There's no place to park around this damn school. I had to park a block away."

Little Tib remembered the rattley truck his father had when they lived at the old place; but he knew somehow that the truck was gone like the old place itself, belonging to the real father locked in his memory. The father of now would have a nice car.

He heard footsteps, and then there was a man he could see walking in front of them—a man so small he was hardly taller than Little Tib himself. He had a shiny bald head with upcurling hair at the sides of it; and a bright green coat with two long coattails and two sparkling green buttons. When he turned around to face them (skipping backwards to keep up), Little Tib saw that his face was all red and white except for two little, dark eyes that almost seemed to shoot out sparks. He had a big, hooked nose like Indra's, but on him it did not look cruel. "And what can I do for you?" he asked Little Tib.

"Get me loose," Little Tib said. "Make him let go of me."

"And then what?"

"I don't know," Little Tib confessed.

The man in the green coat nodded to himself as if he had guessed that all along, and took an envelope of silver paper out of his inside coat pocket. "If you are *caught* again," he said, "it will be for good. Understand? Running is for people who are not helped." He tore one end of the envelope open. It was full of glittering powder, as Little Tib saw when he poured it out into his hand. "You remind me," he said, "of a friend of mine named *Tip*. Tip with a *p*. A *b* is just a *p* turned upside down." He threw the glittering powder into the air, and spoke a word Little Tib could not quite hear.

For just a second there were two things at once. There was the sidewalk and the row of cars on one side and the lawns on the other; and there was Ms. Munson's room, with the sounds of the other children, and the mopped-floor smell. He looked around at the light on the cars, and then it was gone and there was only the sound of his father's voice in the hall outside, and the feel of the school desk and the paper with dots in it. The voice of the man in the green coat (as if he had not gone away at all) said, "Tip turned out to be the ruler of all of us in the end, you know." Then there was the beating of big wings. And then it was all gone, gone completely. The classroom door opened, and a man from the school who sounded important said, "Ms. Munson, I have a gentleman here who states that he is the father of one of your pupils.

"Would you give me your name again, sir?"

"George Tibbs. My boy's name is George Tibbs too."

"Is this your father, George?" Ms. Munson said.

"How would he know? He's blind."

Little Tib said nothing, and the Important Man said, "Perhaps we'd better all go up to the office. You say that you're with the Federal Government, Mr. Tibbs?"

"The Office of Biogenetic Improvement. I suppose you're surprised, seeing that I'm nothing but a dirt farmer—but I got into it through the Agricultural Program."

"Ah."

Ms. Munson, who was holding Little Tib's hand, led him around a corner.

"I'm working on a case now . . . Perhaps it would be better if the boy waited outside."

A door opened. "We haven't been able to identify him, you understand," the Important Man said. "His retinas are gone. That's the reason for all this red tape."

Ms. Munson helped Little Tib find a chair, and said, "Wait here." Then the door closed and everyone was gone. He dug the heels of his hands into his eyes, and for an instant there were points of light like the glittering dust the man in the green coat had thrown. He thought about what he was going to do, and not running. Then about Krishna, because he had been Krishna. Had Krishna run? Or had he gone back to fight the king who had wanted to kill him? He could not be sure, but he did not think Krishna had run. Jesus had fled into Egypt, he remembered that. But he had come back. Not to Bethlehem where he had run from, but to Nazareth, because that was his real home. He remembered talking about the Jesus story to his father, when they were sitting on the stage. His father had brushed it aside; but Little Tib felt it might be important somehow. He put his chin on his hands to think about it.

The chair was hard—harder than any rock he had ever sat on. He felt the unyielding wood of its arms stretching to either side of him while he thought. There was something horrible about those arms, something he could not remember. Just outside the door the bell rang, and he could hear the noise the children's feet made in the hall. It was recess; they were pouring out the doors, pouring out into the warm fragrance of spring outside.

He got up, and found the door-edge with his fingers. He did not know whether anyone was seeing him or not. In an instant he was in the crowd of pushing children. He let them carry him down the steps.

Outside, games went on all around him. He stopped shuffling and shoving now, and began to walk. With the first step he knew that he would go on walking like this all day. It felt better than anything else he had ever done. He walked through all the games until he found the fence around the schoolyard; then down the fence until he found a gate, then out the gate and down the road.

I'll have to get a stick, he thought.

When he had gone about five kilometers, as well as he could

judge, he heard the whistle of a train far off and turned toward it. Railroad tracks were better than roads—he had learned that months ago. He was less likely to meet people, and trains only went by once in a while. Cars and trucks went by all the time, and any one of them could kill.

After a while he picked up a good stick—light but flexible, and just the right length. He climbed the embankment then, and began to walk where he wanted to walk, on the rails, balancing with his stick. There was a little girl ahead of him, and he could see her, so he knew she was an angel. "What's your name?" he said.

"I mustn't tell you," she answered, "but you can call me Dorothy." She asked his, and he did not say George Tibbs but Little Tib, which was what his mother and father had always called him.

"You fixed my leg, so I'm going with you," Dorothy announced. (She did not really sound like the same girl.) After a time she added: "I can help you a lot. I can tell you what to look out for."

"I know you can," Little Tib said humbly.

"Like now. There's a man up ahead of us."

"A bad man?" Little Tib asked, "or a good man?"

"A nice man. A shaggy man."

"Hello." It was Nitty's voice. "I didn't really expect to see you here, George, but I guess I should have."

Little Tib said, "I don't like school."

"That's just the different of me. I do like it, only it seems like they don't like me."

"Didn't Mr. Parker get you your job back?"

"I think Mr. Parker kind of forgot me."

"He shouldn't have done that," Little Tib said.

"Well, little blind boy, Mr. Parker is white, you know. And when a white man has been helped out by a black one, he likes to forget it sometimes."

"I see," Little Tib said, though he did not. Black and white seemed very unimportant to him.

"I hear it works the other way too." Nitty laughed.

"This is Dorothy," Little Tib said.

Nitty said, "I can't see any Dorothy, George." His voice sounded funny.

"Well, I can't see you," Little Tib told him.

"I guess that's right. Hello, Dorothy. Where are you an' George goin'?"

"We're going to Sugarland," Little Tib told him. "In Sugarland they know who you are."

"Is Sugarland for real?" Nitty asked. "I always thought it was just some place you made up."

"No, Sugarland is in Texas."

"How about that," Nitty said. The light of the sun, now setting, made the railroad ties as yellow as butter. Nitty took Little Tib's hand, and Little Tib took Dorothy's, and the three of them walked between the rails. Nitty took up a lot of room, but Little Tib did not take much, and Dorothy hardly took any at all.

When they had gone half a kilometer, they began to skip.

ABOUT THE AUTHORS

GEORGE ALEC EFFINGER currently resides in New Jersey. He is a graduate of the Clarion Writer's Workshop and has sold thirteen books, among them *What Entropy Means to Me, Relatives,* and *Mixed Feelings,* a short story collection. His stories have appeared in *Analog, Amazing, Fantastic, The Magazine of Fantasy and Science Fiction, New Dimensions, Orbit, Wandering Stars, Universe, Bad Moon Rising, The Ruins of Earth,* and other anthologies and magazines. His work has been nominated for the Hugo and Nebula Awards.

FELIX C. GOTSCHALK is a clinical psychologist. He grew up in Richmond, Virginia and is now a resident of Winston-Salem, North Carolina. His work has appeared in *New Dimensions, Orbit, Amazing, Fantastic, Beyond Time, The Writer,* and *SF Emphasis 1.* He is the author of a science fiction novel, *Growing Up in Tier 3000.*

A. K. JORGENSSON's real name is Robert W. A. Roach. He writes: "Supposedly established ways of thinking would have it that I was born on April 29th, 1933, at Chipping Sodbury in Gloucestershire (England) and have since progressed to the position of Chartered Quantity Surveyor." He lives in Algeria.

DAMON KNIGHT is the author of many science fiction novels and short story collections, among them *Hell's Pavement, A for Anything, Beyond the Barrier, Far Out, In Deep, Off Center, Turning On, World Without Children,* and others. His anthologies include *A Century of Science Fiction, First Flight, Now Begins Tomorrow, Cities of Wonder, The Dark Side,* and the *Orbit* series. He founded the Science Fiction Writers of America and became its first president. He received a Hugo Award for *In Search of Wonder,* a book of critical essays. Mr. Knight resides in Florida and is married to writer Kate Wilhelm.

R. A. LAFFERTY is a retired electrical engineer who resides in Oklahoma. His novels include *Past Master, Space Chantey, The Reefs of Earth, Fourth Mansions, The Devil Is Dead, Arrive at Easterwine,* and *Okla Hannali.* He has three short story collections: *Nine Hundred Grandmothers, Strange Doings,* and *Does Anyone Else Have Something Further to Add?* He received a Hugo Award in 1973 for his short story "Eurema's Dam."

URSULA K. LE GUIN received her B.A. from Radcliffe College and her M.A. from Columbia University. Her novels include *The Wizard of Earthsea, The Tombs of Atuan, The Farthest Shore, City of Illusions, The Lathe of Heaven, The Left Hand of Darkness,* and *The Dispossessed. The Left Hand of Darkness* received both the Hugo and Nebula Awards for Best Novel, as did *The Dispossessed.* She has won four Hugo Awards and three Nebula Awards. *The Farthest Shore* received the National Book Award for Children's Literature in 1973. Her most recent book is a short story collection, *The Wind's Twelve Quarters.* Ms. Le Guin resides in Oregon.

VONDA N. McINTYRE graduated from the University of Washington with honors in biology. A graduate of the Clarion Writer's Workshop, she became program coordinator for Clarion West from 1971 through 1973. She is the author of a novel, *The Exile Waiting,* and editor (with Susan Janice Anderson) of an anthology, *Aurora.* She received a Nebula Award for her novelette "Of Mist, and Grass, and Sand." Ms. McIntyre makes her home in Washington.

JAMES TIPTREE, JR., is the author of many science fiction stories which have appeared in *New Dimensions, If, Galaxy, The Magazine of Fantasy and Science Fiction, Again Dangerous Visions,* and other magazines and anthologies. He won a Nebula Award for his short story "Love Is the Plan the Plan Is Death" and a Hugo Award for his novella "The Girl Who Was Plugged In." He has two short story collections: *Ten Thousand Light Years from Home* and *Warm Worlds and Otherwise.* He is currently working on a novel.

GENE WOLFE was born in Brooklyn and resides in Illinois, where he edits the trade publication *Plant Engineering.* He is the author of *The Fifth Head of Cerberus* and *Peace,* a novel. His stories have appeared in *Analog, Orbit, Universe, Again Dangerous Visions, The New Atlantis, The Ruins of Earth, Bad Moon Rising,* and many other anthologies and magazines. He received a Nebula Award for his novella "The Death of Doctor Island."

ABOUT THE EDITORS

JACK DANN was born and raised in upstate New York. He studied drama at Hofstra University and received his B.A. in political science from the State University of New York at Binghamton (Harpur College). He studied law at St. John's University and did graduate work in comparative literature at S.U.N.Y. at Binghamton. His short fiction has been published in *Orbit, New Dimensions, The Last Dangerous Visions, New Worlds, If, Fantastic, Gallery,* and other magazines and anthologies. He is the editor of *Wandering Stars, Faster Than Light* (with George Zebrowski), *Speculative Fiction of the 70's* (with David Harris), and *Immortal.* He is the author of a novel, *Starhiker.* Mr. Dann is currently at work on a novel based on his novella *Junction,* which was a Nebula Award finalist. He has taught science fiction at Cornell University and Broome Community College. He was managing editor of the *Bulletin of the Science Fiction Writers of America* from 1970 to 1974. Mr. Dann resides in Johnson City, New York.

GARDNER DOZOIS was born and raised in Salem, Massachusetts. He sold his first science fiction story in 1966, and entered the Army almost immediately thereafter, spending the next three years overseas as a military journalist. He has been a full-time writer since his discharge from the service in 1969. His short fiction has appeared in *Orbit, New Dimensions, Analog, Universe, Quark, Generation, Amazing, Worlds of If, Chains of the Sea,* and other magazines and anthologies. He has been a Nebula Award finalist five times, a Hugo Award finalist four times, and twice a finalist for the Jupiter Award. He is the editor of an anthology, *A Day in the Life,* and co-author, with George Alec Effinger, of a novel, *Nightmare Blue.* He is currently at work on another novel. For several years he was the chief editorial reader for the UPD science fiction magazines (*Galaxy, Worlds of If,* etc.) and has also been a reader for Dell and for Award Books. He was Guest of Honor at the 1973 Washington, D.C., science fiction convention, Disclave. He is a member of the Science Fiction Writers of America, the SFWA Credentials Committee, the SFWA Speakers Bureau, and the Professional Advisory Committee to the Special Collections Department of the Paley Library at Temple University. Mr. Dozois resides in Philadelphia.